HOPE IS DEAD

A Zack Goodson Novel

BOB ASHER

HOPE IS DEAD

Printed in the United States of America
First Printing 2022
First Edition 2022

ISBN-13: 978-1-958115-01-5

10 9 8 7 6 5 4 3 2 1

This is a book of fiction. The names, characters, organizations, places, events, and incidents are either products of my imagination or are used fictitiously.

Once again, thank you, Sierra Kilo, for your patience and unwavering support while I locked myself up in my office at night to write this story.

CHAPTER 1

DAY 1, FRIDAY NIGHT, JUNE 5

He leaned over and held her head up by a handful of dark blonde hair. The bare dim bulb over them cast shadows on the cracked linoleum floor. His trembling voice broke as he spoke, "Hope! Hope! Wake…wake up, dammit! Don't fuck me over, again! … Shit!" He raised her eyelid with his thumb and saw her cornea had rolled back in her head. He slapped her hard on her bloody cheek a couple of times, but she didn't respond. When he let go of her hair, her head slumped forward again. She wasn't breathing. His mind raced. This wasn't what he'd wanted. He wanted to teach her a lesson, not kill her. *Fuckin' stuck-up bitch!* She thought she was too good for him. He stood back and ran his hands through his grimy hair. *Think, dammit! Think!* He looked down at her limp body tied to the cheap dinette chair. Blood from her battered face had pooled under the chair and mixed with her urine. A red shop towel was duct-taped in her mouth. He didn't realize how angry he had been, but her defiance in the beginning and her whimpering at the end drove him crazy. He regretted being so rough with her now. There was no way to explain this away.

They would lock him up forever—if her father didn't have him killed first.

Fuck it! Her boyfriend could explain what happened to her. This was his trailer, after all. He pulled the syringe from her arm, put the cap back on, and stuck it in his pocket. He grabbed his duct tape and electrical cord off the table. He slammed the flimsy trailer door and leapt from the steps. He fell several times in the darkness as he ran back through the dense woods to where he had hidden his truck. He never looked back. He climbed into the truck cab and started the engine. He saw her blood on his hands and sweaty forearms. He grabbed one of his red shop towels off the passenger seat. He wiped the blood off and threw the towel behind the seat. He drove away as fast as he could. When he got to Highway JJ, he threw the dirty syringe into the ditch. By the time he turned onto southbound Highway 67, he had a cigarette lit and was starting to calm down. Every second that passed, the further he was from the trailer, the more convinced he became that he would get away with his crime. He was rumbling along down the highway on his oversized mud tires a couple of miles south of Highway Y at a steady 80 miles per hour when red and blue lights appeared in his rearview mirror. "Fuck me!" he shouted as he slammed his hand on top of the dashboard.

CHAPTER 2

DAY 4, MONDAY, JUNE 8

It was Monday morning before dawn. The new deputy yawned as he sat in the first row of tables in the squad room directly across from the watch commander's table. He swiveled in his chair and watched as deputies wearing tan short-sleeved shirts and brown trousers began entering the room by ones and twos. The color scheme wasn't his favorite, but he did like the gold six-pointed stars they all wore on their chests. Some of the deputies were from the midnight shift and some were from the day shift, but they all had one thing in common—they all looked tired. He didn't see his training officer yet. It was his first day on the job, and he was a little nervous. The previous Thursday, he met his training officer and was officially sworn in by the sheriff. That was when he received his Glock 22 pistol, badge, and uniforms. He had graduated from the Mineral Area College Law Enforcement Academy a week before. He observed the room, beginning at the off-white painted cinder-block walls. Paint was peeling in places, and the room was furnished with heavy wood tables and chairs that had been rescued from the Farmington Public Library when they remodeled. The building, which included the Sheriff's Station and the jail, had been state of the art when it was built in 1996. The jail was designed to hold 188 prisoners. Now it was vastly overcrowded, mostly due to drug crimes.

The deputy wasn't sure he belonged here. The small-town pace was a bit slow for him. He would've fit in better at a large metropolitan department like St. Louis City or County or, better yet, one of the federal agencies. He had felt out of place for nine months now, like a big fish in a small pond. That was when he left active duty in the Marine Corps after ten years and moved to his wife's hometown, Farmington, Missouri.

Finally, his training officer, Mark Langford, sat down next to him. He was a big man, at least as tall as him and thirty pounds heavier. "Good morning, Zack."

"Hey, Mark."

Mark pulled a half-filled form from his aluminum police clipboard. "I'm going to try to finish up this report before shift change." He started writing.

Zack overheard a conversation coming from two rows behind him that piqued his interest. He had to turn around and focus on the speakers: a large blonde female deputy and a thin balding male deputy.

She pointed to his wrist. "Why do you wear that compass on your watchband?"

He held his wrist in front of them and showed off the compass proudly like it was a recently discovered form of advanced technology. "So if I get turned around, I can look at the compass and tell what direction I'm heading."

She raised her eyebrow quizzically. "It always points north, right? What if you want to go in another direction?"

He cut his eyes to hers to see if she was joking… She wasn't. His thick brown mustache curled up with his grin. "Well, it's like this, Elly May." He pointed to the compass. "If this tiny arrow always points to north, then I can always determine east is to the right and west is to the left and south is opposite of north. If the little arrow just randomly pointed in other directions, it would be useless…like a female deputy."

She clenched her jaw as her face went red and punched him in the arm.

"Ouch!"

"Are you still going to be able to tell the direction after I jam it up your ass?"

Zack turned back to the front and laughed. "Who are those two?"

Mark shook his head. He didn't bother looking up from his report before answering, "Mary Woodall and Bob Wainwright. Bob's our department shit magnet. If you ever get in trouble, just go stand next to him for a minute. Your trouble will be drawn to him. He sucks up trouble like a black hole sucks up…well, everything."

A deputy wearing a white shirt, at least three inches taller and thirty pounds heavier than Zack's six-foot, one-inch and muscular

220-pound frame, entered the room and sat down at the head table. He pushed his gold metal-framed glasses back on the bridge of his nose. "Everyone, take a seat so we can get started. I'm sure these guys would like to go home," Lieutenant Ike McLeod said. It was 0530, and his squad was relieving the night shift watch commander, Sergeant Krote, and his deputies. McLeod and Krote sat behind another heavy wood table at the front of the squad room facing their deputies. After everyone settled in, McLeod said, "Sergeant Krote, before you start, I'd like to introduce our newest deputy, Zack Goodson. Zack's a former Marine helicopter pilot fresh out of the Academy, and he's going to be training with Mark Langford." A chorus of impressed oohs and aahs erupted from the audience. McLeod motioned for the crowd to quieten. "Zack, why don't you stand up and tell us a little bit about yourself?"

Zack turned in his chair to scan the room and was greeted with expectant looks, so he reluctantly stood up and started to speak, but before he finished his first word, all assembled yelled, "Shut up, sit down!" He sat down red-faced. Mark laughed with the others and slapped him on the back. Zack looked down and shook his head. He knew better. He should've seen it coming.

"Welcome to the St. Francois County Sheriff's Department, Zack. Oh, if we ever do anything that bothers you, just let us know," McLeod said with a smile.

Zack smiled back and nodded his understanding. He knew better than to complain about anything. This place was like his first fleet squadron in the Corps. If you ever let anyone know something bothered you, the other pilots would make you miserable. They were like a school of piranhas circling you in the Amazon. Once, another young captain became annoyed because someone had moved the telephone on his desk when he wasn't in his office. It happened a few times in the course of the week, so the next time the officers had a meeting in the ready room, he told all assembled that if anyone used his phone to put it back where they found it. After that, anytime someone walked by his office and saw he wasn't in there, they would move his phone. Some would even unplug it, take it apart, and hide the pieces in his desk.

Another pilot named Barton wanted his callsign to be Bad because his initials were B.A.D. He was the only guy in the unit who liked to wipe down the cockpit controls with antiseptic wipes before flying. He had fair, delicate skin and used facial cream as part of his skin care regimen, whatever that was. The other pilots decided his callsign should be Buffy, but he didn't like Buffy, so he went to the squadron commander and complained. The Old Man immediately called a meeting in the ready room for all pilots who weren't flying. After the room was full, the Colonel entered the room and stepped up to the podium. He scanned the room with a serious look on his face and said, "Gentlemen, I have an important announcement to make. Barton doesn't like being called Buffy. That is all." He left the room as it erupted with laughter.

After that, Barton was doomed. The Buffy callsign would follow him throughout his Marine Corps flying career. There was no way Zack would make that mistake, and if he could help it, the people in the Sheriff's Department would never find out what his callsign was.

"OK, Melvin, what do you have for us this morning?" McLeod asked.

7

Krote cleared his throat. "We only had two calls of note. At 0145, we had another 10-50 J2 on northbound Highway 67 at Highway Y involving a man named Randall Powers and a woman named Jody Brewer. I think that's the seventh one this year. Powers was heading north on Highway 67 when Brewer failed to yield while trying to cross 67 from east to west. Powers T-boned Brewer. Both drivers were transported to Jefferson Hospital in Festus with non-life-threatening injuries. Brewer had neck and head injuries. Powers wasn't physically injured, but he was severely depressed and was suspected of DWI. He was crying uncontrollably and kept saying he was sorry. He kept begging her for forgiveness even though she couldn't hear him. She was in another ambulance. His blood was taken at the hospital. Her vehicle was towed from the scene. His was left on the shoulder.

"At 0230 we had a domestic disturbance at 2509 Watson Road between Teddy and Tina Waller. Mrs. Waller stayed out late drinking with her softball team after their game and came home intoxicated at approximately 0200. Mr. Waller had stayed up waiting for her and immediately began to ask Mrs. Waller a series of repetitive questions as to her whereabouts all evening and who she had been with. Mrs. Waller explained she would talk to him about it in the morning, but she felt sick and just wanted to sleep. Unsatisfied with her answer, Mr. Waller continued to question her. Mrs. Waller again explained her desire to sleep and warned him to leave her alone. Undeterred, Mr. Waller continued to, in Mrs. Waller's words, 'Nag her.' Finally, in a moment of exasperation, she punched him in the face, bloodying his nose. Mr. Waller, mortified and in pain, ran to his phone and called 911. When

Deputies Nickmeier and Mellencamp arrived, they contacted Mr. Waller, who was sitting on the porch steps crying. Mr. Waller stood up on their approach and was observed to stand approximately 6'5" and weighing at least 260 pounds. Blood stained his beard and white T-shirt. Mr. Waller told the deputies what occurred and asked for medical attention. An ambulance was called. Our deputies then contacted Mrs. Waller, who was sleeping on the sofa in the living room. After being roused, Mrs. Waller explained that she had had too much to drink and just needed to sleep, but her husband kept pestering her even after being warned. She said he tended to be a drama queen. Finally, she lost her temper and struck him. She was advised she was under arrest and told to stand up to be handcuffed. At that time, she was observed to stand approximately 5'2" tall and weighing about 110 pounds. As Mrs. Waller was escorted to the cruiser, she complained that Mr. Waller wouldn't stop whining like a little bitch."

The jaded group of deputies made no attempt to stifle their laughter.

Mark and Zack sat in their idling cruiser, a white Ford Police Interceptor, with the AC set on high in a futile bid to cool the interior before their perspiration soaked through their T-shirts into their body armor. Mark adjusted his seat and mirrors. He checked his salt-and-pepper mustache in the mirror and smoothed it with his hand.

"Before we roll, I want to lay out a few ground rules so you know where we stand. We're just getting to know each other, so we may become good friends down the road or we may just learn to tolerate each other, but above all, I'm your field training officer. It's my job to teach you enough over the next twelve weeks for you to be competent to patrol on your own. If at any time you don't understand what's happening or why I'm doing something, speak up. Here's a short list of rules of thumb I call 'Langford's Laws.' I give them to everyone I train. They weren't brought down from Mount Sinai by Moses, but they may help keep you alive and out of trouble."

Mark pulled out of the parking lot and turned left onto Doubet Road. "I'll do everything I can to keep you safe and get you through the training program, but there are things I won't do. First, never ask me to do anything illegal, immoral, or unethical. I won't lie for you, lose my job for you, or go to jail for you. The same goes for you. If another deputy asks you to help him cover up something you know is wrong, don't do it. He's no longer a fellow deputy, he's already crossed over to the other side. That covers the first three laws."

Zack nodded his understanding.

"Also, people react differently to stress. Some are cool and calm, and some freeze up or flip out. I guess I don't have to tell you that. I'm sure you'll do fine. If we're on a call and someone shoots me, first kill that motherfucker, then get on the radio right away and call for help. You don't have to worry about using the proper radio procedure. Just key the mic and tell them where we are and to send help. If you don't know where we are, just look at the map feature on your phone. After a few weeks, you'll learn the roads."

"Ten oh five, barking dog," the Central 911 dispatcher called out over the radio. Her call drowned out the soft country music coming from Mark's favorite radio station, 98.5 FM.

Mark lowered the FM volume with the switch on the steering wheel. "That call is for you. Your department serial number is one zero zero five, but on the radio, you say ten oh five. Just key the handset and say ten oh five," Mark said as he turned right off Doubet Road onto northbound Highway 67.

"Ten oh five," Zack said into the microphone.

"Ten oh five, barking dog complaint at 401 King School Road, Iron Mountain, 0605," the dispatcher transmitted. 0605 was the time, 6:05 a.m. The sun had come up only fifteen minutes earlier.

"Say, 'ten oh five, 10-76,'" Mark prompted.

Being a Marine and used to instantly obeying orders, Zack transmitted, "Ten oh five, 10-76." He knew 10-76 meant "en route" from his training. Despite ten years of experience in the Marine Corps, he was still a little nervous. His FTO was a former brown-water sailor during the first Gulf War, and he didn't want to embarrass himself in front of the old squid. He remembered his first flight in a T-6 Texan II at Navy flight school with his Coast Guard instructor. At the end of the flight, the puddle pirate took the controls and snap-rolled the aircraft a couple of times and then looped it, pulling 6 Gs before nosing it over to cause negative 2 Gs hoping to make the young Marine throw up. He did throw up, but he kept it in his mouth. When the mud duck in the back seat asked him how he was doing, Zack nodded his helmeted head and gave him a thumbs-up as he swallowed the vomit. It took several gulps, but he refused to give the Coastie any satisfaction. He smiled at the memory. He watched the terrain go by and tried to read the road signs as they drove past them slightly over the speed limit.

"The dispatcher's name is Peggy. She's a nice lady and a good dispatcher. She's been working as a dispatcher for over thirty years. This'll be a good call to break you in easy. If the dog's barking when we get there, you can write the owner a warning and we can check that off your training checklist."

"Do you guys welcome every new deputy the way you did me?" Zack studied the area as he stared out his window.

Mark smiled. "No, not all of them. The guy before you was the son of a long-time Desloge police officer named Horace Hubbard. The day before his son, Harold, reported for duty, Horace brought a bunch of the kid's baby pictures to the Sheriff. When the kid sat down in the squad room on his first day, everyone around him was looking at his naked little butt crawling around on a fake bearskin rug. How about you? Do you have any of your baby pictures?"

Zack's eyes widened and he turned to Mark. "Oh, hell no!"

Mark laughed. "We've got another ten minutes before we get to Iron Mountain. Tell me something that's not in your file."

Zack thought for a moment as he returned to staring out the window. "The Sheriff's Department wasn't my first choice."

Mark snuck a quick surprised look at the back of Zack's head as they cruised down the two-lane highway. "Then why are you here? Did your first choice turn you down?"

"Not exactly. I grew up in St. Louis County, so I would have rather worked up there, but my wife grew up in Farmington, and I promised her when I got out of the Corps we would move back to her hometown."

"You were an officer. I'm surprised you didn't go to the FBI or one of the other federal agencies."

"While I was in the Academy, I did apply for the FBI, just to see how I'd do. I took their test, but they said I wasn't a match for the demographic they were recruiting."

"What the hell does that mean?"

"They told me my score was really good for a woman or minority accountant or computer nerd, but because I was a white male military officer, I had to score higher than everyone else. I guess it doesn't matter anyway. There's no way my wife will ever leave Farmington again." He continued looking out his window.

"Are you a Cardinals fan?"

Zack turned around and nodded. "Sure, Cardinals and Blues."

"Well, good. Then there's hope for you. If you'd said you were a Cubs fan, you might've been run out of town on a rail."

"Hey, how come everyone around here calls the county Saint Francis when it's spelled like Francois?"

"Back before President Jefferson bought the Louisiana Territory, this area was owned by the French. It was part of their Upper Louisiana Territory. They settled here to mine the lead and trap fur. That's why some of the towns like Bonne Terre, Desloge, and Terre Du Lac have French names. The French ranged all the way from Canada down to New Orleans and west all the way to the Spanish Territory."

Mark turned their cruiser off King School Road and drove up the 800-foot-long gravel driveway into the trees. "Tell Central you're 10-23."

Zack knew 10-23 meant they had arrived at the scene of the call. "Central, ten oh five, 10-23."

"Ten oh five, 10-23 at 0616," the dispatcher, Peggy, transmitted.

As they climbed out of the car, the steamy June air smothered them. They walked past an old broken-down Camaro partially covered by a blue tarp to get to the run-down ranch home. It was covered with faded white asbestos siding. Before they could knock on the storm door, a heavyset middle-aged woman with a cup of coffee and a cigarette opened it. She stepped out on the porch.

"Good morning, Mrs. Cantwell. I'm Deputy Langford and this is Deputy Goodson. Did you report a barking dog? I don't hear anything now," he said as he scanned the area.

"You don't hear it because it was my dog, Bruno. Every time I let him out in the backyard. he runs to the back fence and barks his head off. He doesn't shut up until I drag him back in the house. He's a retired St. Louis City police dog. I think there might be drugs hidden back there by the creek."

"Has he ever done anything like that before?"

"No, he usually does his business and then patrols the fence for a few minutes before he comes back in. Last night he barked some when I let him out before we went to bed, but this morning he's going crazy."

"OK, ma'am, we'll walk around the side of the house. Why don't you let him out again and we'll watch what he does?"

She went back inside, and they walked around the side of the house.

"Have you ever seen a woman her size wearing yoga pants?" Mark asked.

"I didn't know they made 'em that big," Zack said.

Moments later, she slid the back door open and a large black and tan German shepherd scrambled from the opening and flew off the rear deck. He launched himself to the fence at the back of the yard like a fur missile, barking wildly with slobber flying from his mouth.

"Damn, that's a beautiful dog," Mark said.

"He sure is," Zack said. He thought of his own dog, an Alaskan malamute named King. He had recently lost him to old age.

"OK, ma'am. Take him back inside. We'll go have a look around," Mark said from over the fence. "Come on, let's go see what we can find."

He spun and headed along the outside of the chain-link fence toward the woods. "I guess they told you at the Academy our county is a major hotbed of methamphetamine activity." Mark pointed toward the tall trees and dense brush to the southeast. "That's Middlebrook Creek back there. It runs across King School Road over to Mudd Creek and then it feeds into Iron Mountain Lake. Somebody probably dumped their empty chemical containers in the creek."

They trudged southeast through the thick green brush and trees for 200 feet until they came to the creek. They were already soaked in sweat under their soft body armor and covered in flies and ticks.

"I wish I had a machete," Zack said. "This weather reminds me of the summers at Quantico. I'm already soaked in sweat under my vest." He grabbed the neck of his armor and pulled it out and back several times like a bellows to get some fresh air underneath it.

"Damn flies," Mark said as he took off his brown department ball cap and swung it to no avail at the ginormous horseflies dive-bombing his head. Their bites were vicious. He wasn't watching where he was going and stepped face-first into a giant spiderweb, which sent him spinning into an entirely different stratosphere of gesticulations.

"Goddamn it! Son of a bitch!" he yelled as he flailed about at his invisible enemy.

He heard Zack laugh at him as he stepped around him to take the lead. Zack paralleled the creek as he plodded back northeast toward King School Road. It hadn't rained for over a week, so there was only a foot or so of water in the creek bed. Mark slowly removed the web and composed himself as he followed Zack. He was happy to let the Marine clear a path through the snakes, briars, and poison ivy. From his days as a brown-water sailor, Mark knew it was always good to have a Marine or two around in case someone lobbed a grenade at the patrol. It was slow going through the heavy undergrowth and downed trees, but after about a hundred yards, Zack stopped.

"Mark, do you smell that?"

He stepped up next to Zack and sniffed the air. "Aw, shit. We might have a DB. Follow me. When we get to it, don't touch anything." DB meant dead body.

Thirty feet later, they emerged from the brush into a small clearing next to the creek. They saw a body face down in about a foot of water on the other side of the creek with two turkey vultures on its back feeding.

Zack bent over and dry heaved. "Oh, man, that smells awful." He hadn't smelled a decomposing body since Afghanistan.

On one mission early in his first Operation Enduring Freedom deployment, he had to fly the bodies of four Marines back from their FOB to Bagram Air Base after their Humvee hit an IED. It was 115°F and the bodies were badly decomposed. Even though the bodies were sealed in body bags and the windows and ramp were open, he couldn't out fly the wretched smell no matter how fast he flew.

CHAPTER 3

"Get over there and shoo those buzzards away, but don't move the body." Mark pulled out his cellphone to call the station.

Zack stepped down off the bank into tepid water deeper than the top of his waterproof boots and waded across the creek as he waved his arms. "Ahhh! Get out of here!" The birds screeched in complaint and hopped away about ten feet before stopping. Zack grabbed a baseball-sized rock from the creek bed and threw it at them. They screeched again as they took flight. They orbited impatiently above the trees, waiting for the intruders to leave.

"It looks like a woman, about 5'6" and maybe 130 pounds." He took his desert camouflage bandana from his left back pocket and, making sure he was upstream, dipped it in the water. He squeezed it out and tied it around his face. The dirty creek water didn't smell good either, but the wet bandana helped him breathe. He pulled his iPhone out and began snapping photos of the body and surrounding area, being careful not to get Mark in any of the shots. He knew cops hated getting caught in crime scene photos.

He noticed she was wearing tight faded blue jeans with embroidered back pockets. The style was popular with women from the area. Even his wife wore them.

Mark dialed his cellphone and put it on speaker. "Hey, Don, it's Mark. Our barking dog was barking at a DB in Middlebrook Creek. It's a woman."

Sheriff Don Blair said, "Damn! Is it a suicide or homicide?"

"I can't tell one way or the other. She's face down in the creek. I don't see any obvious wounds except for where the turkey buzzards were picking at her back. Is the lieutenant in the station?"

"No, he's on his way to Lake Timberline to help them deal with a barricaded subject. I'll head out to you after I call Denny and Lester," Blair said before he hung up.

Zack heard the conversation from across the creek. "Who're Denny and Lester?"

Mark put his phone back in his pocket. "Denny is Detective Lieutenant Dennis Close. He's also our internal affairs investigator and the meanest bastard in the county without an arrest record. He'll go out of his way to fuck you over. Stay away from that Lurch-looking motherfucker. Lester Koplin is the county coroner. He also owns and operates Koplin Funeral Home in Park Hills."

"The coroner isn't a pathologist?"

"No, we don't have the money or need for a full-time medical examiner. When we want an autopsy, we contract it out to a pathologist at Parkland Hospital. Lester is elected to the coroner position. He's not a trained investigator, and the job doesn't pay much. I think he does it to help drum up business for his funeral home. Since your feet are already wet, why don't go up and down the creek for a couple hundred feet and check for evidence. If you find something, don't touch it. Snap some photos and mark its position. I'll protect the body from the buzzards until they get here."

Zack nodded and started walking downstream along the creek toward King School Road. He hoped his new patrol boots weren't already ruined. As he sloshed through the water, he was already having second thoughts about his new career. If he wanted to slog through the woods, he would have joined the infantry. He wondered what he'd be doing if he had taken another path. He could have been a flying Customs agent interdicting drugs down in the Gulf, or maybe he could have stayed on active duty in the Marines and flew the President in Marine One. He knew several guys who had. He logged enough flight time to get a job flying for one of the air ambulance companies like Air Evac for more than twice the money the sheriff was paying him or even go to the airlines. Instead, he took a huge pay cut to work for a sparsely populated rural county in southeastern Missouri. It served him right for falling in love with the smartest, most beautiful woman he had ever met. She was the ball and chain keeping him mired in this little backwater town, an incredibly wonderful ball and chain. Why did she have to be from Farmington? He figured he had time, so he followed the creek all the way down to the bridge over King School Road. He saw the sheriff's truck drive over the bridge, so he turned around and headed back upstream.

Sheriff Blair stood next to Mark on the edge of the creek. The sheriff was already sweating through the band of his brown felt cowboy hat. He removed his hat and mirrored Ray-Bans. He wiped his face with his blue paisley handkerchief. "I should have worn my straw hat."

They watched Lieutenant Close walk around in the creek with his camera looking for evidence. He came prepared and was wearing a set of waders. Zack was on the other side of the creek again keeping the buzzards away from the corpse. He had returned from his search of the creek five minutes earlier and told them he had found four empty gallon-sized brake fluid containers in the creek 100 yards downstream. He noticed none of the others were covering their faces and felt kind of embarrassed wearing the bandana. He wiped his face with it and stuck it back in his pocket.

An hour after being notified, the coroner called the sheriff on his cellphone. Blair answered, "Hey, Les. Where are you?" He listened and shook his head. "We're not at the house. We're over in the creek. I'll send Deputy Goodson over to lead you in. Hey, Zack, go get him so we can get this girl out of here."

"Yes, sir." Zack waded back across the creek and disappeared into the brush. Five minutes later, he emerged from the trees and walked across the grass to the black Koplin Funeral Home van parked on the gravel behind the sheriff's dark gray Ford F-150. Koplin and his assistant were sitting inside with the AC going. Zack knocked on the driver's side window, causing Koplin to jump. He turned off the engine and climbed out of his cocoon.

"Sir, I'm Zack Goodson. The Sheriff asked me to show you the way."

"Good to meet you, Zack. Just call me Les," Koplin said as they shook hands. "This is Timmy," he said as Timmy came around the front of the van to shake Zack's hand. Zack looked up at him and took his hand. He must have been at least 6'8" and 350 pounds.

"Good to meet you, Timmy."

"Are you the Marine?" Timmy asked as he smiled.

"What?" Zack wondered how Timmy could know he was a Marine. He didn't have any tattoos.

"The other deputies have been talking since last week about a hotshot Marine coming to work for the Sheriff."

"Well, I am a Marine." Zack followed the men to the rear of the van and helped them with their equipment. They also had the foresight to dress for the environment. Les and Timmy began climbing into their waders. "I didn't know they made waders that long," Zack said.

"I was an Eagle Scout. Always prepared," Timmy said.

Les handed Zack a black body bag. Timmy pulled an orange plastic litter out of the van.

Zack was relieved. He was expecting an ambulance-type gurney with legs and wheels.

Timmy saw his expression. "We can carry this one or drag it if we're on a smooth surface. It can help a lot over long distances."

"OK, this way, gentlemen." Zack led them toward the trees. Ten minutes later, they emerged from the brush at the creek. Lester pulled on his nitrile gloves. He stepped down into the water and waded across. He leaned over to look at the body and then checked its back pockets for evidence. There was none. Then with Zack and Timmy's help, they rolled the body and carried it over to the body bag lying next to the water. The face was grotesquely bruised and bloated. The left side had been partially eaten by the turtles and other scavengers. Zack gagged at the sight but, again, recovered quickly.

Les checked the other pockets. "There's no ID on the body. I guess this one will have to be a closed casket," he said matter-of-factly.

Lieutenant Close stepped in with his camera and examined the body. "Back out of my shot, Probie," he said dismissively to Zack as he bent over and took photos of the body.

"Yes, sir." Zack stepped back immediately, but he was thinking Close was a grade-A asshole. He had met plenty of dickheads like him in the Corps.

Close pointed with his black nitrile-gloved finger. "She was gagged and her hands were bound. I can see the ligature marks on her wrists and some adhesive on her face. We'll definitely need an autopsy on this one. I'll come by later and take her prints."

The sheriff pulled an old pocket watch out of his jeans and noted the time. "After eight already. OK, Mark, you and Zack help Les get the body back to his van and then take Zack back to town to get some dry shoes. Denny, since you're in your waders, you can

24

collect the brake fluid jugs. I'll see you boys later. There's a big stack of pancakes with my name on 'em waiting for me at Granny Annie's. It's good to be king." Blair strolled away laughing at his own joke.

"OK, gentlemen, since I'm the only one with dry shoes, I hope you won't mind if I stay on this side while you guys get the body over here," Mark said.

Zack took charge. "How about you guys take the front of the litter and I'll take the back until we get to the other side of the creek?"

They agreed, and Les, Timmy, and Zack strapped the body bag to the litter and carried it across the shin-deep water. After they were on dry land, Zack and Timmy took the front of the litter and Les and Mark took the rear. They slowly made their way back through the thick undergrowth, stepping over downed trees and getting their feet caught in poison ivy vines for twenty minutes. Finally, they slid the litter into the van, and Mark and Zack walked back toward Mrs. Cantwell's house to tell her what they had found. Mark was sweating profusely and breathing hard.

"Are you going to make it?" Zack asked with a big grin on his face.

"I'm still a little shook up from the spider web." Mark reached for the doorbell, but Mrs. Cantwell opened the door first.

"Did you find a body back there? I saw the coroner's van."

"Yes, ma'am. It was a woman. She was probably in the creek for a few days. Do you know of anyone who is missing from the area?" Mark asked.

"No, I don't, but that don't mean nothin'. Livin' back here in the trees, I don't see the neighbors much."

Mark handed her his business card. "Lieutenant Close from our Detective Bureau will be contacting you, but if you find out anything before he does, please, call me. Thank you for calling this in. There's no telling how long that girl would have been out there if you hadn't, and please, give Officer Bruno a special treat. He's a fine dog."

"Don't worry about that old boy. He's spoiled rotten. He was my son's dog."

"Is your son a City policeman?" Zack asked.

"He was. He got shot dead a couple of years ago up on Cote Brilliante by a fourteen-year-old drug dealer."

"We're sorry for your loss, Mrs. Cantwell. Thank you, again, for calling us," Mark said before they turned and walked back to the cruiser.

"Now I feel like a dumbass," Zack said as he rubbed the back of his neck.

"Don't sweat it. I'm sure she thinks about him every day anyway."

Zack came down the stairs and into the kitchen.

"How do you feel?" Mark asked. He was sitting at the granite-topped island drinking a glass of orange juice. He had driven Zack back to his house in Farmington so he could put on some dry boots and trousers.

"I could have sucked it up for the rest of the day, but it does feel a lot better to get dried off. Thanks."

Mark stood up and put his empty glass in the sink. "You have a nice house."

"Thanks. My wife, Patty, picked it out and decorated it. I have a man cave in the basement for all my unsightly guy stuff," he said as he grabbed two bottles of water from the refrigerator. He handed one to Mark. "So, what's next?"

"Now we go patrol the south sector in our mobile observation platform and deter crime." He turned and Zack followed him out the door to the cruiser. Moments later, he backed out of the driveway onto West Columbia Street and drove west toward Highway 67. "Your field training is twelve weeks long. You'll ride with me for most of that time. If one is available, you'll ride with another FTO for a couple of weeks so you're exposed to more than one way of doing things. We'll follow a crawl, walk, run approach. In the beginning, I'll drive while you learn the streets. I'll ask you from time to time where we are, and I expect you to know. As we get calls throughout the day, I'll take the lead and show you how to deal with the victims, witnesses, and suspects we encounter. You'll write all the reports, summonses, and tickets. If an interesting call comes out in another sector, we may jump it so you can use it for your training. After a few weeks, you'll start to drive. By the end of your training, I'll be sitting on the passenger side evaluating you as you do everything. I'll back you up, but I won't help unless you need it."

"Ten oh five, contact nine eighty-two at the station," Peggy transmitted from Central Dispatch.

"Ten oh five, 10-76," Zack responded on the radio then turned to Mark. "Who's nine eighty-two?"

"He's the undersheriff, Jim Baderman. He handles all the administrative jobs the Sheriff doesn't like to mess with. He doesn't leave the station very much." Mark turned left onto Highway 67, and a couple of minutes later, they parked beside the station.

Mark knocked on the open door of Baderman's office. "Do you want to see us, Captain?"

"Yes, come in Mark. You must be Zack," Baderman said. He stood up from his desk and held out his hand.

Zack shook it. "Yes, sir."

"The Sheriff told me the ladies out front couldn't get the ID card machine to work last week when he swore you in. The machine's getting old and finicky. Sometimes I have to give it some special attention. I'm sorry I missed your ceremony." He handed the ID card to Zack.

"Thank you, sir." Zack looked at it, remembering last week when he put the uniform shirt and tie on over his street clothes so the clerk could take his photo.

"I heard you got off to an interesting start this morning. We don't have many bodies dumped in the county. Denny will be excited to have an interesting case to investigate."

Zack nodded. He would have expected the captain to be a little less cheerful on learning a young woman had been brutally murdered.

"We better get back out there, Captain. Come on, Zack." Mark peeked in the sheriff's office as they walked by. "He must still be eatin' pancakes."

They went back out to their cruiser.

"Ten oh five, 10-8," Zack transmitted, indicating they were back in service. "What's the deal with the Captain?"

Mark gave Zack a knowing look but said, "What do you mean?"

Zack smiled. "He's built like G.I. Joe but acts like Ken. He looks like a Sheriff's Department recruiting poster but talks like an office manager. It's like his uniform is really a costume—all show, no go."

"I think you have a clear picture. Years ago, when he was a road deputy, a local shitbum shot him in the calf with a 22. Being shot actually gave him some street cred and helped him get promoted. He took an office job in the station doing D.A.R.E., public relations, and supply, all the jobs no one else wanted. Once he tasted life in the station, he was hooked. Since then, he has done everything he could to get jobs inside. He would much rather buy cruisers and uniforms than come out on the road and risk getting hurt. He's strictly nine to five. He spends his afternoons lifting weights to maintain that buff look. He wants to be part of the team, but he's afraid to patrol."

"So, he's the Sheriff's house mouse," Zack said.

Mark laughed and shook his head. "That's it. That's him exactly."

CHAPTER 4

"Ten oh five, suicide in progress," Peggy transmitted from Central Dispatch.

Zack keyed the mic. "Ten oh five."

"Ten oh five, suicide at 1017 Knob Lick Road, apartment A. Caller advises the apartment is on the second floor of her house and the entrance is up the stairs on the side of the building. She heard the female tenant screaming at her husband. He threatened to kill himself," Peggy transmitted.

"Ten oh five, 10-76," Zack transmitted.

"Ten oh five, 10-76 at 0917," Peggy responded.

"Nine eight four, en route to assist," Lieutenant McLeod transmitted.

"Nine eight four, 10-76 at 0917," Peggy responded.

Mark flipped on the lights and siren and turned south onto Highway 67. "This is one of the most dangerous calls we can get— an attempted suicide combined with a domestic dispute. Be very careful when we get there. Men usually use guns to kill themselves.

If we get in the way, he might try to take us with him. If he loses his nerve, he may try to get us to shoot him."

Five minutes later, Peggy transmitted again, "Ten oh five, caller advised she just heard a single gunshot upstairs and now the woman is screaming hysterically."

"Ten oh five, understood," Zack replied.

Two minutes later, they pulled onto the street. Mark pointed and said, "That's it, the gray two-story with the stairs. Put us twenty-three."

Zack transmitted, "Ten oh five, 10-23."

Mark turned off the siren as they pulled into the gravel driveway and lurched to a stop. "Bring the shotgun." He exited the cruiser and cautiously proceeded to the stairs. Zack chambered a round into the Remington 870 and followed him.

"Cover me from the bottom of the stairs, and when I get to the top, I'll cover you," Mark said. He hustled up the rickety old stairs with his eyes and Glock trained on the door. As he came to the top step, the door burst open and he prepared to fire. A woman rushed out sobbing uncontrollably. She ran past him and down the stairs. He took a quick peek through the doorway with his Glock held close to his chest with both hands. "The kitchen is empty. Come on up." Zack took the stairs two at a time. "Stay behind me, and whatever happens, don't shoot me in the back," Mark said softly. He entered the kitchen and inched forward into the hall. He looked into the small bathroom on the left. "Clear." He advanced to the next room on the right. The air was heavy with the acrid stench of burnt gunpowder and the coppery tang of blood. He brought his Glock around the edge of the doorframe, and it came to a stop pointed at a man lying across the unmade bed in nothing but his boxers. His feet were on the floor. His right hand held a large frame blue steel revolver, and it rested on the mattress next to his thigh. A hole was blown through his right temple, and his right eye was bugged out grotesquely.

Mark yelled out to the man, "Drop the gun or I'll shoot!" but the man didn't move. Mark yelled again, "Drop the fucking gun, now!"

Zack stacked behind Mark with the shotgun pointed to the ceiling. He put his left hand on Mark's shoulder. "What's happening?"

"I think the guy's dead, but the gun is still in his hand. I'm going to feel really stupid if I go in there and this dead man kills me. Go around me to the other side of the doorway and cover me."

Zack sidled as quickly as he could past Mark in the narrow hallway and pointed the shotgun at the body. "OK, I got you."

Mark crept cautiously across the room and snatched the revolver from the man's hand, but the man didn't move. From his new vantage, Mark could see the left side of the man's head was missing. Blood, bone, and brain matter were spattered on the headboard, wall, and window. A large flow of red and gray goo had run off the bed and was pooling on the rug near the man's bare feet.

"Ten oh five, we have a man in custody with an apparently self-inflicted gunshot wound to the head. Respond an ambulance and supervisor," Mark transmitted on his walkie.

"Ten oh five, ambulance is en route. Nine eight four just went 10-23," Peggy replied.

Zack stepped up to the foot of the bed. "Isn't it too late for this guy?"

"Yeah, but we don't get to decide. The ambulance crew will. Keep an eye on him and don't touch anything. I'm going to talk to the woman who ran past us. Hopefully, Ike has her. Here, give me the shotgun and I'll secure it in the cruiser. Take some photos before the paramedics get here. They'll make a big fucking mess of the scene."

"Roger that. The safety's on, but a round's chambered." He handed it over.

Five minutes later, the EMTs arrived. Mark was right. A large man and a small woman entered the bedroom with their lifesaving equipment.

"Jesus, half of his head is missing. What can we do for him?" the woman said.

"Nothing. We'll hook up the EKG and run a strip to show he's dead," the man said.

She attached the leads and started the machine. She looked at the results. "Shit, he still has activity. Now what? Should we wrap him up and transport?" She handed the strip of paper to her partner.

The man studied the results. "No. Wait five minutes and run another strip." Seven minutes later, the EMTs had packed up their equipment and headed down the stairs. They left the adhesive EKG attachments stuck to the body and the wrappers lying all over the bed and floor. Zack stepped around the red pool on the rug and noticed the holes in the double-paned window. He lined them up with the hole in the screen and determined the fatal round must have lodged about twenty feet up the trunk of the massive white oak in the yard. Zack stepped out on the landing at the top of the stairs to get some air. It was cooler inside, but the air was better outside.

The hysterical woman had finally calmed down a little and was sitting at the bottom of the stairs talking to Mark and McLeod.

"Ma'am, can you tell us what happened?" Mark asked.

She looked up at Mark through tear-filled eyes. "He was supposed to be at work by eleven o'clock at Beckwith Motors. You know, they're the used car dealer next to the highway in Bonne Terre with the giant pink elephant out front. So anyway, I woke him up to get ready. Then I went into the kitchen to make his breakfast. Ten minutes later, I went to check on him and he was still in bed. He had too much to drink again last night. He was supposed to go into alcohol rehab again tomorrow."

"How many times had he been already?" Mark asked.

"This would have been the fourth time. So, I told him I wasn't leaving until he got out of bed. He said 'OK, you win' and he sat up on the side of the bed and looked at himself in the mirror for a minute. Then, he reached under the mattress and pulled out that big gun. He lined it up against his head in the mirror and pulled the trigger right in front of me. We've been married for twenty-three years. That's the meanest thing he's ever done to me." She started to cry again.

"Ma'am, is there anyone we can call to come get you?" Mark asked softly. "You won't be able to go back into the apartment for a day or two." Mark heard a car stop behind them.

"That's my momma. I can go with her," she said through her tears.

Mark helped her stand up. She walked over to the car and talked to her mother through the open passenger side window before she got in and they drove away. Mark and McLeod mounted the steps, and all three of them went inside.

"What kind of gun did he use?" Zack asked.

Mark pulled it out of his waist and showed it to Zack and McLeod. "It's a Smith and Wesson Model 29. That's a .44 magnum with a six-inch barrel."

"Yeah, I reckon that'll do it," McLeod said.

"I lined up the holes in the window and screen. It looks like the bullet is stuck in the oak tree." Zack pointed. McLeod looked out the window and estimated how far off the ground the bullet must be. "Well, I'm sure as fuck not climbing up there to get it. This sounds like another job for our crack Detective Bureau. Road dawgs like us aren't smart enough. Clouseau's on his way to take over the investigation. As soon as you guys brief him, you can clear. He and Les can deal with the body. Two DBs in one morning.

That's impressive. Maybe it would be safer for the citizens of the county if we put you guys on the front desk for a while," McLeod said with a smile.

"Sir, did you just call Lieutenant Close 'Clouseau,' like Inspector Clouseau?"

Mark groaned like he knew what was coming.

"Yeah, he picked up that moniker right after he got promoted to sergeant and was put in charge of the Detective Bureau. Back then it was just him and Mark. We had a spate of car cloutings, and he decided he would come out at night and try to catch whoever was doing it. So, I think it was the third night of zero action, around 2:00 a.m., he and Mark were cruising a subdivision looking for the car clouter. That's someone who steals from vehicles. Anyway, they saw a guy riding his ten-speed zip past them on the sidewalk. Denny, using his highly developed investigative skills honed over his two weeks as a dick, recognized immediately the man was breaking the law because, as we all know, anyone over fifteen is not allowed to ride on the sidewalk, and if he was sixteen or younger, he was violating the curfew law, so they attempted to stop him.

"Instead of complying, he kept pedaling, and Denny called out in medium-speed pursuit. The young man made it about a half mile through the subdivision and dropped his bike in his front yard like he'd made it across the Canadian border. Denny and Mark slid to a stop in front of his house and grabbed him before he could get inside. They were on both sides of him in the front yard, each holding an arm to control the guy. He had a plastic shopping bag in his hand. Denny told him to drop it and asked him what he was doing. The guy said he went to the gas station to get some snacks. He reeked of Mary Jane and was high as a kite. Denny asked him why he didn't stop for them, and the guy said he didn't recognize their authority.

"Mark told the guy he was going to pat him down for weapons. As Mark got to his chest, he felt something hard in the inside breast pocket of his jacket, but before he could react, the guy yanked his hand away from Mark's grasp and then dove his hand into his pocket to grab the object. Denny grabbed a handful of the guy's hippy hairdo and Mark grabbed the guy's wrist with his left hand and his jacket with his right hand. Mark yelled at him to let go of the object, but the guy kept resisting. Mark was afraid it was a weapon and pulled out his Glock and pressed it against the side of the guy's head. He told him to drop the object or he would blow his fucking head off. Denny shouted, 'Wait! Let me move my hand first!' At this point, the guy figured they were serious and dropped the object. When it hit the ground, they saw in the dim light being put out by their blue and red light bar it was a pink plastic bubblegum container. It popped open and a one-hitter pipe and a tiny amount of marijuana fell out. Relieved it wasn't a weapon, they threw the guy to the ground and tried to get his hands behind his back to get the cuffs on him, but he kept resisting. Mark was pulling on his arms trying to get the other cuff on as Denny was kidney punching the kid.

"He was yelling for help the whole time. Finally, the porch light came on and his mother came outside in her nightgown. She yelled, 'What the hell is going on out here?' and the guy yelled back, 'What's it look like? I'm getting my ass kicked!' She yelled, 'It looks like you're being stupid to me!' Then she went back in the house and switched the porch light off. So, Mark almost blew the kid's head off because of a pipe and a trace of weed. All because Inspector Clouseau was so eager to catch a car clouter," McLeod said with a laugh.

Zack laughed too and asked, "So what's Mark's nickname?"

Before McLeod could speak, Mark said, "None o' your fuckin' business."

McLeod laughed. "OK, I'm going to clear before Denny gets here and starts whining about being overworked and understaffed."

CHAPTER 5

"Ten oh five, caller locked his keys in his truck at 2653 Wycliff Drive," the dispatcher, Peggy, transmitted.

Zack looked at Mark questioningly and he nodded. Zack replied, "Ten oh five, 10-76."

"Ten oh five, 10-76 at 1003," Peggy said.

"Are we locksmiths too?"

"People around here can't afford to call a locksmith every time they lock themselves out of their vehicle. So, we try to help them as long as they sign a waiver saying they won't blame us if we damage their vehicles. We have a slim jim in the back of the cruiser. If it's an older model car, we can probably get in. If it's a newer model with electric locks, we may tear it up trying to get in. We're here."

"Ten oh five, 10-23," Zack transmitted.

"Ten oh five, 10-23 at 1008," Peggy replied.

Mark stopped in front of the house. They walked back to the rear hatch, and Mark opened a large gray plastic tub. "Put this waiver form on your clipboard and bring it with you." He pulled the slim jim out of the tub. They approached a young man wearing a Taco Bell shirt leaning against an old Ford Ranger pickup. The engine was running. "What can we do for you?"

"I'm late for work and I locked myself out of my truck."

"What's your name?"

"Darrin Lynch."

"What year is your truck?"

"'95."

"Does it have electric locks?"

"No."

"OK, Mr. Lynch. Do you understand we can't guarantee we won't damage your truck while trying to get into it?"

"Yeah, I get it."

"Alright, just sign the waiver form Deputy Goodson has for you and we'll see what we can do." Lynch signed it. "Zack, have you ever used one of these before?" Zack looked at the long thin strip of metal called a slim jim and shook his head. It was a tool designed to open car doors. "Come over here and watch what I do. This truck is pretty straightforward. It has manual locks and manual windows. I'll just slide the slim jim inside the door in front of the glass and feel around for the metal bar that leads to the door latch. Sometimes you can feel it take hold and you can just pull it up to unlock the door. Other times you wind up pulling up and down on the slim jim while you repeatedly pull on the door handle and hope it pops open." He made one pull on the slim jim and then the handle. The door came open.

"Sweet. Thanks, Deputy. Excuse me, but I need to get to work," Lynch said as he tried to get past Mark and into the truck.

"Hold on a minute, Mr. Lynch. Zack, do you see that pill bottle on the passenger side floorboard mixed in with the red shop towel and the Taco Bell trash?"

Zack peered over his shoulder. "Yeah, I see it."

"Go around to the passenger side and see if you can read the name on the bottle without opening the door."

Zack walked around the truck and spun the bill of his cap around backward. He stuck his hands up to the glass to shade his eyes. "It's an oxycodone prescription for Beatrice Clawson in Park Hills. It's about half full."

"Mr. Lynch, why would you have Beatrice Clawson's pills?" Mark asked.

"I didn't put those in there. I've never seen them before."

"Really? So, when we fingerprint the bottle, we won't find your prints on it?"

"I don't know. I might have touched it accidentally. That's my Taco Bell trash all around it."

"Are you currently prescribed any drugs by a doctor?"

"No."

"Didn't you think it was odd someone's drugs were in your truck?"

"I told you, I didn't know it was in there."

"Did Beatrice sell you her pills?"

"No."

"Who's been in your truck that could have dropped it?"

Lynch raised his hands and said, "I don't want to get anyone in trouble."

"Mr. Lynch, right now, you're in trouble, and according to you, someone else put you there. You don't want to go to jail for something someone else did, do you? Wouldn't you rather we went and talked to them?" Lynch didn't answer. "Do you want us to get that stolen property out of your truck?"

"Yes."

"Zack, glove up and put the pill bottle in an evidence bag. Mr. Lynch, why don't you reach in there and get your keys?" Lynch turned off the engine and put the keys in his pocket. Zack came back from the cruiser with a bag and put the bottle inside. "I'll take the bag. Handcuff him and then search him real good. He may have more pills."

"Shit, man! I'm going to get fired!"

"If you want, we can roll through the drive-thru on the way to the station and talk to your manager for you." Mark winked at Zack. Mark reached into Lynch's pocket and retrieved the truck keys. "We'll need to inventory the property in your truck before we tow it to the impound lot. Are there any more pills in there? If there are, we'll find them anyway when we get the dog over here."

Lynch looked up in frustration and said, "Fuck me. Yeah, there's two more bottles in the glove box."

An hour later, Mark and Zack were patrolling their sector again after booking Lynch into the jail.

"So now what happens with Lynch?" Zack asked.

"Your report will be sent to the drug task force, and they'll try to flip him to get people higher up his supply chain," Mark replied.

"Do we have deputies in the task force?"

"Yeah, we usually have at least one. The Mineral Area Drug Task Force is made up of troopers, officers hired by the task force, and deputies from surrounding counties. They all go through advanced training with the Patrol and DEA. Since it's based here, they're all deputized by the Sheriff."

"Did you ever work for the task force?"

"No. It would have been fun for a while going after the shitheads responsible for our drug problem, but once the Sheriff gets you trained up for the task force, he expects you to stay there for at least three years. That's three years of looking like and pretending to be a shitbum even when you're not undercover. Do you want to show up at church or your boy's T-ball game looking like a drug addict with greasy long hair and dirty clothes? Now, being the man behind the curtain running the task force would be great, but he's usually a trooper."

"Why's that?"

"Because the state and the Feds provide money, they like to oversee it. About fifteen years ago, their civilian secretary got caught after she stole over $75,000 from the task force." Mark looked at the time on the dashboard. "It's after eleven o'clock. Are you hungry yet?" Mark asked as they drove past the Dollar General store in Doe Run.

"I'm always hungry. The first thing they taught us in flight school was never pass up a chance to get fuel or food." He twisted in his seat to watch an old man pushing a baby stroller down the gravel shoulder of the highway. "He shouldn't be out here with a baby. Should we go talk to him?"

"Naw, don't worry about him. That's not a baby. He lost his driver's license to DWIs about a year ago, so now he pushes that stroller up to the Dollar General every morning to get a case of beer. For a while he rode an old Craftsman riding lawnmower with a little garden trailer, but it broke down. We'll head for Park Hills and get lunch at Granny Annie's."

"I remember the Sheriff talking about their pancakes. Is the food good?"

"Oh yeah, it's real good. The servings are big, and the prices are reasonable. Plus, I get the friends and family discount. Annie's started out as a bakery. Her baked goods are terrific. About five years ago, people started asking for breakfast sandwiches, and it wasn't long before she opened up for breakfast and then lunch. She has two bakers who come in and bake all night. They unlock the back door around three in the morning when the cops start showing up. Annie gives them free coffee and donuts. It's not uncommon to see cars from five or six jurisdictions, including the troopers, lined up out back. It gives the cops a chance to shoot the shit, pass intel, and get to know the new guys from other towns."

About ten minutes later, Mark pulled into the parking lot of a worn-out strip mall, being careful not to hit any of the potholes in the crumbling asphalt, and drove to the end of the building. A brightly painted wooden sign with "Granny Annie's Kitchen" on it was mounted above the door. He parked a few rows away from the entrance. "Ask for J4 at Granny Annie's."

Zack keyed the mic. "Central, ten oh five, requesting J4 at Granny Annie's."

"Ten oh five, cleared for J4."

They climbed out of the cruiser.

"Here's your first lesson. Don't approach a business and walk in like a civilian. If you can, try to observe what's going on through the windows before you go in. You don't want to walk in on an armed robbery if you don't have to." They walked inside. "Number two, always sit as far from the entrance as you can get and never sit with your back to the door. You don't want to repeat Wild Bill Hickok's mistake." Mark pointed to the far corner and led Zack to a table marked reserved near the kitchen door. They sat down, and Zack reached for a menu standing on its edge between the napkin holder and the condiments. "Number three, always scan the room to see who could be a threat."

Shortly, a comely woman in her forties came over with two glasses of ice water and set them on the table. She placed her hand on Mark's shoulder. "Good morning, sweetie." She bent over and kissed him on the lips. "Who's your friend?"

Mark wrapped his arm around her waist. "Hi, babe. This is Zack Goodson. It's his first day on the department. We'll be riding together for a while. Zack, this is my wife, Annie."

She smiled and held out her hand. "I'm pleased to meet you, Zack."

Zack stood up. "I'm pleased to meet you too, Mrs. Langford." He shook her hand.

"Please, sit down and call me Annie. Mrs. Langford sounds like an old lady. What would you like to have?"

"I don't know. What are you having, Mark?"

"I don't know either. I usually eat whatever she puts in front of me. Just like at home."

"I'll have a bacon cheddar cheeseburger, medium well, with fries and a Coke, please." Zack returned the menu to the center of the table.

"You got it." Annie turned for the kitchen.

"I thought Annie was a granny. She's not old enough to have grandkids. You, sure, but not her," Zack joked.

"Funny. She's only two years younger than me. Granny Annie is her grandma. Annie is named after her, and she named the restaurant in her honor. Most of the recipes came from her grandma. Our boys are in high school, so it won't be too long before we see some grandbabies. Back to the lessons. Do you have a spare handcuff key?"

"No," Zack said as he shook his head.

Mark reached behind his back and unsnapped one of his duty belt keepers. He pulled out a handcuff key that was designed to be hidden inside the keeper. "Get one of these. How about a backup pistol?"

"No."

"I carry a Glock 27 on my ankle. It's the compact version of the Glock 22 we carry so our 15-round magazines work with the 27. That way, if your extractor breaks or you have some other malfunction on your 22, you can run all your ammo through your backup pistol. I carry two extra 15-round magazines, so I as sit here, I'm carrying 56 rounds and two pistols. It's cheap insurance. I don't plan to get into a shootout, but if I do, I'm ready. Do you carry a personal flashlight?"

"No."

Mark pulled a small flashlight off his belt. "I carry this SureFire G2X light. It puts out 600 lumens and is only five inches long. How about knives?"

Zack pulled out the folder clipped to his pocket and flipped open its four-inch blade to show Mark.

"That's good, but this would be better." He produced his tactical folder. "This one has a seatbelt cutter and glass breaker on the end. I've used it several times on 10-50s. I also keep a small pen knife in my pocket. I'm sure you've heard two is better than one. Two cops, two guns, two lights, two knives, or two sets of cuffs."

"Is there any chance the Sheriff will pay for any of this?"

"Not likely. He has a hard enough time finding money for cost-of-living raises every year."

"Getting back to the calls we had this morning, is it a common occurrence to find bodies dumped around the county? Are there many murders?" Zack asked.

"We get our fair share, but nothing like St. Louis. They have gang violence and carjackings on top of the drug problem. Most of our violent crime involves the meth labs and an occasional husband or wife killing their spouse. We only have one or two murders a year. Usually less than a hundred assaults, and a lot of them involve a couple of guys drinking too much and going out to the parking lot to duke it out. You'll probably go your whole career without firing a shot."

"What about suicides? Are there that many?"

"No, not a lot. Maybe one a month. But the ones involving men can be really dangerous. Like I said earlier, the vast majority of men tend to use guns to kill themselves, and if you get in the way, they'll take you with them. Sometimes they're too chicken shit to kill themselves, so they go the suicide by cop route. The second-most used method I've seen for men is asphyxiation by carbon monoxide poisoning. Women mostly like to overdose on drugs so they don't disfigure themselves. Sometimes they pop open a bottle of wine to go with their pills."

The kitchen door swung open, and Annie appeared with a tray holding their lunches. She balanced the tray on the edge of the table. "Bacon cheddar cheeseburger, medium well with fries and a Coke for Zack." She placed the plate and glass in front of him.

Zack smiled. "Thanks, Annie. This looks great."

"You're welcome, hon, and roast beef with potatoes and carrots with a chocolate shake for my man." She smiled and left to take care of her other customers.

Zack stared at the huge platter of mouthwatering food in front of Mark and watched him pull the tender roast apart with his fork. "Next time, I'll have what you have."

CHAPTER 6

Mark was slowly cruising through another subdivision smiling and waving at people like he was running for office. Zack sat next to him fighting a food coma when the radio came alive.

"Ten oh five, missing child," Peggy transmitted.

Zack snatched the mic from the radio stack. "Ten oh five." He sat tall in his seat. Now he was wide awake, ready to leap into action. Rescuing kids was one of the reasons he got into law enforcement.

"Ten oh five, four-year-old white male reported missing from 2510 Buck Mountain Road, Doe Run, by his mother, Debra Morton. She was getting ready to take him to day care before going to work when she saw him last."

"Ten oh five, 10-76." He looked at Mark's right hand, expecting him to turn on the emergency lights and siren.

Instead, he cautiously and slowly turned the cruiser around and headed for Doe Run. Mark fought to stifle a yawn.

"Shouldn't we run code?" By code, he meant code three with the light bar and siren activated.

"No. We would if she saw some perv throw him in the back of a panel van, but we'll probably find him in the house. We'll be there in about five minutes."

Zack remained silent, but he was pissed at Mark's blasé attitude. The boy's life could be in danger.

Right on time, Mark turned off Highway 221 onto Buck Mountain Road. "I'll talk to the mother. I want you to go into the house and check everywhere a kid could hide. Put us 23."

"Central, ten oh five, 10-23."

"Ten oh five, 10-23 at 1215," the dispatcher responded.

Mark pulled onto the gravel driveway. As they approached the front door, they could hear a woman calling out for her son, Billy, from the backyard, so they walked around the house. "Hello, ma'am. I'm Deputy Langford, and this is Deputy Goodson. Are you Mrs. Morton?"

"Yes, please help me find my baby!" Tears ran down her face from her red eyes. "I can't find him anywhere!"

"Has Billy ever run off from the house before?" Mark asked.

"No, but he must be out here somewhere. He's not in the house."

"Ma'am, have you seen any strangers in the area recently?" Zack asked. Mark shot him with an overly polite smile that Zack instantly translated into 'shut up, dumbass.'

Mark turned his attention back to the lady. "Is anyone else home?"

"No, my husband is at work."

"Is it alright if Deputy Goodson goes inside just to double-check while I ask you some questions?"

"I already looked in the house."

"Please, ma'am, indulge me."

"Alright! Yes, go ahead! Please, just help me find Billy!" She scanned the area for her son.

Zack quickly hoofed it over to the back door and entered the kitchen. "Billy, are you in here, buddy?" There was no response. He opened the doors under the island and found it full of pots and pans. He checked the pantry and found food. "Billy, your mom's getting worried about you. Where are you?" Still no response. He went to the family room and looked behind and under the furniture. Next, he walked down the hall and turned into the first bedroom. It had a set of bunk beds against the far wall and the floor was littered with toys. "Billy, can I play with some of your toys?" He searched in the closet. It was jam-packed with clothes. He opened a large toy chest and found more toys. "Hey, Billy, can I take some of your toys home with me so my son, Danny, can play with them?" Still no sign of him. He slowly rotated, scanning the room. He saw four brightly colored toy boxes on casters about the size of milk crates lined up under the bed. He got down on his hands and knees and pulled one of the boxes away. He found a little boy holding a teddy bear lying backed up against the wall. The boy started to giggle.

Zack smiled back. "Hey, buddy, I'm Zack. Have you seen Billy under here?" Billy nodded his head as he continued to laugh. "Are you Billy?" The boy laughed and nodded again. "Do you want to come out of there?" Billy shook his head, still laughing. "OK, buddy." He pushed the box back into position. He stood up and pulled the curtain back on the window. He tapped on the glass and motioned for Mark and Mrs. Morton to come inside.

Mrs. Morton rushed into the bedroom, followed by Mark.

Zack smiled and pointed under the bed. "He's playing hide and seek."

Mrs. Morton got down on her knees and pulled a box out of the way. She reached in and grabbed Billy by the arm and dragged him out. She sat on the bed and wrapped him in her arms. She started rocking, mostly to calm herself. "You scared the crap out of me, boy. Why'd you do that?"

Billy shrugged.

"I'm sorry you had to come out here and waste your time. I thought for sure he got out of the house."

"It's alright, Mrs. Morton. We usually find them hiding in the house somewhere. Sometimes they find a good place to hide and then fall asleep. Have a good day. Catch you later, Billy."

They walked back out to the cruiser.

"How'd you know he'd be in the house?"

Mark shrugged. "Thankfully, it just usually works out that way. In this county, it's rare to have a pedophile snatch a kid. Those guys don't have a very long life span around here. Most kids that are taken are actually grabbed by their mom or dad after they lose custody in court. Those Amber Alerts you get on your phone are mostly parents taking their own children. Put us 10-8, NRN, and tell them the boy was found in the house."

"What's NRN?"

"No report needed."

"Central, ten oh five, the boy was located in the house, 10-8, NRN."

"Ten oh five, 10-8, NRN, 1223," Peggy replied.

"Now what?" Zack asked.

"We continue to fight crime by using our most effective tool."

"What's that?"

Mark smiled. "Officer presence. We will patrol our area and deter crime."

"Ten oh five, domestic dispute at 2647 Willow Street in Doe Run. Caller stated her sixteen-year-old daughter is refusing to mind her parents," Peggy transmitted.

Mark busted out laughing. Zack pulled the mic off the radio stack, but Mark grabbed his wrist to keep him from responding until he could compose himself. He slowly recovered and let go of Zack's wrist. "OK, go ahead."

"Ten oh five, 10-76."

"Ten oh five, 10-76 at 1235."

"That's hilarious. This should be good. Try not to laugh in front of them when they're telling their story," Mark said. He tried to stop giggling.

"I'll try," Zack said stone-faced as he observed Mark.

They arrived ten minutes later and were met at the front door by a visibly upset mother. Mark flipped his internal switch and became Mister Professional. "Good afternoon, ma'am. What's the problem today?"

"Our daughter, Mandy, is driving us crazy. She is rude and disrespectful. She refuses to do what she's told. My husband and I are at our wit's end. We don't know what to do. Her disobedience is beginning to influence her little sister." She dabbed a tissue at her eyes.

Mark shook the ink pen in his chest pocket to remind Zack to take notes. "What's your name, ma'am?"

"Nikki Paxton."

Zack wrote it down.

"And your husband's name?" Mark asked.

"Roscoe."

Zack wrote it down.

"Is he here?" Mark asked.

"Yes."

Zack wrote.

"Would you ask him to join us?"

She walked past the stairs and opened the basement door. "Roscoe, the deputies want to talk to you." She rejoined Mark and Zack. "He's embarrassed that we had to call you."

The man climbed the creaky wooden stairs and offered his hand to Mark and then Zack. "Thanks for coming," he said.

"When did Mandy start misbehaving?" Mark asked.

"About a month ago after her sixteenth birthday. We bought her a used Ford Escape so she could drive herself to school this year and help us with her little sister. Now she hops in the car and runs around at all hours. Her friends call her day and night to give them rides. She doesn't do her chores anymore," Mrs. Paxton said.

Mark was confused. "Why don't you discipline her?"

"She said if we touch her, she'll call the child abuse hotline on us," Mr. Paxton said.

"When she was little, did you ever spank her for disobeying you?" Mark asked.

They shook their heads.

"Why not?" Mark asked.

"My wife wouldn't allow it," Mr. Paxton said.

She gave him an icy look and turned to Mark. "It stunts a child's creativity and free spirit if you strike them," Mrs. Paxton said.

"I completely disagree with you, but that's a discussion for another day. I assume you called us because you want us to help you straighten out your daughter," Mark said.

They nodded.

"Is Mandy home now?"

They nodded again. "She's up in her room," Mrs. Paxton said.

"Would you tell her to come down here, please?"

"She won't come down. She refuses to open her door," Mrs. Paxton replied.

"Sir, would you get me a flat-head screwdriver and a hammer? Ma'am, can you take us to Mandy's room?" Mark and Zack followed her upstairs to Mandy's bedroom. Mark knocked on the door. "Mandy, this is Deputy Langford and Deputy Goodson. Your parents called us because they are very concerned about your recent behavior. Open the door so we can talk to you."

"Fuck off! Leave me alone!" she yelled through the locked door.

Mark turned to Mrs. Paxton and pointed at the knob. "Ma'am, this is a privacy lock. You can put a penny in that little slot like this and unlock it." He demonstrated and opened the door.

Mandy screamed at the top of her lungs, "Get out! Get out of my room now!"

Mr. Paxton arrived and gave the screwdriver and hammer to Mark. "Thank you, sir. Zack, hold the door steady for me." Mark tapped the pins out of the hinges and the door came loose. "Just lean it against the wall out there in the hall. We can take it down to the basement on the way out." Mark strolled in and scanned the room. "C'mon in, everybody. This is a very nice room, Mandy. You have a TV, an Xbox, a laptop, a cellphone. The only thing missing is a mini fridge. Where'd you get all of this stuff?"

She sat silently on her bed scowling.

"Did you buy all of this for her?"

"Every bit of it," Mr. Paxton replied.

"Well, let me explain the law to you. You are her parents, and you are responsible for her well-being while she's a juvenile. You have to feed her, clothe her, and provide a roof over her head. Other than that, you have a lot of options. You can take everything out of this room and leave her a mattress on the floor in the corner, or you could move her in with her little sister. She has no right to privacy while she is a child in your house. You can take away her cellphone, her laptop, her TV, and her car. Instead of designer clothes, you can buy her the cheapest clothes and shoes you can find at Walmart or Goodwill. You can tell her what to do, and if she doesn't do it, you can force her."

"I'll report you to the state if you touch me," Mandy said hatefully to her parents.

"Sis, see this badge? I am the State of Missouri's duly sworn representative. If your parents want to bend you over and spank your fanny, I'll watch them do it, and if they get close to the line, I'll tell them to dial it back a bit."

All 5'2" of holy terror jumped off her bed and kicked Mark in the shin. He displayed no pain and instead grabbed her by the collar of her blue jean jacket with one hand and raised her feet off the ground.

He looked her eye to eye. "Have you ever been to the Juvenile Detention Center? That's what it says on the building, but it's really a jail. They've got girls in there twice as big as you and a whole lot meaner. They don't kick people in the shin. They grab a big handful of hair with one hand and start punching you in the face with the other." Mandy's eyes went wide in horror, and she started crying. He sat her back down on her bed.

Mark turned to her parents. "If she were mine, I'd ground her right now for a month. I'd put that door in the basement and take the car keys away from her. If her attitude doesn't improve, I'd take her phone and laptop next. If she doesn't straighten out, I'd keep taking things away from her until she's left with her mattress in the corner. Then, I'd sell that car, and when school starts, I'd make her take the bus back and forth. Do you want us to carry the door downstairs?"

"Yes, thank you," Mrs. Paxton said.

"Can we talk to you downstairs?" Mark asked the couple. He and Zack carried the door down to the basement, and then they all walked outside to the cruiser. Mark leaned on the hood and crossed his arms.

"If you want to turn her around, the two of you have to present a united front. Be firm but fair with her. Reward good behavior and immediately punish bad behavior. She's a smart girl. She'll figure out pretty quick who makes the rules."

Mr. Paxton held out his hand. "Thank you. With the world changing the way it is, I was afraid I'd get locked up for disciplining her."

Mark shook his hand. "That might happen somewhere like New York City, but not out here in God's country. We still expect parents to control their children. Good luck to you. C'mon, Zack." They backed out of the driveway.

"You know, if they had spanked that little girl when she was three years old, today she'd be a respectful, responsible young lady."

"Is the Juvenile Center really that bad?"

"No. They only have eleven beds so they can't have too many hardened criminals in there at one time," Mark said with a grin.

CHAPTER 7

Zack parked his truck in the garage and entered the kitchen. It was only 1430. Patty wouldn't be home with Danny for three hours. He went upstairs to the bedroom and removed his gun belt. He rolled it up and put it on the shelf in his closet. He stripped off his sweaty uniform. The department only issued him three, and he used two of them today. He thought about ordering a few more but still wasn't sure if he was going to stay on in the department. He thought about the first day of his fledgling law enforcement career. He didn't arrest a bank robber or drug kingpin; instead, he found a young woman face down in a muddy creek with buzzards feasting on her. Then he saw a guy lying dead with a hole big enough to put a fist through in the side of his head. Even the missing kid wasn't really missing.

He changed into his running clothes. He always felt better after he went for a run. Probably because he had just stopped running. After he put his uniforms in the washing machine, he went for a three-mile run through the neighborhood. It was his habit to run three times a week. On alternate days, he hit the weights and pull-up bar in the basement. He still maintained a perfect score on the Marine Physical Fitness Test. At thirty-three, he was in superb condition. He completed his run in just under eighteen minutes, even with June's heat and humidity. Despite the insane number of miles he had run in his life, it never seemed to get any easier. He stepped up onto his wide front porch and saw a UPS package in front of the screen door. He sat down on the porch swing under the fan and watched traffic go by on West Columbia Street while he recovered. He returned the waves of all the strangers driving by. This certainly was a friendly town.

After cooling down, he grabbed the package and went inside. He put it on the kitchen island and went to take a shower. Ten minutes later, he put on a gray Cardinals T-shirt and red gym shorts and went to the kitchen to find something to make for dinner. Patty had left ground chuck in the refrigerator to thaw. She had staged a jar of pasta sauce, a box of spaghetti noodles, and a loaf of Italian bread on the counter next to the stove before she left for work. He could get dinner ready before she got home and still have time to check the internet for news on the Marine Corps.

He had been off active duty for nine months, but he maintained his subscriptions to *Leatherneck Magazine* and the *Marine Corps Gazette*. He still thought of himself as a Marine. The transition to civilian life was more difficult than he thought it would be. He searched the internet for information on the massive "K" model CH-53 heavy-lift helicopter that was planned to replace the "E" model he had flown. Development and testing were taking longer than expected. The cost per helicopter had ballooned to over $130 million. He would've loved to have flown that monster. To take his mind off his troubles, he checked the Cardinals website.

They were in Pittsburgh, so the game would start a little after 1800. He could watch the whole game and still get around seven hours of sleep.

Zack nodded off in front of the evening news and was sound asleep when his wife came home. He heard her open the kitchen door from the garage. He got up from his recliner and went to greet her. "Hey, babe," he said as he kissed her and took Danny from her. He held him up over his head and entertained him with funny faces for a moment. "Hey, big boy. Did you have fun at Grandma's today? Do you want spaghetti for dinner?"

"Yay, schetti," Danny replied as Zack gave him a zerbert on his belly.

"How was your day?" he asked Patty as she washed her hands in the sink.

"OK. I guess it was better than yours. I heard you found a body today." She pulled plates out of the cabinet for dinner.

Danny was kicking to go play so Zack let him down. "Actually, it was two bodies. We found a woman in a creek and a man committed suicide in his bedroom. How did you hear about it?" He went to the refrigerator and pulled out the salad he had put together and took it to the table.

"It's a small town. The coroner notified Dr. Patel he would be bringing a body to the hospital for autopsy. He told him Deputy

Langford and Deputy Goodson found the body in a creek. Dr. Patel told me."

"We found the young woman face down in Middlebrook Creek in Iron Mountain. She had been there long enough for the scavengers to begin working on her face. I almost threw up when we rolled her over." He brought the spaghetti over to the table. "My training officer, Mark Langford, figured it might be drug related, since meth is so prevalent in the county."

Patty picked Danny up off the floor and put him in his chair. "What do you think?"

"I don't know. It was only my first day. Mark's been a deputy for over twenty years. He's pretty sharp. Making the right decisions just seems to come easy for him. He's probably right, but seeing her dumped face down in the creek like that seemed real personal to me. Like the killer wanted to disfigure her or else wanted to make IDing her difficult, but at the same time, he carried her about 300 yards up a creek in the woods so she wouldn't be found anytime soon. The only reason we found her was because a lady nearby owns a retired police dog that smelled the body decomposing.

"The girl wasn't big but still had to weigh around 130 pounds. The guy who carried her through the woods had to be in terrific physical condition. Mark and I had a hard time just walking through the dense undergrowth in broad daylight. I'd think a pissed-off drug dealer would just dump her in the ditch along a deserted stretch of gravel road."

"Why did the man kill himself?"

"He was a used car salesman who was about to go into alcohol rehab for the fourth time. I don't think he was getting along with his wife. They were living in a crappy little apartment in Knob Lick. I think he just gave up on living. We did have one call that had a happy ending. A lady reported her four-year-old boy missing from the house. When we got there, she was in the backyard yelling his name. She was panicked. I was ready to call out the National Guard to look for him, but Mark insisted we start by looking in the house. So, he sent me inside to look for him while he talked to the mother. Sure enough, he was hiding under his bed behind a bunch of toys. He thought it was really funny, but he scared the shit out of his mom. Mark was right again. It's a hard job, but he makes it look easy."

Patty hung a bib around Danny's neck. "OK, enough talk about work. Let's eat."

"Sounds good to me. How about you, Buddy?" He tickled Danny. "Oh, I forgot. That package on the island came for you today."

Patty pulled a paring knife from the drawer. "Good, I've been expecting it." She cut the box open and passed the inner box to Zack.

He examined the box. "Why do we need another clock radio?"

"It's also a high-definition nanny cam. Eventually, we'll want to leave Danny home with a babysitter so we can go out alone. I want to be able to check up on what's going on while we're gone. With this one, we can dial in from our phones and see and hear what's happening at home. It even has night vision."

Zack took a closer look to see if he could spot the camera lens in the picture. "That's cool. Maybe we should get one for his room and one for down here."

CHAPTER 8

Nico"Nick" Pagano had just landed at Farmington Regional Airport in his company's Gulfstream G550. He slept most of the way home from London except for a brief stop at St. Louis Lambert International Airport to go through Customs. He was growing tired of the constant international travel required from him as the CEO of his international security company, a company he had started at his kitchen table. Since the towers came down on 9/11, his small security firm had grown into a multibillion-dollar enterprise. He was considering retiring and letting the board pick another CEO. The company had already ruined his marriage.

The plane rolled to a stop, and he quickly transferred to the back seat of one of his black armored Cadillac Escalades. He picked up the latest edition of the local newspaper, the *Daily Journal*, and started reading as his driver exited the airport and drove northbound on Highway 67. Two additional bodyguards sat with him in his SUV, and another four were in an identical Escalade three car lengths to their front. Being a retired police chief, he always went to the crime section of the paper first. The main story said Sheriff Blair was running unopposed for his sixth four-year term. Pagano figured if his company hadn't taken off after 9/11, he'd be the sheriff now. His cellphone rang. "Hello."

"Hi, Mr. Pagano, this is Lindsay Miller." Lindsay was one of his daughter's roommates.

"Hi, Lindsay, what's up?"

"Well, we haven't seen or heard from Hope in three days, and we're getting worried about her. Do you know where she is?"

He put the paper down. "No. I haven't talked to her in about a week. I've been out of the country. I guess you called her cellphone?" He was concerned. He had been divorced for a year, and Hope was his only child.

"Yeah, but it goes right to voice mail. She's never been gone this long before."

"Are you guys home now?"

"Yes."

"OK, I'm coming to talk to you before I go to the police. Thanks for telling me." He hung up and dialed Hope's cellphone. Like Lindsay said, it went straight to voice mail. He was immediately filled with dread. After the divorce, his wife took her huge settlement and moved to Palm Beach. The divorce wasn't his idea, but Hope blamed him, and their relationship had been strained ever since. He only saw her once or twice a month for holidays and other special occasions like their birthdays. He should have used some of the vast resources available to him to keep better track of her. Over the years, his little security company had grown into a multinational private military and intelligence corporation operating on four continents. Hope wanted to be independent and asked him to give her space. Now he wished he had had one of his guys at least put trackers on her phone and car. "Change of plans, Jesse. Take me to my daughter's house."

Jesse, the leader of his security detail, sat next to him. "Yes, sir." He keyed the microphone in his sleeve and transmitted to the lead vehicle, "Change of plans. Take us to Hope's house."

Fifteen minutes later, Nick arrived at the house Hope rented with her best friends forever, Krista Snyder and Lindsay Miller. His men waited outside as he hurried up the stairs to the porch. Krista opened the door and invited him in.

Pagano began questioning them right away. "You girls have been friends since the fifth grade. Have the three of you been getting along lately, or have you been fighting?"

"No, Mr. Pagano, we've been getting along great, but for the last month or so, Hope's been staying out overnight a lot. Sometimes two days in a row, but she always answers her phone. We think she has a new boyfriend, but it's a big secret. She wouldn't tell us anything about him," Krista said.

"How about you, Lindsay? Has Hope said anything that would give you a clue who she's seeing?"

"No, she's really enjoying keeping us in the dark. We ask her constantly, but she won't say. Every day we ride to class with her, and then we work some evenings and weekends at Colton's. I've never seen her talking or hanging around with anyone new, but when he calls, she goes to another room so we can't hear what's said."

"OK, I'm going to the police station to file a report. One of the Desloge officers will probably be coming to see you. Thanks again for calling me." He closed the door. He hustled down the stairs and climbed in the open rear passenger side door of his vehicle. Jesse closed the door and got in. "My daughter's missing. Take me to Desloge PD."

"Sir, do you want us to find her?"

"No. Apparently she has a new boyfriend. They're probably off somewhere having a good time for a few days. I'll have the police put a want out on her and her car."

CHAPTER 9

DAY 5, TUESDAY, JUNE 9

Zack pulled his gray Ram 1500 4x4 truck into the employee parking lot next to the station and parked at the end of the line of deputies' personal vehicles. He hopped down from the cab and reached for the sky to stretch his stiff body before heading for the back door.

"Hey, Zack! Come here a minute!" Mark yelled from his SUV halfway down the row.

Zack walked over as Mark climbed out of his six-year-old Suburban. "Good morning. What's up?"

"Here, take this." Mark handed him a box of donuts from Granny Annie's.

"Is this another new-guy gag?

"Well, sort of. I was supposed to tell you yesterday to bring in donuts for roll call and I forgot. When you bring them in, they'll all call you a brownnoser, but if you show up empty-handed, it'll be a lot worse."

Zack carried the donuts inside and set them on the table in front of Lieutenant McLeod without a word and sat down at the first row of tables like a new deputy was expected to do. There was a pecking order of sorts. New deputies sat up front, experienced deputies sat in the back, and the old-timers sat wherever they wanted.

"Well, thank you very much, Zack. This is a pleasant surprise. You're a good man. These donuts look wonderful. Have I ever told you you're my favorite?" McLeod said with a smile right before he stuffed half of a chocolate-covered long john in his mouth. Frosting dangled from his bushy brown mustache.

Deputy Bob Wainwright got up from his chair in the back of the room and hurried to the lieutenant's table in front of the rush of deputies to grab a donut before all the good ones were gone. He grabbed a sugar-coated raspberry jelly donut and took a big bite. On the way back to his seat, he slapped Zack on the shoulder. "Thanks a lot, kiss ass." He didn't notice the giant glob of jelly creeping slowly down the front of his shirt like lava. The red stain contrasted sharply with his tan shirt, a bold fashion statement.

Deputy Kurt Sada pointed at the stain and faked a frown. "C'mon, Bob, the least you could do is wear a clean shirt to work."

In less than a minute, the box was empty. McLeod said, "Alright, everybody, listen up so Sergeant Krote can brief us before you all go into a sugar coma."

"Thank you, sir. Last night at approximately 2200, a man named Rodney Ernold hobbled into the Parkland ER bleeding severely from his groin. He used a dish towel in an unsuccessful

73

attempt to staunch the flow. He had lost a considerable amount of blood. The doctor advised the man's penis had been bitten and was partially severed."

A chorus of uncomfortable groans interspersed with a few "fuck"s and "damn"s filled the room as the men squirmed in their seats. The two female deputies snickered.

Krote continued, "At approximately 2230, a woman named Lynette Cook called 911 and reported she had been assaulted and was bleeding from her head. Deputy Nickmeier and a county ambulance responded to her house and brought her to the ER. The doctor advised she had numerous small puncture wounds in rows of four to her scalp. The wounds were scattered randomly about the top of her head. She also had blood in and around her mouth but no wounds to her mouth. I'll let Clint explain from here."

Clint cleared his throat and said, "Yeah, uhhh, so when we got to the ER, the doctor told me about the guy, Ernold, who had been bitten, so I asked Ernold what had happened to him. He said he had been on a date with a young lady; it was their second date. He had taken her to dinner at the Shogun Steak House, and things went very well. After dinner, she asked him if he would like to come back to her house for dessert. He agreed, and after they got there, she led him to the kitchen table and served him a slice of homemade apple pie with a scoop of ice cream."

"What flavor?" Deputy Wainwright interrupted.

Nickmeier looked back at Wainwright and said, "What?"

"What flavor was the ice cream?"

"Ummm, it was vanilla," Nickmeier answered dismissively and then faced the others to continue his story.

"Thanks," Wainwright said with a smile.

Nickmeier looked at him again and then faced front. "So, uhhh, anyway, Ernold said the pie was really good and he told her so. She thanked him and slid off her chair down to the floor between his legs and began rubbing him through his trousers.

"Rubbing what?" Wainwright asked.

Nickmeier turned around. "What?"

"What was she rubbing?" Wainwright asked.

"She was, uhhh, rubbing his crotch." Nickmeier turned back around.

"Thanks."

Nickmeier regarded Wainwright again and then faced front. "Ummm, so, he quickly became aroused and she, uhhh, undid his belt and trousers and pulled his junk out."

"Pulled what out?"

Nickmeier looked at Wainwright, but before he could summons some words, McLeod said, "Shut up, Bob!" from the front of the room. "Go ahead, Clint."

Nickmeier turned back around. "Yes, sir. So, uhhh, she went down on him as he was finishing the ice cream, and everything was going great, but just as he was about to, ummm, spurt, she bit down on him and went crazy. She started shaking her head back and forth like a rabid animal. He squeezed her head between his legs and tried to pry her jaws apart, but she didn't budge. He said the pain was excruciating, and he was afraid she would bite it off, so he grabbed his fork and started stabbing her on the top of her head. Finally, she passed out and released him. He grabbed the dish towel off the table, waddled to his car, and drove to the ER.

"Uhhh, when Miss Cook woke up, I talked to her, and her story matched his except all she remembers is going down on him and then waking up on the floor with her head bleeding profusely. She called 911 and passed out again. It turns out she has epilepsy that's usually controlled with medication, but she still has seizures on rare occasions. By the time I left the ER, they were both alert and talking to each other. No one wanted to press charges."

As the laughter subsided, Wainwright said, "Ole Rod will have to change his name to John Wayne Ernold."

Kurt said, "More like Stubby Ernold. I guess next time he'll ask his date to submit a medical history form."

"Did you want us, Sheriff?" Mark asked from the office doorway. Zack was standing behind him.

"Yeah, come in, boys. Have a seat. How was your first day, Zack?"

"I guess I would say eventful."

"I bet. Usually a new deputy doesn't see that much excitement in months. I called you in because we might have an ID on the body you found yesterday. Last night, Nick Pagano got a call from his daughter Hope's roommates, Krista Snyder and Lindsay Miller. They told him they hadn't seen her in three days. They said it wasn't the first time she had disappeared for a while, but never for that long. Pagano went over to the house they rent and talked to them and then reported her missing with the Desloge PD. Jimbo heard about our DB and called me a few minutes ago. Here's a copy of the report." He handed it over. "We pulled her driver's license photo, and it could be a match, but with the damage to her face, we can't be sure."

"What about the prints?" Mark asked.

Before Blair could answer, the jailer, Barry, stuck his head in the door. "Mornin', you hook-nosed motherfucker." He showed his snaggletoothed grin then walked away laughing.

Blair grinned and yelled back, "Fuck you too, Barry! You're fired, you old bastard!"

They heard Barry cackle as he shuffled down the hall.

"Where was I? Denny printed her over at Koplin's, but they weren't on file. I'd send him since it's his case, but he won't be in until around nine and I don't want Pagano to hear about the DB from somebody outside the department. I want you guys to go talk to him and take him over to Parkland to view the body."

"OK, Boss, we're on it. C'mon, Zack." They rose and headed for the door.

Zack waited until they got to the parking lot before he asked, "What's the deal with Barry and the Sheriff? They don't get along?"

"No, just the opposite. Barry was a crusty old fuck when Blair got here. He showed Blair the ropes when he was a rookie. He wears nine of those five-year stars on his shirt, and he knows where all the bodies are buried. Now he's like our crazy old uncle we keep locked up in the attic."

"I'm surprised he hasn't been forced to retire."

"If the Sheriff was going to do that, he would have done it when Barry popped off a round in the locker room."

"What? How did that happen?"

"Back in the old days, we wore our duty belts threaded through large belt loops in our trousers. They looked sharp and you didn't need to wear belt keepers, but if you needed to take a dump, your leather gear wound up getting scuffed up on the floor. Barry was allowed to keep carrying his .357 magnum revolver when the rest of us switched to the Glocks. One morning during shift change, he went to the locker room to take a dump. He dropped his trousers, but he didn't want his gun and holster to slide around on the floor, so he hung the revolver by the trigger guard from the coat hook on the stall door.

"He sat down and went about his business. Somehow the little door bolt gave way and the door swung open. Barry stood up over the toilet holding his trousers with his left hand and grabbed the barrel of his gun with his right to pull the door closed. He accidentally pulled the trigger, and the round zipped past his head and through the wall into the ladies' locker room. One of the clerks, Miss Francine, was standing at the sinks adjusting her makeup when the mirror exploded. She screamed for her life, and everybody at shift change came flooding into the locker rooms. Barry was in the stall on the toilet with gun smoke swirling around his head, and Miss Francine had lipstick running from her mouth to her ear. After that, the Sheriff had gun lockers installed outside the locker rooms. Some smart ass added a wooden plaque above ours that says, 'Barry Lutz Memorial Gun Locker.'"

After Zack stopped laughing, he said, "You acted like you know Pagano. Is he a big deal?"

Mark leaned against the hood of their explorer. "Have you heard of Iron Mountain International?"

"Sure, IMI, it's a huge paramilitary contractor with a ton of government contracts. They have that big training facility east of Iron Mountain where we found the body."

"Well, Nick Pagano is the founder and CEO. He started IMI over twenty years ago when he was the chief of the Farmington Police Department. Back then, it was a tiny company offering security guards and alarm systems mostly to the mining companies when they were having union problems. His employees were all off-duty cops and deputies. I worked part-time for him for a few years myself. After 9/11, he started applying for government contracts. He got one after another. Five years later, he had offices on four continents and employed thousands of people working in places like Iraq, Afghanistan, and East Africa. He has a cattle ranch with hundreds of acres east of Bonne Terre on Highway D. We'll head over there and see if he's home." Mark pushed off the hood and headed for his door.

"If Pagano's a VIP, why isn't the Sheriff going to see him?"

"Back in the late nineties when Pagano was the Farmington chief, he and Blair got into a fight over jurisdiction on a case on the edge of the city. I mean a real fight—they were throwing punches and rolling around on the ground. Blair came away with a broken nose, and Pagano lost two of his molars," Mark said with a smile. "They haven't seen eye to eye since."

Zack laughed. "What was the case about?"

Mark shrugged. "I don't remember."

"What about Jimbo? Who's he?"

"Jimbo is the Sheriff's brother, James Blair. He's chief of the Desloge Police Department." Mark started the car and drove off.

"Why do you think Pagano will be home?"

"Because its 0615, and he has more money than God. He doesn't have to set his alarm to be at work on time. When he does go to work, he'll probably be picked up by one of his helicopters. Hey, did you eat before you came in?"

"No."

"We'll roll through Burger King on the way. It'll be hours before we get another chance to eat."

Mark turned off of Highway D and rolled to a stop 100 feet up the two-lane asphalt driveway at the large air-conditioned guard shack. He looked at the heavily tinted bulletproof glass but couldn't see inside. "That guard shack's bigger than my first apartment," he quipped.

A minute later, a guard wearing a black IMI polo shirt under his plate carrier and khaki cargo pants emerged from the shack and approached the car. He smiled broadly as he repositioned his Oakley sunglasses to the top of his head. He held his M4 at low ready. "Good morning, gentlemen. What can I do for you?"

"Good morning. I'm Mark Langford and this is Zack Goodson." Mark motioned to Zack.

Zack saw the Eagle, Globe, and Anchor tattoo on the guard's left forearm. "Semper Fi."

The man leaned over and eyeballed Zack. "Who were you with?"

Zack smiled. "HMH-361 Flying Tigers."

"No shit! You guys saved our asses outside of FOB Delaram. I'm Jeremy Soto."

"Hi, Jeremy. Good to meet you. We're here to talk to Mr. Pagano about his daughter, Hope."

Before Jeremy could respond, his radio came to life. A voice said, "Send them up, Jeremy."

He activated the remote attached to the ammo pouch on his plate carrier then keyed his radio mic. "Aye, sir."

The heavy metal gate parted in the middle, and Jeremy waved them through. A quarter of a mile further up the driveway, it ended at a circle at the top of the rise. Mark and Zack walked to the twelve-foot-high arched entrance. Pagano was standing in the open doorway.

"Sir, I'm Mark Langford and this is Zack Goodson." Mark held his hand out to Pagano.

Pagano shook his hand and then Zack's. "I remember you, Mark. Pleased to meet you, Zack. Do you have information about my daughter?"

Mark nodded with an uncomfortable look on his face. "Sir, there's no good way to say this. We have a body at Parkland that we need you to view. No ID was found with it."

Pagano's face saddened and he looked to the sky. "I was afraid you had bad news. How bad is it? You could probably ID her from her DL photo unless there was damage to her face."

Mark nodded. "We found the body face down in Middlebrook Creek. Can you come with us?"

Pagano shook his head. "I'll have my guys drive me. We'll follow you over." He turned back into the house.

Mark and Zack walked back to their cruiser, and Mark drove it around the circle to the beginning of the straightaway.

"My son Danny's only two years old. I can't image the pain I would feel if something happened to him."

"Yeah, it doesn't matter how old they are. You never stop worrying about them." Mark turned up the volume on his favorite country station.

Ten minutes later, two black up-armored Cadillac Escalades came from around the house and drove up behind them. As Mark started rolling forward, Jeremy opened the gate.

Zack gave him a thumbs-up as they drove by. "If we got into a big shootout, do you think Pagano's detail would help us?"

"Hell no. They'd use those up-armored SUVs to push our cruiser out of the way and go about their business. They might call 911 for us if they weren't too busy."

Zack chuckled. "Yeah, that's what I figured."

CHAPTER 10

N ick Pagano stood silently before a stainless-steel table in the small morgue under Parkland Hospital. Two of his bodyguards stood behind him, one on each side. Mark and Zack stood off to the side.

The pathologist, Dr. Patel, said, "I am terribly sorry to put you through this, Mr. Pagano, but this young woman's face was disfigured before she was found. She was also pregnant. Do you know if your daughter is pregnant?"

Pagano couldn't take his eyes off the sheet. He shook his head. "If she was, she didn't say anything."

"Does your daughter have any scars or identifying marks on her arms or legs you would recognize?"

Pagano swallowed hard. "Hope has a small triangular scar a couple of inches above the back of her left wrist."

Dr. Patel solemnly pulled the sheet away from the body's left side, exposing its left wrist.

Pagano saw the triangular scar and reached for the cold gray hand. Tears filled his eyes and his face reddened as he lowered his head. He sobbed openly as his knees sagged. His men grabbed his arms to hold him up. He stiffened and jerked his arms free. He looked at Mark. "Who did this? Tell me! Tell me who did it!"

"I'm sorry for your loss, sir. We don't have any suspects yet, but now we know where to focus our investigation. Lieutenant Close is in charge of the investigation. He'll be in contact with you. Gentlemen, please, take Mr. Pagano back home."

Mark waited for Pagano and his men to leave the room before he turned to the pathologist. "Dr. Patel, do you have the cause of death yet?"

"No, Deputy Langford, but based on the injection mark in her right arm, I suspect it was a drug overdose of some sort, although I didn't find any evidence of prior drug abuse. I won't get the toxicology results back for a day or two. I can confirm she was dead when she was put in the creek. There was no water in her lungs."

"What about the damage to her face?" Mark asked.

"She was badly beaten, but I don't think it was enough to kill her," Patel replied.

"What about the marks on her face and wrists, Doc?" Zack asked.

"The ligatures weren't with the body when I received it, but I suspect her mouth was covered with duct tape. There was a small amount of adhesive on the undamaged side of her face between her mouth and right ear. I did recover a three-inch length of red cotton string stuck between her teeth, possibly from a sock or rag. The wrist marks look like they were made by some sort of electric cord."

"The ligatures weren't on the body when Zack and I found it in the creek either. OK, thanks, Doctor. Oh, uh, how far along was she?"

"About four weeks."

"Thanks, Doctor. C'mon, Zack. Let's go talk to the Sheriff."

Pagano's entourage drove around his house to the garage and parked the Escalades. He just sat there for a few minutes thinking before he turned to Jesse. "I need some time to myself. I want you to talk to the Board of Directors for me. Have them pass control of the company to the president until I'm ready to come back to work. I don't want a hundred people calling me to express their sorrow. I want you to send the boys and domestic staff home. I don't want any staff in the house or on the farm except the front gate. Keep it manned so they can turn away anyone who shows up to see me. I don't want to be disturbed by anyone. I'll call you when I'm ready to go back out."

"Understood, sir. We'll stand by at home. I'm really sorry. Please, call me if you need anything at all," Jesse replied.

Pagano nodded and walked into the house.

"You got a minute, Sheriff?" Mark asked.

"Sure, come on in. Did you find out anything?"

Mark and Zack entered the office and sat down in front of the sheriff's desk. Blair was cleaning his AR-15. The air smelled of solvent. The rear pin was pulled, and the bolt carrier group sat on a red shop towel on top of the desk blotter.

"Pagano ID'd the body as his daughter, Hope. He took it really hard."

The sheriff sighed. "I'm not surprised. He's living out there in that huge house all by himself. His wife, Carol, divorced him a year ago and left town, then Hope moved out after she finished high school. She blamed her dad for her mom leaving," Blair said as he fed a bore snake through the barrel and pulled it out through the muzzle.

"How do you know so much about what's going on with him? Have you guys been talking?" Mark asked.

"Hell no! He's still an arrogant asshole, but we have some of the same friends and word gets around." Blair held the rifle up to the light and looked through the barrel. Satisfied, he slid the bolt carrier group into the upper receiver and slammed it shut. He pushed the rear pin back in and leaned the rifle against the cabinet behind his desk.

"Is it alright if we go talk to Hope's roommates? I know it's Clouseau's case, but it'll be good training for Zack."

Blair nodded. "And you want to play detective some more. OK, go ahead. If Denny complains, I'll tell him I sent you over to make notification to the roommates before they hear it from somebody else."

"Thanks, Boss." He and Zack got up to leave. They walked outside and climbed into their cruiser. "Put us 10-8." Mark started the cruiser.

"Central, ten oh five, 10-8."

Mark and Zack pulled out of the station parking lot and turned left on Doubet Road headed for Highway 67.

"Yesterday, Lieutenant McLeod said you were a detective when you worked with Lieutenant Close and just now the Sheriff said you wanted 'to play detective some more.' What happened back then?"

Mark seemed uncomfortable. "I've been a deputy since before Don got elected twenty years ago. Back then, guys like Close, McLeod, and me were all road deputies. After Don became sheriff, one by one we all started moving up. Close became a detective sergeant, and I worked for him as a detective. Back then, the two of us were the Detective Bureau. I worked for him for about eight years. Then he screwed up a couple of times even after I warned him, and we blew the cases in court. Instead of manning up, he blamed me and kicked me back to patrol. Like I told you, he will screw you over in a heartbeat. Never turn your back on him. Working for him was like being locked in a room with a wild animal. As long as you are awake with your back in the corner, you'll be OK, but if you fall asleep, he'll eat you."

CHAPTER 11

Nick Pagano sat down the road from Lindsay and Krista's house in a copse of trees waiting for them to leave for school. He was sitting in a rusted-out fifteen-year-old brown Ford F-150 that he used when doing chores around the farm. Mud conveniently obscured the license plates. After he sent his bodyguards home, only Jeremy Soto stayed to man the front gate to send away any sympathetic friends. When the coast was clear, he changed clothes, got in his truck, and left the farm by the back gate. It was a blind spot without any cameras, but normally he had four men randomly patrolling the fields. He drove to the girls' rental house on the outskirts of Desloge.

As expected, the girls left the house on time and as soon as they were out of sight, he pulled into the gravel driveway and drove around the house so he could park out of sight in case the UPS man pulled up to deliver a package. The house sat on a two-acre lot surrounded by trees. This wasn't his first time entering a house illegally to conduct a search. In the old days when he was a detective with Farmington, they were called black bag jobs. It was a trick local cops learned from Hoover's FBI. If they thought someone was guilty of a crime but didn't have enough evidence to convince a judge to sign a search warrant, they would search houses or offices illegally and look for evidence to confirm their suspicions. Some of the more corrupt cops would even plant evidence.

He put on a pair of latex gloves as he exited the truck and climbed the stairs. The back door was locked. He looked under the mat for a key, but there was none. He checked the window next to the door and saw it was not locked. He popped the screen loose and slid the window open. He stuck is arm inside and unlocked the door. He put the screen back in place and stepped inside and closed the window. He walked through the kitchen, across the front room, and straight into Hope's bedroom. He found her cellphone under her mattress. It had been turned off. He resisted the urge to search the phone right away. A laptop sat on her dresser next to the door. A row of framed family photos were lined up next to the laptop. They depicted a family in much happier times. He picked up a photo of him holding Hope in his arms when she was three years old. He touched her face and fought the urge to cry. He put the photo down and searched the rest of the room quickly. He was careful to leave everything as he found it, except for the phone and laptop. He was out of the house in less than five minutes.

Mark and Zack were sitting in the Mineral Area College cafeteria. Mark had called and arranged for Hope Pagano's roommates to meet them between their classes. Mark was drinking coffee and Zack a Coke when two young ladies approached them.

They stood up to greet them and Mark said, "Hello, ladies. Are you Lindsay and Krista?"

The taller one said, "Yes, I'm Lindsay and she's Krista."

"I'm Deputy Mark Langford and he's Deputy Zack Goodson."

Zack smiled and said, "Hello."

"Please, have a seat," Mark said. After they dropped their book bags and sat, he and Zack did the same. "It's always hard to do this, but I find it's best to just say it. Hope is dead. Her father identified her body this morning."

The girls immediately leaned over to hug each other and began crying. He waited and watched their reactions. Zack made eye contact with Mark and gave him a "what should we do now?" look. Mark held his hand up in a just stand by gesture. After several minutes, they began to regain their composure.

"I'm sorry for your loss, and I know this is a really awful time, but we need to ask you some questions. Do you know of anyone who would want to harm Hope?"

The girls looked at each other and then Lindsay turned to Mark. "Everyone loved Hope. We've known her since grade school. She was always the most popular girl in our class. She and her old boyfriend, Grant Cunningham, were prom king and queen. Her dad's so rich she could have gone away to college anywhere she wanted, but she stayed here and went to MAC so we could be together. We planned to be nurses and stay here and help our friends and families." Lindsay pulled a couple of paper napkins from the stainless-steel holder in the center of the table and dabbed her eyes.

Krista sniffled as she rubbed Lindsay's back. "Hope was seeing someone, but she refused to tell us who he was. For some reason, it was a big secret. She would be gone overnight two or three times a week, sometimes more than one night."

"Where could they have met? Here at school, or did she have a part-time job?" Zack asked.

"All three of us work at Colton's Steak House as servers. The servers get hit on all the time, but I guess she could have met him here or Colton's. Most of the servers and cooks are taking courses here," Krista said. "What happened to Hope?"

"The cause of death hasn't been determined yet," Mark answered and quickly changed the subject. "Do you know if she knew anybody over around Iron Mountain?"

Both girls shook their heads.

"How long have the three of you lived together?" Mark asked.

"We moved in together about a month before classes started last year, so it was almost a year," Krista said.

"Thank you for meeting with us. Lieutenant Close from our department is leading the investigation and will be contacting you soon. Again, we're sorry for your loss." Mark and Zack stood and left the cafeteria.

They walked back out to the cruiser, which they had left parked in the fire lane next to the building. "What do we do now?" Zack asked.

"You write up what the girls said and we send it to Denny and the Sheriff, then we go back on patrol," Mark replied. "Put us back in service."

"Central, ten oh five, 10-8 with a supplemental report."

"Ten oh five, 10-8, and a call. Assist Highway Patrol with a 10-50 J2 southbound Highway 67 just south of Hefner's Furniture," Peggy replied.

"Ten oh five, 10-76."

Mark flipped on the light bar and siren as he ran the red light on the Highway 32 overpass and accelerated down the ramp onto Highway 67. "This won't be good. Accidents with injuries on the highway can be really bad. Put your gloves on. We'll be there in a couple of minutes."

Moments later, Zack saw the trooper's cruiser on the right shoulder with the front of his vehicle canted to the left to block half of the right traffic lane. An old blue Chevy Silverado was parked in front of the trooper's cruiser. Mark stopped 100 feet back from the cruiser. They got out and approached the scene. They saw the pickup was up on a jack. The trooper was pulling an emergency blanket from the rear of his Explorer.

"Hey, Phil. This is Zack Goodson. Zack, this is Phil Woolsey."

"Hi, Zack, good to meet you." Phil held out his gloved hand.

"Same here, Phil." Zack shook his hand.

"What do you have?" Mark asked.

"The driver's J4."

"He's what?" Zack asked. He didn't remember this ten code.

Woolsey explained to Zack, "He's 10-50 J4 or DRT, dead right there. He's off the shoulder in the grass about fifty feet from the truck. The reporting party said he was driving northbound and saw the man stand up from changing his left front tire and stumble back into the traffic lane. A red Peterbilt hauling a livestock trailer hit him and kept going. I've got Troop E down the highway watching for the truck. The driver's right arm is missing. His shirt sleeve is still there, but I can't find his arm. It may still be stuck in the grill of the truck, but can you guys walk the shoulder and see if you can find it?"

"Sure, no problem," Mark said as they began walking. "Zack, we'll walk the right shoulder for a few hundred yards and then cross over to the center median on the way back."

As they passed the victim, Zack saw the man, probably in his forties, was wearing highly polished cowboy boots, tight blue jeans, and a blue and white long-sleeved cowboy shirt. Like Woolsey said, the right sleeve was empty. His eyes were open, and he had bled from his ears, mouth, and nose.

"Where's his cowboy hat?" Zack asked, half joking.

"I saw it in the truck. He probably wanted to keep it clean," Mark replied.

Zack nodded. "How often does this happen?"

"Fatalities on the highway are pretty common, between drunks and people racing, but having a person struck is rare. Thankfully, the troopers handle most of them."

They heard more sirens approaching and turned to see a red pumper truck from the Leadington Fire Department pull to a stop behind their cruiser to block the right lane of the highway.

"Good, that should slow people down while we're out here," Mark said.

Zack checked his watch and said, "They took their sweet time getting out here."

"That's because they're mostly a volunteer department. They may have only had one or two guys in the station when the call went out, so as soon as they had enough people show up to the station to man the truck, they rolled out. A lot of the small towns in the county rely on volunteer firefighters. Some of the towns have reserve police officers too."

Fifteen minutes later, Mark and Zack made their way back to the scene. "Sorry, Phil, no of sign of the arm."

"Thanks. It's probably still stuck to the truck," Phil replied. "You guys can clear. The fire department's going to stay until I get another car here."

"OK, good luck," Mark said.

"One fifty-three, robbery just occurred at Linda's Laundry, 217 North Washington Street. Suspect fled northbound on Washington in a black Subaru Brat," the dispatcher, Peggy, transmitted.

"One fifty-three, 10-76," the officer replied.

Mark and Zack were patrolling north of Farmington driving south on Highway D when dispatch put out the call. "One fifty-three is a Farmington car, and I'd bet good money the suspect is Chuckie Frazier," Mark said. "He has the only black Subaru Brat that I know of in the county. He lives in a trailer with his mom up near Highway K. Let's pull into the lot at the Old Time Pantry and see if he comes by." Less than a minute later, the Brat zoomed by going at least 20 MPH over the speed limit. "That's Chuckie alright." Mark flipped on the lights and siren and accelerated out of the lot. After half a mile, Mark said, "Chuckie's not stopping. Put us in pursuit."

"Central, ten oh five in pursuit of one fifty-three's robbery suspect northbound Highway D passing Timberfield Drive," Zack transmitted.

"Ten oh five in pursuit on Highway D passing Timberfield Drive," Peggy repeated.

"Ten oh five, the suspect just turned west on Highway O."

Peggy repeated the call to the listening units.

Highway O curved off to the left, but Chuckie continued straight onto Farmer Road rather than trying to make the turn.

Farmer Road ended at Hillsboro Road in a quarter mile, and Chuckie was approaching the intersection too fast.

"He's not going to make it," Mark said as he began slowing down. Chuckie's Brat slid across Hillsboro and slammed to a stop against a large oak tree.

"Ten oh five, suspect is 10-50 J2. Request an ambulance at Hillsboro and Farmer," Zack transmitted. Mark skidded to a stop, and Zack ran to the driver's side of the Brat. Chuckie was bleeding from a cut to his forehead and a badly broken nose.

"Are you OK, Chuckie?" Zack asked.

"Who the fuck are you? I know all of the County Brownies," Chuckie said as he held the hem of his dirty T-shirt to his nose.

"I'm Zack Goodson. I'm new."

Mark walked up and looked over Zack's shoulder. "Damn, Chuckie, that looks bad. Why didn't you stop? You know we all know you drive this piece of shit."

"I have a date tonight. I've been trying to go out with this girl for weeks, and she finally said yes. I figured you could arrest me tomorrow."

"The ambulance is on its way. Just sit still until they get here. It might help if you tilt your head back. Zack, go ahead and read him his rights."

Zack pulled his Miranda card from his breast pocket and read it to Chuckie.

"Chuckie, how's your mom doing?" Mark asked.

"She's good. She's thinking about moving back to Germany."

"What for?"

"After fifteen years of wedded bliss, ole Fred died from liver disease last year. He's the only reason we came to the States. Now that he's gone, she's thinking of moving back to be near her family."

Ten minutes later, while Chuckie was sitting on the gurney in the back of the ambulance wearing a cervical collar and getting his head and nose bandaged, the Farmington officer arrived. Mark and Zack were standing outside the back door.

"Hey, Mark, how've you been?" The officer shook hands with him.

"Pretty good, Orville. Zack, this is Orville Cobb. Orville, this is Zack Goodson."

"Good to meet you, Zack."

"Same here, Orville."

"I see you caught our desperado."

"What did he do?" Mark asked.

"You know Linda's Laundry, right? The front and side walls are all glass. Well, Chuckie rolls up in his piece-of-crap Brat and everyone inside watches him walk into the shop, but he doesn't have any laundry. So, he walks up and down the aisles a couple of times trying to act natural while everybody eyeballs him. On his next pass, he grabs a purse and runs for the side door, but the people know he just pulled up in the Brat out front, so they go out the front door and intercept him. They tell him to hand over the purse, and he reaches behind his back and says he has a gun. They hesitate for a second and then say, 'No, you don't.' Chuckie realizes he's screwed. He throws the purse at them and runs around them to his car and takes off."

"Is the lady who owns the purse pressing charges?" Mark asked.

"Yeah, and the shop owner is pressing charges because Chuckie broke the glass in the side door when he threw it open during his escape."

From inside the ambulance, Chuckie yelled, "Hey, man! That's bullshit! I took the purse, but I didn't break no fucking glass door. That shit's expensive. I ain't paying for that."

"Oh, Orville, FYI, Zack already read him his Miranda rights," Mark said. "How do you want to divvy this up?"

"I'll go with Chuckie to the hospital and then book him. You can write the 10-50. Can you tow the car and put a hold on it, just in case I need it for something? You can add your charges on top of mine."

"OK, sounds good. He's all yours. Zack, call for a hook. You can start on the accident report while we wait." They returned to their cruiser.

"Central, ten oh five, request a 10-51 to our location," Zack transmitted.

"Ten oh five, 10-51, 10-76," Peggy replied.

"The way Chuckie smacked into the tree, I thought he was toast," Zack said.

"Naw, Chuckie's what we call a good shitbum, and you can't kill a good shitbum. He's one of the best. He's like one of those cockroaches you step on and then it runs off when you raise your foot."

Ten minutes later, the red Mailer's tow truck rolled up, and the driver climbed down from the cab. He began preparing the Brat to be dragged up on the flatbed.

"C'mon, I'll introduce you to Tiny."

Zack looked through the windshield at the man. "You gotta be shitting me." Zack laughed. "He's fucking huge." The man was at least 6′3″ and 350 pounds. His jeans hung down under his beer belly.

They approached the driver as he was dragging the chains down the flatbed.

"Hey, Tiny. This is Zack Goodson."

Tiny removed his dirty work glove and shook Zack's hand. "Good to meet you, Zack."

"Good to meet you too, Tiny."

Tiny dragged the chains over to the Brat and got down on his knees to hook the chains on the rear axle. His jeans sagged enough to expose half of his hairy ass. Mark and Zack got a clear view of the moonshot. It was a revolting sight, but they still had difficulty looking away.

"Tiny, how do you like driving for Mailer's?" Mark asked.

"It's not bad, but I don't think I'll be doing this forever."

"Have you ever thought about being a plumber?" Mark asked. He exchanged a smile with Zack.

Tiny stopped what he was doing and stuck his head out from under the car. "Yeah, I have actually. My uncle's a plumber. I thought I might work for him." Then he ducked under the car again.

"I'm telling you, Tiny, from where I'm standing, I think you'd make a hell of a plumber."

"Thanks, Mark."

Zack turned and ran back to the cruiser, trying to mask his laughter. Mark slowly followed him and climbed inside.

"You have an ornery side," Zack said.

Mark just grinned.

A few minutes later, Tiny walked up to Mark's door. "Sign here, Mark."

"Put a hold on it for Orville Cobb at Farmington, OK?" Mark said as he signed it.

"Sure thing. See you later," Tiny said before walking away. He climbed up in the truck cab and drove away.

"I'll find a place to sit so you can write up the interview with the girls."

Five minutes later, they pulled into the parking lot in front of Granny Annie's. Zack looked at Mark with a big grin.

"What? You can write while you eat, can't you?"

CHAPTER 12

Pagano drove back home the way he came, straight to his back gate. He slipped into the house and went to his office to search the phone and laptop. He opened the laptop and found it password protected. He quickly gave up on guessing correctly. He had better luck with the cellphone. Hope used the month and day of her birthday as her pin number just as she had in high school when she was on his family plan. He tapped the message icon, and the first thing he saw was a message string between Hope and Randy Powers.

"Motherfucker!" he yelled. He was flummoxed. Randy Powers was a retired Special Forces master sergeant who worked for him as an instructor at Iron Mountain. He had to be at least forty years old. He was old enough to be her father. "You fucking bastard!" he yelled so hard it hurt his throat. He began reading. The messages soon escalated from flirting to invitations to dinner and movies and then sleeping over at his place. Then he warned her they had to keep their relationship a secret because if her father found out, he would fire him and have some of his boys beat the shit out of him. He told her to stop texting him and delete his number from her phone. He would buy her another phone just for their communications. She promised she would.

Pagano checked the time on the phone. He could still make it if he hurried. He could get to the facility and put eyes on this asshole before he left work. This time he took his Escalade and left through the front gate. Half an hour later, he parked in his parking spot outside his office. He arrived in time to see Powers standing 100 feet away in front of a couple of picnic tables debriefing the Springfield Police Department SWAT team. He was gesticulating wildly, and the cops were laughing. It infuriated Pagano that Powers was having a good time while his daughter and grandchild were on a slab in the morgue, and this was the bastard who killed them. He climbed out of his vehicle and went inside.

"Hello, Nick. I'm so sorry," the receptionist said before he threw his hand up to stop her.

"I'm not here. No visitors," he said before disappearing into his office and closing the door. He sat down behind his computer and looked up Powers's address. He already had his phone number from Hope's phone.

Pagano watched him from his office window. A few minutes later, Powers dismissed his class and climbed into his Jeep and drove away. Pagano hurried to his Escalade and followed him. Powers drove straight to the Bonne Terre VFW Hall. Pagano had learned from the texts that his daughter would frequently meet him at his trailer after the VFW closed. He watched him go inside before driving back to the farm to switch vehicles.

Zack walked through the house from the garage to the front door and opened it to retrieve the mail from the letterbox attached to the wall. He wondered why it was still called a letterbox when letters were so rare anymore. He thumbed through the bills and junk mail and put them on the kitchen island. He went to the bedroom to change from his uniform into his workout clothes. Five minutes later, he was in the basement in his home gym. He flipped on the TV and selected an old *Adam-12* episode from the DVR. He started his workout with three sets of twenty dead hang pull-ups, then three sets of fifty push-ups, followed by three sets of eighty crunches. Now that he was sweating and breathing hard, he went to his weight bench to complete his workout. He banged it out in forty minutes and went back upstairs to sit on the front porch to recover and wave at the cars going by.

The Aurora tone alerted him he had a new text on his iPhone. He looked at the text from his Marine buddy Bruce Anders, callsign Gumby. He was assigned to HMX-1, the president's squadron. Gumby had sent Zack a photo of himself standing in front of the Eiffel Tower with a hot French woman. He always sent a photo when he went someplace interesting with the president. Zack sent his standard response, "Fuck you!" and received the standard reply, a series of laughing emojis.

Gumby was something of a legend in the Flying Tigers. Zack remembered the time he and Gumby flew a CH-53E Super Stallion helicopter to Nellis AFB for the base's annual air show. Gumby was the aircraft commander and was wearing a cross-country name tag on his flight suit with a nom de guerre instead of his real name. It identified him as Major Richard Weed. They stood out in front of their helicopter answering questions and giving people tours of the cockpit and cargo compartment.

An attractive young reporter from one of the local TV news shows came by with her cameraman and asked Major Richard Weed if he would consent to an interview on the air and talk about his helicopter and experiences in the Marine Corps. He agreed and asked her to please call him Dick, so at the beginning of the interview, she introduced him as Major Dick Weed of the United States Marine Corps. She asked her questions, and Dick Weed gave his answers with a straight face. When they returned home to MCAS Miramar from the air show, there was already a copy of the interview in the ready room that had been downloaded off the internet. If he hadn't been christened Gumby years earlier, he would have been stuck with Dick Weed for the rest of his life. Zack always smiled when he thought about that air show. Now he wished he could make more of those memories.

When a horn honked, Zack looked up in time to see a couple in a pickup wave to him as they drove by. He smiled and waved back. *Man, this is a friendly town.*

Three hours later, dinner was over, the dishes were in the machine, and Zack was sitting in his recliner watching the Cardinals play game two of their three-game series with the Pirates in Pittsburgh. Danny was sitting on the rug playing with his toys. Patty sat with her feet up on the sofa reading from her tablet.

"There's an article in the *Journal* that says the body you found was Hope Pagano," Patty said.

"Yeah, we brought Mr. Pagano in to identify her. He took it really hard. That guy's a billionaire, but all that money didn't protect his daughter from a tragic end. You'd think he would have had her better protected," Zack replied. "Afterward, we went to talk to her roommates. They said she had a new boyfriend, but they didn't know who he was."

Patty put her tablet down and stood up. "Well, I know you'll figure it out. Come on, Danny, time for bed," she said as she picked him up off the floor. She kissed Zack and said, "Don't stay up too late."

Just as before, Pagano got in his truck and snuck out the back gate. He drove to Powers's trailer on Rouggly Road. He rolled up the driveway and, not seeing Powers's Jeep, turned around and drove back down the driveway to hide his old truck in the trees.

Pagano had come prepared. His pack included food, water, duct tape, handcuffs, a waist chain, leg irons, flex cuffs, gloves, and two pistols. One was a Glock 23 he built himself from an 80 percent polymer lower using a rotary tool. Therefore, there were no serial numbers to lead law enforcement back to the owner. The second pistol was a silenced .22LR High Standard pistol. He took it from a speeder one night in the late '80s in Farmington when he was a patrolman. The man was passing through town on his way from Chicago to New Orleans. For some unknown reason, he was driving down Highway 67 instead of the faster, more direct route on I-55. The owner said he won the pistol from a Green Beret during a poker game in Vietnam in 1972. Pagano gave him a choice: surrender the pistol or be arrested for having an illegal weapon. Then, of course, he would have to search the car and seize whatever drugs or money that might be secreted inside. The man quickly gave up the pistol, thanked him, and went on his way.

Pagano slowly walked up the curved gravel driveway. He was concealed from the road. He checked for motion sensors and trail cameras. He circled the trailer and checked the metal garden shed. He found the key Powers kept in the shed for Hope under an old coffee can full of nails. He had read about it in one of the texts. He entered the trailer and immediately smelled bleach. He searched the trailer and found a scoped Remington 700 leaning up against the wall behind the bedroom door. Then he saw some of Hope's clothes in the bedroom. His hands trembled as he picked up one of her high school T-shirts from the bed. Then he saw lace panties on the floor next to the bed and started hyperventilating.

He went back to the kitchen table and sat down facing the window. He tried to calm himself. Eventually, the sun went down. He sat there in the dark waiting for hours. He imagined the horrible ways his daughter might have died. The fire in him grew hot again. Around midnight, the stress and emotions of the day caught up to him. He started nodding off. His chin would drop to his chest, then he would jerk awake. He would stand up and pace around for a while before he tired and sat down, fell asleep, and his head dropped again. He was asleep when light coming through the window woke him. He saw headlights approaching slowly from the driveway. He really didn't believe, but he prayed Powers was alone. He didn't want to kill an innocent person. Powers parked next to the trailer. He staggered to the stairs and stumbled on the first step. He went down hard on his left side and smacked his head on the gravel.

"Fuck me," was all he said as he rolled over to his hands and knees. He stood up and fumbled with his keys before he got the door unlocked. He pulled the door open and stepped inside. Before he could flip the light switch, he saw a flash of light and heard a loud crack. He felt an intense burning pain coming from his left thigh as his leg collapsed beneath him and he fell to the floor. He involuntarily yelled out. Pagano flipped the kitchen light on in time to see Powers reaching for the Glock in his waist holster with his bloody right hand. Pagano shot him again, this time in the right forearm near his elbow. Powers screamed again. Pagano kicked him in the head, knocking him unconscious, and took his pistol. He pulled the door closed. Then he collected his spent brass and put them in his pocket.

When Powers woke up, he found himself flex-cuffed to one of his own kitchen chairs. Slowly, his eyes focused, and he saw Pagano sitting across the room from him with the silenced .22. Powers shook his head. "I didn't do it, sir! I swear, I loved her!"

Pagano stood up and stepped forward. He shot him in the other forearm. Powers screamed in pain. Pagano sat back down and patiently waited for him to quiet down. "Why did you kill her? Was it because she was pregnant?"

Powers eyes grew wide. "What?! She was pregnant? I didn't know! You gotta believe me. I loved Hope. I wouldn't hurt her."

Pagano stood up and leaned over him menacingly and exclaimed, "Bullshit! I smelled the bleach as soon as I got in here!"

Powers shook his head. "She was supposed to meet me here when I came home from the VFW, but when I got here, I found her tied to a chair. She was dead, but I didn't kill her. I loved her. I had no reason to hurt her."

"She was half your age, and she was pregnant! You would've lost your job and been stuck paying child support for a kid you didn't want! So, you killed her and dumped her in that damned creek!"

"Sir, I admit I put her in the creek, and I cleaned up the blood on the floor, but I didn't hurt her. Please, you have to believe me. I've done some shitty things in my life, but I didn't hurt her."

Pagano took several deep breaths and said calmly, "Why was there blood on the floor?"

"Whoever killed her smacked her around first. I'm sorry for what happened, but it wasn't me. Some fucker set me up!"

Pagano was unconvinced. Missouri's prisons were full of people who swore they were innocent. He had put over fifty of them in there himself over the years. "Where's Hope's car?"

"I hid it in an abandoned barn a couple of miles from here."

Pagano stepped forward and hung a couple of blue chem lights around Powers's neck. Then he flipped open his knife and cut Powers free from the chair. "Let's take a walk."

"If I go with you, you'll kill me," Powers sobbed.

"If you don't walk, I'll kill you right here. As long as you walk, you'll be alive. You might even be able to escape. Let's go!"

Reluctantly and with great difficulty, Powers got to his feet and gingerly limped to the door and down the stairs to the gravel. His left thigh was so swollen, it strained against his pant leg. His arms were near useless.

"Go behind the trailer and start walking toward the trees. Keep walking until I tell you to stop. I doubt if anyone would hear you, but if you yell for help, I'll cut your tongue out and chain you to a tree. Then the scavengers can finish you." Pagano shook a set of leg irons.

CHAPTER 13

DAY 6, JUNE 10, WEDNESDAY

"Everyone, take a seat and quiet down so Sergeant Krote can get his people out of here," Lieutenant McLeod said from the front table of the squad room. "Alright, Mel, tell us what you have."

"Thanks, Lieutenant. At approximately 2345 last night, we had a call for an Assault–First Degree at 764 Wortham Road. The reporting party, Audrey Wilkins, reported her husband, Rudolph Wilkins, was chasing her around the house and attempting to kill her with a hammer. Deputies Nickmeier and Mellencamp responded and took Mr. Wilkins into custody. I'll let Clint explain what transpired."

Deputy Bob Wainwright groaned from the back row.

Clint swiveled in his chair to look at Bob. Bob smiled back at him and motioned with his arms for Clint to please proceed. Clint turned back around. "Uhhh, so when Steve and I arrived on the scene, we observed Mrs. Wilkins standing in the driveway behind her Cadillac waving at us. Mr. Wilkins was at the front of the Cadillac trying to catch Mrs. Wilkins."

"What kind of Cadillac was it?" Bob asked.

"Uhhh…what?" Clint asked as he turned in his seat.

"The Caddy—what model was it?" Bob asked.

"Uhhh, it was a Coupe DeVille," Clint replied and then turned back to the front.

"Thanks," Bob said.

Clint glanced back at Bob and then addressed the rest of the room. "So, ahhh, Mr. Wilkins was trying to catch his wife and kill her with the 16-ounce claw hammer he was holding, but he is physically and mentally impaired due to a stroke he suffered about a year ago. He is partially paralyzed on his left side. So, he was taking a step with his right foot and then dragging his left foot in a sort of…ummm…slow step-drag, step-drag motion. Mrs. Wilkins would watch him until he got within about five feet and then she would step back out of reach. We took the hammer away from Mr. Wilkins and sent him to Parkland in an ambulance. I asked Mrs. Wilkins what happened to set him off. She said after the stroke, the doctors put him on a fistful of medications and a strict diet. He woke her up and mumbled that he wanted some bacon. She told him he couldn't have any because of the diet. He mumbled to give him some bacon or he would kill her. She told him to go back to sleep. She heard him get out of bed and step-drag himself through the house and out into the garage. He banged around out there for about five minutes until he found the hammer. Then, he step-dragged himself back into the bedroom. She saw him standing in the doorway with the hammer and told him to stop acting a fool. She said he roared, 'I want bacon,' like a crazy man as he step-dragged over to the bed. She rolled over to the other side of the bed and left the room before he could change direction and catch her. She went to the kitchen and called 911. She waited in there until he step-dragged himself to the kitchen, and then she walked out the front door. He followed her outside, and they made a few laps around the Caddy before we got there."

"So, the invasion has begun," Bob said.

"Uhhh, what?" Clint asked.

"The invasion. The bacon-eating, hammer-wielding, killer zombie invasion," Bob replied with a smile.

McLeod shook his head. "Shut up, Bob. Go ahead, Mel."

"Thank you, sir. At approximately 0345, Deputy Mellencamp conducted a traffic stop on Berry Road at Lake Timberline Drive for a broken headlight that became a DWI arrest. I'll let Steve explain."

"I was waiting at Highway Y to turn south on 67 when I saw a vehicle traveling southbound on 67 with one headlight. The driver turned right onto the Y cutoff and then left onto Berry Road. I followed her down Berry and stopped her for failure to maintain her lane and the headlight. When I approached the car, I saw the driver was a young lady wearing a Hooter's uniform. About this time, Clint arrived to back me up. I asked her if she had been drinking, and she said she had stayed after work with the team and had a couple of beers. I asked her to get out of the car to perform a few field sobriety tests. I asked her to do the one-leg stand and walk-and-turn tests, which she failed. She was obviously intoxicated, and I told her I had one more test for her, and if she passed it, I would give her a ride home instead of arresting her. I said, 'Is Mickey Mouse a dog or a cat?' She thought about it for a minute and said, 'A cat.' I told her that was incorrect. I brought her back to the station and booked her. Just before shift change, her boyfriend came up and posted her bond. Before she left, I asked her again if Mickey Mouse was a dog or a cat. She shook her finger at me and said, 'Oh, no. I remember. Mickey Mouse is a dog.'"

"What's her phone number?" Bob asked.

"Shut up, Bob," McLeod said.

"One fifty-three, a two-year-old choking at 407 Center Street, ambulance en route," the dispatcher, Peggy, transmitted.

"Central, one fifty-three, I'm five minutes away. See if someone's closer!" Officer Orville Cobb of Farmington PD transmitted over the wail of his siren.

Mark was about to pull into Burger King but turned toward Center, and when no Farmington cars responded, he said, "We're a minute away. Put us en route."

"Central, ten oh five, we'll take the call at 407 Center. We're a minute out," Zack transmitted. Mark turned off West Karsch, raced down Center, and then slammed on his brakes.

"Ten oh five, 10-23," Zack transmitted. He jumped from the cruiser and sprinted to the open front door. He ran into the house and yelled, "Sheriff's Department!" He heard a woman crying down the hall.

"Help me!" she screamed.

He followed her wailing and found the woman sitting on her bed rocking her lifeless son.

"Oh, Lord, please don't let him die! Don't let him die!" she prayed aloud. She looked up with tear-filled eyes and said, "He won't breathe!"

Zack took the boy from her and stuck his finger in his throat as Mark entered the bedroom behind him. "I can feel something in his throat, but I can't get it," he said. The boy was turning blue.

"Give him to me," Mark said as he reached for the limp little boy. He held him upside down by his feet with his left hand and slapped him on the back with his right hand. A shiny wet nickel came flying out of his mouth and landed on the rug. The boy gasped for air and then started crying. Mark gently rolled him over and gave him back to his mother. The boy wrapped his arms around her and continued crying.

She took one hand off her son and grabbed Mark's forearm. "Oh, thank you! Thank you for saving my baby!" She looked appreciatively at Mark and Zack. "God sent you to save him! How can I thank you?"

Mark bent over and picked up the nickel. He smiled. "This should about cover it." He put the coin in his right breast pocket and keyed his walkie. "Central, ten oh five, the boy's airway is open and he's breathing."

"I hear the ambulance. I'll go show them back here." Zack walked outside. It gave him a chance to wipe his eyes.

The EMTs grabbed their bags from the ambulance and hurried to the porch. "He's in the bedroom," Zack said as he led them into the house and down the hall. Mark and Zack went out to the family room to give the EMTs space to work. "Where'd you learn that technique? They don't teach it at the academy."

"When I was a kid, I saw my dad use it on my cousin when he choked on a piece a hot dog."

"If that was my son, I don't know if I would've been able to save him. I'm afraid I might've frozen up trying to decide what to do."

"Sometimes there's no time to think, there's just action. Say you have three young kids, and somehow, they all fall off the dock into the lake at the same time. You don't stand there and calculate which one's the worst swimmer, you just jump in and rescue the closest one, and then the next, and hopefully you get to them all in time. Here's one where you do have a choice. Say you're at the zoo and a little girl you don't know falls into the lion exhibit. Are you the type of person who would jump in to save her, knowing you might die doing it, or would you stand there and watch the little girl get killed?" Mark asked. "That's the kind of stuff you think about when you're driving around at oh dark thirty on Sunday morning waiting for a call to come out."

A Farmington car pulled up, and Orville Cobb climbed out. He walked into the house. "That's the second time in two days you guys have responded to my call. I'm starting to think you want to come work for us."

Mark chuckled and said, "No thanks, I'm a road dawg. I need room to run." Then he pulled the nickel from his pocket to show Cobb. "Besides, you guys don't pay enough."

"Well, for sure, we can't put a price on what you guys did today."

"Ten oh five, 10-50 J2, 637 Osage Avenue, ambulance en route," Peggy transmitted.

"Ten oh five, 10-76," Zack replied.

"Ten oh five, 10-76 at 0830," Peggy replied.

"That's odd. Osage is in a subdivision. The speed limit's probably twenty miles per hour," Mark said. He activated his lights and siren. They arrived on the scene seven minutes later. They could see a gray Dodge Ram pickup stopped in the road and a John Deere riding lawn mower laying on its side in the grass. "That's not good," Mark said.

"Ten oh five, 10-23," Zack transmitted.

"Ten oh five, 10-23 at 0837," Peggy replied.

Zack hurried down the passenger side of the truck and Mark went to the driver's side. They arrived at the front together and saw an old man lying on his back in the street twenty-five feet from the truck. He was bleeding from his head, and his left leg was bent at an unnatural angle between his knee and ankle. His left tibia was protruding from his ripped trouser leg. His wife was on her knees next to him trying to hold a dish towel to his bloody scalp, but he kept pushing it away.

"Hold still, you old fool!" she scolded him.

A younger man was pacing back and forth in front of the truck, talking on his cellphone.

"Zack, you talk to him, and I'll talk to the victim," Mark said.

"Sir, you need to hang up so I can talk to you," Zack told the man.

"Hey, I gotta go. The deputies are here," he said into his phone.

"Sir, were you driving the truck?"

"Yes, I was," the man said nervously as he peeked over his shoulder at the old man and his wife.

"I need to see your driver's license and proof of insurance," Zack said. The ambulance drove past them and stopped in front of the old man.

The driver pulled his license out of his wallet. "Here it is. I think the proof of insurance is in the truck." He went around to the passenger side and rummaged around in the glove box. He came back and handed it to Zack. "The truck belongs to my boss."

Zack stuck the license and insurance card to his clipboard. "Is this your current address, Mr. Martin?" he asked as he wrote down the man's information on a Missouri Uniform Accident Report form.

"Yes, sir."

"Would you tell me what happened for the report?"

"I was driving down Osage looking for an address. I have an appointment to measure a lady's kitchen for new cabinets. I was only going about twenty miles per hour. I dropped my phone on the floorboard and bent over to pick it up. It only took a second, but the guy drove his lawn mower out into the street, and I hit him just as I looked up. I didn't have time to react."

Zack wrote it down on the report and noted the airbags had not deployed. "Wait here, sir." He walked over to Mark.

Mark was writing down the old man's information. "What's your name, sir?"

"His name is Jasper Bock," his wife said as she held the bloody towel to his head. The man nodded at Mark.

Mark looked at her and then him and wrote it down. He returned his gaze to Jasper. "And your address, sir?"

"His address is 637 Osage Avenue," his wife said. The old man nodded.

Mark nodded and wrote it down. "Can you tell me what happened, Mr. Bock?"

"He had his headphones on and wasn't paying any attention to the traffic. He drove out there right in front of the truck to turn around and got hit. He almost killed himself and left me behind all alone. Stupid old fool!" she said as she unsuccessfully fought off tears.

The old man shrugged and nodded his head.

"Can I have your name, ma'am?"

She lost control and was openly sobbing.

"Her name is Lena Bock," the old man said.

She nodded as she held the bloody towel to his head with one hand and wiped her eyes with her other.

Jasper patted her on the knee. "I'm sorry, Hon. Don't worry, I'll be alright. It'll take a lot more than that truck to kill me. The only place I'm going is to the hospital."

The EMTs quickly bandaged the man's head, put a cervical collar on his neck, and splinted his leg. They loaded him into the ambulance, and Mark helped his wife up into the cab.

Mark picked up Bock's cap and handed it to the EMT before closing the doors. The ambulance made a left onto Silver Street and headed for the entrance to the subdivision.

"Zack, let's see if we can push the mower back up on its wheels," Mark said. They gave it a push and it rolled back onto its wheels, but the damage was extensive on the left side. It would never mow another lawn. They turned to walk back to Mr. Martin.

"Did you get a statement from the victim?" Zack asked.

"Yeah, he said he was going back and forth, north and south cutting the lawn. He was wearing earmuffs to protect what's left of his hearing, so he didn't hear the truck coming. He made twenty or so passes without seeing a car. He guessed he must have stopped looking."

"Do you think he'll be alright?" Martin asked.

"Well, he has an Army Combat Jump Wings tattoo with two gold stars on his forearm, and he was wearing a Korean War ball cap with purple heart and combat infantry badge pins stuck to it, so I think he's pretty tough," Mark said.

"I hope so. Are you guys done with me? I have an appointment with a lady who lives on this street to measure her kitchen for new cabinets," Martin said.

"What's her address?" Mark asked.

"637 Osage."

"Sorry, pal, your customer just left in the ambulance with her husband."

"Damn."

CHAPTER 14

"Ten oh five, call the station for nine eighty," Peggy transmitted.

"Ten oh five, 10-4." Zack made the call on his cellphone and was transferred to the sheriff. "Sir, this is Zack. You're on speaker with Mark."

"Hey, boys, thanks for calling so fast. We just got a call from some bounty hunters up from Texas. They're chasing a shitbird who beat a man in Fort Worth half to death and stole his collection of rare coins. They think he's hiding out at an old girlfriend's house at 5393 Whittaker Road. Why don't you boys head over there and check on these cowboys, make sure they're on the level."

"OK, Boss, we'll check them out," Mark said, and Zack hung up. "Tell Central we're en route for an investigation."

"Central, ten oh five, 10-76 to 5393 Whittaker Road for an investigation," Zack transmitted.

"Ten oh five, 10-76 at 0945," Peggy replied.

Five minutes later, they rolled up about fifty feet behind a White Ford F-250 with a camper shell and Texas plates at the end of the driveway. Three men climbed down from the truck and waited at the tailgate. They were all wearing black body armor with embroidered gold badges and lettering indicating they were Fugitive Recovery Agents. They carried semiautomatic pistols in drop-leg holsters and wore Oakley sunglasses.

"Unlock the shotgun and hang back behind your door. Try to record us with your cellphone. I'll do the same. I'll go up and talk to them, feel them out. If any of them go for a gun, kill 'em all," Mark said before they climbed out of the cruiser. Mark stopped about fifteen feet from the men and said, "Good afternoon, gentlemen. I'm Deputy Mark Langford, and he's Deputy Zack Goodson," he said with a smile.

The man in the center with a Fu Manchu mustache and man bun smiled back. "Good afternoon, Deputy. I'm Terrance Caldwell, but my friends call me Buster. This is Eric Rios and Tyrone Moore."

Mark nodded to the men. "What can we do for you fellas?"

"A low-down coward named Johnny Hammond is hiding out in that house down there. He jumped his bail in Fort Worth, and we're here to bring him back to face justice. We're going to go down there and drag him out of whatever hole he's hiding in."

"Are you boys licensed in Texas?"

"Yes, sir. We're all commissioned security officers approved by the Private Security Board of Texas."

Mark nodded. "Does Hammond own that house?"

"No, it's his girlfriend's."

"What makes you think he's in there?"

"His bail bondsman got a call last night saying he was here."

"Have you been down to the house to talk to the lady yet?"

"No, we waited for you to get here."

"That's good. Alright, you fellas stay here, and we'll go down and talk to her," Mark said as he turned to go back to the cruiser.

"We'll go with you," Caldwell said as he and his boys turned for his truck.

"No, sir. You'll stay right here until we come back," Mark said with a friendly smile that brooked no disagreement.

"C'mon, Zack," Mark said as they climbed back into the cruiser. Mark pulled around the truck and drove down the 400-foot-long gravel driveway to the house. Mark knocked on the front door and a woman of about thirty answered.

"Good afternoon, ma'am. I'm Deputy Langford and this is Deputy Goodson. Can I have your name?"

"Brenda Francis."

"Miss Francis, have you noticed those boys down at the end of your driveway?"

"Yes, I did. I was getting ready to call the Sheriff when I saw you drive up."

"They're bounty hunters from Texas chasing a man named Johnny Hammond. Is he here?"

"No. I haven't seen or heard from him since I moved back home from Fort Worth three years ago."

"Would you be willing to let us in to search for him? That way we can go back and tell them he's not here and send them on their way."

"What if I don't let you search?"

"Well, they might come down here after we leave and search for him themselves. We can't sit here all day guarding your house, but they can park out there on the road as long as they want. We can't make them leave, but if we search ourselves and tell them he's not here, they won't have any reason to search, and we'll lock them up if they trespass on your property."

"OK, come on in." She opened the door wider.

"Before we do, are you sure he's not here? Because if he is and he shoots us or we shoot him, you'll be charged with a felony."

"Yeah, I'm sure. Really, I told you the truth. He's not here. C'mon in."

Mark and Zack thoroughly searched the house and attic, and as she said, Hammond wasn't there.

"Miss Francis, do you have any firearms?"

"Yes, I have a Ruger 10/22 rifle that my daddy gave me years ago."

"Are you a pretty good shot with it?"

"I was back then."

"Can I see it?"

"Alright. It's in my bedroom closet." She led them back into the bedroom. She pulled it out of the closet and handed it to Mark.

The rifle had a twenty-five-round magazine in it. He removed the magazine and saw it was empty. He checked the chamber, and it was also empty. "Do you have any ammunition for it?"

She nodded and pulled down an open 525 round box from the shelf. It was almost full.

"These are jacketed hollow-point rounds. That's good. Can we load it for you?"

"Alright. Thank you."

"Zack, grab that other mag off the shelf." They both loaded a twenty-five-round magazine, and Mark attached his magazine and chambered a round. He didn't want the woman to be left there defenseless after he and Zack left. "OK, you have twenty-five rounds in the rifle and another full magazine. The safety's on. I recommend you keep it by the bed when you turn in tonight and keep your cellphone with you. If those yahoos try to break into your house, you have every right to defend yourself. Now, we'll go shoo those boys away. If they come back, give us a call. Do I have your permission to tell them if they come on your property, they'll be arrested for trespassing?"

"Yes, sir. Please do." She opened the door for them.

Mark drove up the driveway and stopped about fifty feet from the truck. The men had added AR-15s to their armaments. He got out and walked up to the men as Zack covered him from behind his door. "Well, we talked to her, and she said she hasn't seen Hammond or talked to him in three years. She let us search the house, and he's definitely not there. I'm sorry you boys wasted your time, but this is a dry hole."

"Well, Deputy, we do appreciate your efforts, but you won't mind if we check for ourselves?" Caldwell said as if it wasn't really a question.

"Yes, sir, we do mind. Now, you've been told he's not here. You need to move along and not harass this nice lady. She told us to inform you that if you step foot on her property, she will prosecute you for trespassing. Also, if you force your way into her home with weapons, that's called Burglary First Degree in this state. Under the castle law, she'll have every right to blow you out of your socks. You won't have a right to self-defense."

"Look, Deputy, Hammond is worth two hundred grand to us. We'll cut you in for an even share. That's forty grand for each of us."

"I'm sure you know we can't except the bounty money."

"Hey, man, I'm not going to put you on the payroll, I'll just leave a fat envelope in your mailbox. How you report your income is your business."

"No thanks."

"We're not gonna just tuck tail and leave. We've got too much invested in bringing Hammond back."

"How can I dissuade you from this false notion that your avarice somehow trumps my authority?"

"C'mon, dammit! He's a dangerous felon! Don't you want him out of your county?" Caldwell asked angrily.

"Of course, we do. And as long as you fellas stay on this side of the line, you'll have no trouble from us, but if you cross the line, we'll lock you up or put you in the ground. You might be hot shit in Texas, but up here, you're just three more knuckleheads."

"That's big talk for a hick-town Barney Fife out here deep in the woods. Are you sure you can back it up?" Caldwell was getting more pissed by the second. He shifted is weight back and forth on his feet.

The more agitated Caldwell got, the cooler Mark became. "Well, this is the Show-Me state, and if you're hell-bent to find out, we'll show you, but if you have the sense God gave a goose, you'll get back in that truck and start headin' south."

Caldwell eyed Mark for a minute. "I'm pretty good at readin' people, but when I look at you, I don't see anything in there, just cold, dead eyes."

"Maybe that should tell you somethin'. This ain't my first rodeo," Mark replied stone-faced.

The men stood their ground staring down Mark. From behind his door, Zack jacked a round into his Remington 870. The men turned their attention to the shotgun.

Mark shouted, "I'm tired of hearing you jaw jackin'! Kick rocks, now!"

The men leisurely backed away and then turned to walk back to the truck. Buster made a slow U-turn and drove off.

Zack watched until the truck disappeared and then removed the round from the chamber and stowed the shotgun. "Damn, I thought I was watching Wyatt Earp coming up against the Clantons."

"Fuck them shitheads. This is our county. They don't get to come up here and bow up on us." Mark's scowl became a smile. "I suppose they sparked my competitive spirit." He got in the cruiser. "Put us 10-8 and then call the Sheriff. We need to alert the other departments in the county to be looking out for these nimrods."

"Nine ninety-four, assault with a knife just occurred at 2039 Patience Avenue in Eagle Estates. The suspect called 911 to request an ambulance for his brother," Peggy transmitted.

"Nine ninety-four, en route," Deputy Wainwright transmitted.

"Zack, put us en route to assist," Mark said as he flipped on his lights and siren.

"Central, ten oh five, 10-76 to assist nine ninety-four," Zack transmitted.

"Nine ninety-four and ten oh five, 10-76 at 1100," Peggy replied.

"Have Bob go to four," Mark said as he raced west on Highway Y toward Highway 67.

"Nine ninety-four, go to channel four for ten oh five," Zack transmitted and then switched to channel four.

"I'm up, Zack," Bob transmitted.

"Key the mic for me," Mark said. Zack did so and held it up for him. "Bob, where are you coming from?"

"I'm northbound on 67 approaching DeClue Lane."

"OK, we're on Y approaching 67. We'll meet you there. Go back to one," Mark transmitted. "Zack, glove up now; it could be bloody." Zack pulled a pair of black nitrile gloves from the leather pouch on his belt.

Four minutes later, Wainwright transmitted, "Nine ninety-four, 10-23."

"Nine ninety-four, 10-23 at 1105," Peggy replied.

"Ten oh five, 10-23," Zack transmitted.

The deputies approached the trailer with their Glocks held down beside their legs. One man sat on the porch at a small glass-topped table drinking a beer. Another sat on the porch steps holding a bloody red shop towel to his abdomen.

"What's the problem, gentlemen?" Wainwright asked as he zeroed in at the man sitting at the table.

Before he could speak, the man on the steps said, "He came home from work and stabbed me."

"Shut up, stupid ass. He ain't talkin' to you. Officer, my name is Antwan Hayes, and that lazy ungrateful bastard over there is my brother, Andray. He lost his job three damn months ago, 'cuz he's a thief and an alcoholic. He's been livin' here off me ever since."

"What's the problem this afternoon?" Bob asked.

"I fried pork chops for our dinner last night and there was one left over. I told him he could eat anything he wanted today except that damn pork chop. I was gonna eat that pork chop when I got home from work. I come home, and sure enough, he ate my pork chop. I saw the bone settin' on the table. He didn't even clean up his mess. When I asked him why, he laughed at me and said he forgot. So, I stabbed his stupid ass. Maybe next time he'll remember," Antwan explained.

Wainwright nodded. "Where's the knife?"

"I left it in the sink."

Wainwright turned. "Andray, how are you doing?"

"I'll be alright. The knife wasn't that long. I just need some stitches."

"Why'd you take his pork chop?"

"I got tired of him lordin' over me. Telling me what to do. I won't be here forever. I just hit a rough patch. You don't stab somebody over a damn pork chop, especially your brother."

"Do you want to press charges?"

"Naw, he's my brother. I shouldn't have egged him on."

"Well, after you get out of the hospital, you'll need to come down to the Sheriff's Station and sign a form for us saying that. I hear the ambulance coming. We'll have you on your way in a minute."

Wainwright motioned for Zack to follow him up on the porch. "Antwan, I'm placing you under arrest. Stand up and put your hands behind your back."

Antwan was exasperated. He chugged his beer before he stood up and allowed the handcuffs to go on.

"I need your car keys," Andray said.

"What? I ain't givin' you my car!" Antwan replied.

"I'll need it to come down and sign the form to get you out of jail," Andray explained.

"Damn." Antwan faced Wainwright and said, "They're in my right front pocket. You're gonna get me fired too, Andray. Then we'll have to move back in with Momma and quit drinkin' and start goin' to church again."

The ambulance arrived as Wainwright was reading Antwan his Miranda rights. The EMTs bandaged Andray's wound and took him to the hospital.

"Watch him, Zack. I need to seize the knife." Wainwright went inside.

Zack walked Antwan over to Wainwright's cruiser and put him in the back seat.

Wainwright came out with the knife and walked over to the cruiser. He pulled an evidence bag from his patrol bag and dropped it inside. "Thanks for the assist, gentlemen." Wainwright started the cruiser and headed back to the highway.

"That's the kind of call I like. Just stand back and watch you young bulls work," Mark said. "I'm glad it worked out that way. It could have been a lot worse. I hate knife calls. Some naked idiot on PCP running around with a knife is my worst nightmare. They keep fighting even when their bones are broken. At the Academy, do they still demonstrate that a man can cover twenty feet and stab you before you can get your gun out and shoot him?"

"Yeah, that was a real eye opener," Zack replied.

Two hours later, Mark and Zack were patrolling the northern most part of the county. Mark was taking baby steps with Zack. "Where are we?"

"Eastbound Highway Y approaching Highway D."

"Good. What little town is up ahead?"

"French Village."

"Right again. I'll have to start making the questions tougher."

"Ten oh five, go to channel four for nine ninety-four," Deputy Wainwright transmitted.

Zack punched up channel four on the radio. "Go ahead for ten oh five."

"Hey, can you guys contact me at the Dollar General in French Village?"

"10-4, we'll be there in a couple," Zack replied.

Minutes later, Mark and Zack rolled up into the parking lot and stopped behind Wainwright's cruiser. It was blocking a car parked in the handicapped spot.

Wainwright came up to Mark's window. "I stopped across the street at BJ's to take a leak, and when I came out, an old guy told me the car in the handicapped spot at Dollar General was parked illegally so I came over here to check it out. Sure enough, there was no hang tag displayed. I looked in the windows and didn't see one between the seats or stuck in the visor, so I wrote a ticket on it. Just as I finished, an old lady came out of the store with her bags and got in the car and started it up like she was going to leave. I stopped her and told her I wrote her a ticket for parking in the handicapped spot. She reached over and pulled her hang tag out of the glove compartment and hung it from the mirror. I told her it was too late and that I couldn't just tear up the ticket, but if she came to court and showed the judge her hang tag, he'd throw out the ticket. She got pissed and refused to sign the ticket. What should I do with her? I wouldn't have written her the ticket if I knew she had a hang tag."

Mark rubbed his chin like King Solomon. "Well, Bob, she broke the law, there's no doubt about that. It doesn't matter if she actually had a hang tag or not; it has to be displayed properly. You had every right to ticket her, and if she refuses to sign the ticket, you have every right to arrest her. If she resists arrest, you can drag her out of the car window, drop her on the ground, cuff her up, and hope no one records it for CNN or…you could just write 'refused to sign' on the bottom of the ticket, throw it in her window, and run away before she can catch up to you. It's your call."

Wainwright nodded his understanding. He would take the path of least resistance: retreat and live to fight another day. Mark pulled out of the lot and drove over to BJ's to watch from a safe distance, hidden by another vehicle. Wainwright approached the lady's car and motioned for her to roll down her window. When she did, he dropped the ticket in her lap and took off at a run for his cruiser. He spun his tires in the loose gravel as he exited the lot heading east on Highway Y. The woman chased him on foot waving the ticket in the air.

Mark and Zack could hear her cussing him from their hideout.

"Come back here, Goddamn it!" she yelled. She threw the ticket on the ground and stomped back to her car. Mark and Zack shared a good laugh at Wainwright's expense.

"I told you, ole Bob's a shit magnet." He waited for the lady to drive out of sight before he crept out of hiding and headed in the opposite direction.

CHAPTER 15

"Ten oh five, trespassing at 5393 Whittaker Road. Caller reports armed bounty hunters are trespassing in the woods surrounding her house," Peggy transmitted.

"Ten oh five, 10-76," Zack replied. "I guess they didn't take the hint," he added to Mark.

"Sounds like they want to go the 'Show Me' route. Call Miss Francis and ask her what's going on." Mark said.

"Central, show nine eight-four and nine ninety en route to assist ten oh five," Lieutenant McLeod transmitted.

Zack dialed her number and put it on speaker. When she answered, he said, "Miss Francis, this is Deputy Goodson. Deputy Langford and I are en route to your house right now. Where are the bounty hunters, and what are they doing?"

"They're creeping around my house through the trees. I see them stand up and change positions every so often. Their vests say police on them, but I know it's the bounty hunters because I can see the front end of their white truck sticking out beyond the trees at the end of my driveway."

"Stay in your house, but if you can, snap a picture of them wearing the police vests and send it to me. If they come to the house, lock yourself in the bathroom with your rifle. We'll be there in about five minutes. Call me back if they try anything." Zack hung up. "Do you believe that shit? They're impersonating the police."

"If we catch them in the act, that will be the end of their bounty hunting days." Mark drove their cruiser up Highway D as fast as he could without using his siren. He didn't want to tip them off that they were coming.

Zack heard his phone notification and looked at his phone. "Hey, she got 'em. She took photos of every one of them. Their vests clearly say 'police' on them."

Minutes later, they rolled up behind the white pickup.

"Ten oh five, 10-23," Zack transmitted. He climbed out of the cruiser with the shotgun and chambered a round.

Mark went to the back seat and reached into his police patrol bag. He pulled out two tire caltrops. They were hardened steel with four sharp spikes sticking out in all directions. They were designed to flatten car tires. He handed one to Zack. "Here, put one in front of the right rear tire. I'll get the other one."

After placing the caltrops, they headed toward the house, being careful to stay inside the tree line next to the driveway.

Zack called Miss Francis. "This is Deputy Goodson again. Do you still see them?"

"They just split up. It looks like they're leaving one guy behind the house and the other two are circling around to the front. They're trying to stay hidden."

"Central, nine eight-four and nine ninety, 10-23. Ten oh five, go to four," McLeod transmitted.

They flipped their walkies over to channel four, and Zack said, "Go for ten oh five."

"Kurt and I are behind the house over on High Line Road. Do you want us to start making our way toward the house?"

"Miss Francis said one is covering the back of the house and the other two are making their way around to the front. They're wearing police banners on their vests. Come on up, but be careful. They have rifles. Stay on four," Mark said.

"Roger that," McLeod replied.

Mark and Zack stopped inside the trees about a hundred feet from the front of the house and watched. Caldwell and Moore came creeping out of the trees to the left of the house.

Zack called Miss Francis. "Get in the bathroom, now!"

Caldwell and Moore staged on opposite sides of the front door. Caldwell nodded and pulled the pin on a stun grenade. He yelled, "Police! Search warrant!" as Moore kicked in the door.

Mark yelled, "Sheriff's Department! Drop your weapons and get on the ground!"

Caldwell and Moore turned around but didn't see anyone.

Mark yelled again, "Sheriff's Department! Drop your fuckin' weapons and get on the ground! This is the last warning!"

"What about this stun grenade?" Caldwell asked. He hadn't released the spoon yet.

"Goddamn it! Throw it over where you came from and drop your guns!"

Caldwell threw the grenade away, and he and Moore dropped their rifles and proned out on the ground. They did it like it wasn't their first time. Mark and Zack waited for the grenade to blow and then ran forward. Mark handcuffed them while Zack provided cover.

"Watch out for number three," Mark said. He transmitted, "Ten oh five has two in custody." He searched both men and took their pistols from them.

McLeod transmitted on four, "We have the other one in custody. We'll bring him around front." Minutes later, McLeod and Sada emerged from around the side of the house. McLeod carried an AR-15, and Sada held Rios by his handcuffs. Somehow, Rios had managed to hurt himself. Blood was running from his forehead into his left eye.

Zack was smiling. "What happened to him?"

"Don't look at me. When he heard Mark yelling 'Sheriff's Department,' he turned to run and saw us. He tried to run to the southwest but tripped and smacked his head. So, it's Mark's fault. Have a seat, Mr. Rios." Sada sat him down next to the other two.

"Read them their rights, Zack. I'll go check on Miss Francis," Mark said.

Zack pulled the card out of his pocket and read it to the men. Mark came out of the house with Miss Francis.

"Do you want to prosecute these yahoos for trespassing and destroying your property?" Mark asked.

"Yes, sir," she said as she stood next to the lawmen with her arms crossed.

Mark turned to Caldwell. "What police department do you fellas work for?"

"Lawyer," Caldwell replied.

"How about you, Officer Moore?" Mark asked.

"Fuck you, Barney," Moore said.

"Mr. Rios?" Mark asked.

Rios just looked at the ground and tried to wipe his bloody face on his shirt sleeve, which was near impossible with his hands cuffed behind his back. "Does anybody want to say anything that would help explain why you came back here armed and impersonating police officers and then kicked in this woman's door after we told you Johnny Hammond wasn't here?" Mark asked. "Just so you know, we ran Hammond after we talked to you this morning, and it turns out he was arrested in Dallas. It was awful clever of him to come up here and then double back home right away. Miss Francis, could we use your hose and trouble you for some paper towels for Mr. Rios?"

She went back into the house and returned with a handful of paper towels. Rios was lying on his back on the lawn, and Sada was running the water over his head. Zack gloved up and dabbed the towel on his head and found a small cut near his hairline.

"Kurt, take him to Parkland to get stitched up. Mark and Zack can take the other two back to be booked. I'll collect that stun grenade, bring their guns back, and wait for the tow truck," McLeod said. "Miss Francis, are you going to be able to find someone to repair your door?"

"I'll get my brother over here. He's a carpenter," she replied.

McLeod walked back up the driveway with Mark, Zack, and their prisoners. He borrowed a vehicle inventory form from Mark and opened the truck's camper shell and lowered the tailgate to inventory its contents. A large wooden box was bolted to the truck bed. McLeod opened the lid to look inside. "Hey, check this out!" McLeod called out to the others.

Mark and Zack belted their prisoners into the back seat of their cruiser and walked over to the back of the truck. McLeod raised the lid again.

"What the fuck? I'm pretty sure that's illegal," Mark said. He stepped back so Zack could take a look.

Zack saw a set of leg irons bolted to the far end of the box. It was just large enough for a man to lie down in. By the smell, he could tell the box was used regularly. The scene made Zack think of the Robert Burns poem, "Man's Inhumanity to Man." "They were gonna make that guy ride all the way back to Fort Worth in that shitty little box."

"These hombres will never collect another bounty." Mark observed them through the window. "Maybe we should chain these shitbums to the back of the cruiser for the first couple of miles back to the station."

Mark and Zack worked their scheduled day shift and were offered four hours of overtime to cover for a deputy who called in sick. They had just left the station after dropping off the fugitive they had picked up at De Soto PD in Jefferson County on a Failure to Appear warrant when Zack saw an old man with a cane limping along on the shoulder of Highway 32 in front of Walmart. "Should we stop and check on that old guy?" Zack pointed at him.

Mark's eyes followed where Zack pointed. "No, that's Laverne Skaggs. He's OK. He walks over to the Bread Company to get a smoothie and one of their Kitchen Sink cookies most afternoons. He's not that old either—probably around fifty."

"Shit! He looks more like seventy. What happened to him?"

"He lives back there behind Walmart in a run-down century house with his wife. He always liked to carry a little .22 automatic in his pocket, and whenever his wife started ragging on him, he'd pull it out and threaten to shoot himself in the head to shut her up. One time, about ten years ago, he accidentally squeezed off a round and it zinged around inside his skull a couple of times. It left him partially paralyzed and made it hard for him to talk. When he came home from the hospital, the first thing his wife said to him was, 'You cain't even kill yourself right.'"

"Damn, that's harsh," Zack replied, still watching Laverne.

"Yeah, his parents probably doomed him to a shitty life as soon as they named him Laverne." Mark pulled over to the side of the road and pulled out his phone. "Phil Woolsey just sent me a text." He read the message. "They found the cowboy's arm from yesterday."

"Was it stuck to the truck?"

"No. Dr. Patel found it. When he started the autopsy, he saw fingers sticking out of the body's right shoulder. It looks like the guy tried to stiff arm the semi and his arm collapsed back into his chest cavity. The broken bones destroyed his heart and lungs."

CHAPTER 16

Pagano woke up in a panic, soaked in sweat. It was 2:10 p.m. He had been sleeping since he returned from the trailer around four in the morning. He had just realized that if someone reported Powers missing, like his chief instructor at IMI, eventually the Sheriff's Department would wind up searching his trailer and Jeep and find Hope's clothes, hair, fingerprints, or DNA inside them. That would link her to Powers and give Pagano a motive to kill him. If, or more likely when, Powers's body was found, he would be a suspect. He dressed quickly and checked the monitor for the front gate. He saw Soto kicked back with his feet on the desk watching TV. No vehicles were waiting to enter. He went to the barn and climbed into his truck. He drove it out the back gate again and headed over to the trailer as fast as he could.

Pagano drove slowly up the driveway and looked around the area from the cab of his truck. Everything appeared as it had last night. He pulled up in front of the trailer and climbed out. He knocked on the door in case someone was inside. No one answered.

He retrieved the key from the shed and an almost full five-gallon gas can sitting next to the lawn mower. He went into the trailer and began spreading gas in every room. As he got back to the kitchen, he froze. He saw a white Ford Crown Victoria with a radio antenna attached in the rear emerge from around the curve in the driveway. He recognized it immediately as a police vehicle. His heart leapt to his throat, and he spun in a circle hoping for an escape hatch to appear. The car stopped next to his truck, and Lieutenant Denny Close climbed out. Close walked around to Pagano's truck and stuck his head inside the open driver's side window. He flipped the visor down to see if anything would fall from it. Nothing did. Close faced the trailer and tried to smooth his rumpled brown sports coat as he walked.

Pagano had known Denny for over twenty-five years and considered him a friend. He waited inside the front door until Close approached the steps. Pagano pushed the door open and said, "Hey Denny," with a big smile on his face. Close smiled back and was about to speak when Pagano shot him three times in the chest before he could react. Pagano bounded down the steps, ready to shoot again. As Close lay on the gravel, he looked at Pagano in utter confusion and disbelief. Pagano said with true regret in his eyes, "I'm sorry, man." Close died seconds later.

Pagano holstered his Franken-Glock and picked up the three spent shell casings. He put them in his front pocket. He took Close's Glock and stuck it in his back pocket. Pagano grabbed him under the arms and slowly dragged him up the stairs. He laid him out on the floor and poured gas on his body. It occurred to him he could blame Powers for this as long as no one ever found Powers's body. He went back to the bedroom and grabbed Powers's rifle. He stepped outside and put the rifle in his truck. He lit a roll of paper towels and tossed it through the doorway. He closed the door and drove away in his truck. He fought the urge to speed all the way to the back gate.

The radio came to life. "Nine eighty-three, 10-89?" the Central 911 dispatcher, Denise, called to Lieutenant Close. It had been twenty minutes since he called out at a trailer on Rouggly Road to follow up on a missing person's report. There was no response. She tried again, "Nine eighty-three, what's your status?" Again, no response.

Mark said, "Tell Central we'll go by and check on him."

Zack grabbed the mic. "Central, ten oh five, we'll go check on nine eighty-three."

"Ten oh five, 10-76 at 1503," Denise replied.

"Clouseau's a dumb ass. He probably forgot to turn on his walkie." Mark pulled into a driveway on Highway Y and turned around to head back westbound.

"Doesn't he have a cellphone?"

"Yeah, but he's a cheap bastard. It's one of those pay-by-the-minute phones. He refuses to use it for work."

Five minutes later, they were driving through dense forest on both sides of Rouggly Road when Mark said, "Shit, there's smoke coming from the trees up there." He stomped on the brakes and turned up the winding gravel driveway leading to the trailer. When the cruiser emerged from the trees, they saw the trailer was burning out of control. "Zack, grab that hose and put some water on the trailer! Do not try to go in there!" Mark yelled. He took a deep breath and keyed the mic, "Central, ten oh five, we're 10-23. The trailer is on fire. Lieutenant Close's vehicle is here, but there's no sign of him. Get the fire department and an ambulance out here, ASAP, and notify Lieutenant McLeod and the Sheriff." Mark moved the cruiser out of the way to open a path for the coming fire truck.

Zack ran to the garden hose connected to the spigot at the wellhead and dragged it as close to the fire as he could bear and sprayed water into the trailer's ruptured windows. Orange flames surrounded by thick acrid black smoke billowed from every opening. He could smell gasoline and plastic burning. Then he smelled something totally foreign to him. It was a sweet, putrid pork smell. He realized it must be human flesh and instinctively backed up a few steps to get away from it.

Mark ran over to Close's unmarked Crown Vic and checked to see if he was inside. He wasn't. Then he saw a 500-gallon propane tank sitting fifty feet off to the side of the trailer. Flames were steadily licking at the weeds surrounding it. "Zack, get back from the trailer!" he yelled, but Zack didn't hear him over the roaring inferno. Mark ran over to Zack, took the hose from him, and threw it toward the window. He grabbed Zack by the arm and pulled him behind their cruiser.

"There's a body burning in the trailer!" Zack yelled.

Mark nodded and said, "Yeah, I smelled it too."

Five minutes later, the silver paint on the propane tank was burned black.

"Get down! The tank's gonna blow!" Mark yelled as he took a knee behind the cruiser. He stuck his fingers in his ears and opened his mouth. Zack crouched down next to Mark but watched the tank through the rear window. Seconds later, the tank exploded, sending a huge fireball into the sky. The basketball-sized metal dome from the top of the tank fell from the black cloud and landed behind them. Mark took out his cellphone and called McLeod. He put it on speaker.

McLeod answered the phone, "How bad is it, Mark?" over the sound of his wailing siren.

"The propane tank just exploded. I can't find Denny. I think he's in the trailer. There's no sign of the resident either," Mark said somberly.

"Damn. I'll call the Sheriff. I'm coming from Leadwood, so it'll be a while," McLeod replied as the siren continued.

Mark hung up, and he and Zack stood there watching the trailer burn for the next ten minutes while they waited for the Big River Volunteer Fire Department and County ambulance to respond from Bonne Terre. By the time the firemen started putting water on the trailer, it was a burned-out shell. Five minutes after the fire was out, the firefighters confirmed there was a body inside the trailer. They didn't move it, but they could see a deputy's star attached to the belt next to an empty holster. Sheriff Blair,

McLeod, Mark, and Zack all took turns leaning in through the doorway to look at the body, but the smell quickly turned them away. No one was eager to go inside.

"I asked Sheriff Marsh at Jeffco to send a couple of his CSIs to process the scene. They will be here in a few minutes. I also asked Troop C to send us their SWAT Team and Metro Air Support for a helicopter. Les is on his way too. Ike, call Jeffco back and ask them to put cars on Boyd Branch Road. Then call Bonne Terre, Desloge, Park Hills, Leadington, Leadwood, and Farmington and ask them to send cars up here to help form a perimeter from Highway 67 to Highway Y to Highway D. I want everyone to work in teams of at least two. Nobody operates alone. And see if we can get a K-9 unit," Blair said.

McLeod replied, "Yes, sir," and walked away to make his calls.

"Boss, why do we need SWAT? What was Close doing out here?" Mark asked.

"The guy who lives here is Randall Powers. His landlord made an appointment with him to come over this morning to pick up the rent because she likes cash. But when she got here, Powers was gone. The door was unlocked. She went inside and said the floor had been cleaned and smelled like bleach. She said Powers is a retired Green Beret and an instructor at Iron Mountain. The Jeep over there is the only vehicle registered to him. Did you guys see him when you got here?"

"No," Mark replied as he looked into the trees surrounding them. "But if he killed Denny, he could be hiding out there in the trees right now ready to snipe us, for all we know."

Zack spoke up, "I worked with Special Forces guys in Afghanistan. If he's retired SF, we won't catch him in the woods, and he may kill some of us if we go in there looking for him. I bet he grabbed his go bag and bolted. He'll probably get caught a couple weeks from now sleeping in a cash-only motel a thousand miles from here."

The lawmen tried to remain cool but couldn't resist the urge to scan the trees. The thought of an invisible apex predator running loose was, to say the least, disconcerting.

"Well, we'll leave him alone until the SWAT boys get here. Then we'll sweep the woods for him," Blair said.

"Sir, do you think Powers killed Lieutenant Close and Hope Pagano?" Zack asked.

"Why Hope? Denny probably stumbled onto Powers doing something illegal and got killed for it, but what's his motive for Hope?"

"I don't know, but they're connected by IMI. Powers worked there, and Hope's dad owns it. And her roommates said she had a secret boyfriend. What if Powers and Hope were a couple? Maybe she threatened to tell her dad about their affair and the baby, and he knew Nick Pagano would fire him or worse. I know I'd be pretty hot if I had a nineteen-year-old daughter hooking up with a guy twice her age. Maybe he thought Pagano sent Lieutenant Close over here to smack him around or lock him up on a bogus charge. The county only averages one or two murders a year. Now we have two in less than a week. The IMI connection can't be a coincidence," Zack replied.

By the time Koplin showed up with his van, the firefighters had already rolled up their hoses, stowed their equipment, and headed back to their station house. The sheriff arranged for the ambulance to stand by at the scene in case anyone looking for Powers was wounded. Within half an hour, the MD 500E helicopter from Metro Air, callsign Air-2, arrived and the officers McLeod requested were surrounding the woods where they believed Powers was hiding.

Sergeant Kevin Mitchell was the SWAT Team leader. He arrived five minutes after Air-2 in his Highway Patrol Explorer. He was already wearing his green operational camouflage pattern uniform. He approached the circle of lawmen and held out his hand to Blair. "Afternoon, Sheriff. I'm sorry for your loss."

Blair shook it. "Thank you, Kevin, and thank you for coming out to give us a hand. Our suspect's not your ordinary shithead. His name is Randall Powers, and he's a retired Green Beret with extensive combat experience. With Jeffco and our local police departments' help, we've set a perimeter from Boyd Branch Road to Highway D to Highway Y to Highway 67. Metro Air's helicopter, Air-2, just arrived and is checking the area. Here's a copy of his driver's license. Do you guys have a dog coming?"

The wail of multiple sirens approaching penetrated the trees, and within a minute, a train of six troopers' cars rolled up the driveway and staged next to Mitchell's car.

"No, sir. All of the Patrol's K-9 units are already tasked elsewhere. I'll brief my team as we suit up, and we'll be ready in about ten minutes." Mitchell walked off to talk to his men.

"Damn, I'd give my left nut for a dog right now. Ike, you'll have to take over here for a while. I need to go notify Denny's wife. I don't want her to hear about it from someone else. I'll come back when I'm done," Blair said.

"Sheriff, do you want Zack and me to go with the troopers?"

"No, why don't you boys go do an area canvas before it gets dark?"

"C'mon, Zack." They climbed in their cruiser and drove back out onto Rouggly. "We'll take the closest house and then head west toward 67, then we'll come back and go east. When we approach these houses, I want you to be alert. Powers could be holding the residents hostage in one of the houses we approach. We have to be prepared to react. Always tell dispatch where we are before we get out of the car so they know where to send help."

They stopped at the first house on the north side of Rouggly about 200 feet from the entrance to Powers's driveway. Mark approached the front door and told Zack to stay back behind his open car door in case he needed to call for help. No one answered the door, so Mark wrote a note asking the owner to call Zack or him at the station and left it stuck in the doorjamb.

Mark walked back to the car. "Take a minute to call your wife. Tell her you're OK, but don't tell her about Denny. I'm gonna do the same." After they were finished, they got back in the car. "Let's go check the next one." Three hours later, they had checked the homes in both directions. The sun was low on the horizon when they arrived back at the trailer. Blair had returned and was talking to McLeod. Mark and Zack joined them.

"The people we talked to didn't see or hear anything unusual, until they saw the smoke and the tank exploded. How'd it go with Ginny?" Mark said.

"About like you'd expect. She's devastated. They still have two boys in high school. I got her sister to come over and help her. My wife will go over there tomorrow. I hope I never have to do that again. We'll need to arrange a proper funeral for him. I think I'll put Baderman on it," Blair said.

Minutes later, Sergeant Mitchell and his team silently materialized from the tree line. Mitchell approached the sheriff and his deputies while his men walked to their cars and began peeling off their weapons and armor. He removed his helmet and clear ballistic shooting glasses and vigorously rubbed his sweaty scalp.

"We didn't see any sign of him in the woods. There's a little clearing back there where he had set up a small pistol range, probably fifteen yards long. We covered the area all the way down to Highway Y and over to Highway D. He must have gone north toward Boyd Branch Road. If he did, he might have breached the perimeter before Jeffco got set up."

"That's too bad. I would've liked to wrap this up today. Thanks again for coming out, Kevin, and tell your team I really appreciate it," Blair said as he patted him on the back.

Mitchell joined his team, and in minutes, they were on the road.

"This guy, Powers, is a real danger to the community. He murdered a deputy. In this state, that means death by lethal injection. Now he has nothing to lose. He'll kill anybody that gets in his way. As far as I'm concerned, this asshole's paid for," Blair said. "I'm going to call out the Major Case Squad. I'll get them spun up tonight so they can get started. Our only remaining detective is assigned to the Mineral Area Drug Task Force, and they're working on a case with the DEA, so we can't pull him back. Mark, you and Zack go home and get some sleep. Tomorrow morning at 0900, you two report to Sergeant Deer at the Troop C office in Park Hills."

"Will do, Boss. C'mon, Zack." They climbed in their cruiser and headed out. "Tomorrow, wear your department polo shirt and cargo pants. We'll meet at the station at 0830 before we go to the Patrol's building. Being a good Marine, I bet you have your own AR-15 and plate carrier."

Zack nodded. "Yup."

"Good. Bring 'em. Act like you're going to war because you are."

"What did the Sheriff mean when he said Powers was paid for?"

"Powers is a cop killer, so he's used up all of his favors. Treat him like a dangerous animal. There won't be any warnings to 'drop your gun or we'll shoot.' Shoot first and keep shooting until he stops moving. He'll have no hesitation to kill you or anyone else. If the troopers find him before we do, he'll probably commit suicide before they can arrest him. That's what usually happens. Seriously, don't give him an opportunity to shoot first; if you do, he'll kill you. Just remember this phrase: 'I was in fear for my life.'"

"Roger that," Zack said as he looked out the window.

CHAPTER 17

DAY 7, THURSDAY, JUNE 11

Zack walked through the back door to the station at 0825 and found Mark seated in the sheriff's office. The sheriff motioned for him to come in and have a seat.

"Morning, Zack. I was just telling Mark we got Hope Pagano's toxicology report back. No surprises. She died of a massive meth overdose." Blair turned to Mark. "How would you like to be the new sergeant running our Detective Bureau?" Blair asked as he slid a sergeant's star across his desk.

Mark picked up the shiny gold star and studied it for a moment. "I'd like that, Boss. The circumstances sure suck, but I did enjoy the work."

"I know you'll do a first-rate job. It's no secret you were always a better investigator than Denny. That star comes with a $500 a month bump in salary. Zack will stay with you until this case is over, and then we'll put him with Kurt Sada. Unlimited overtime is authorized for you two until we get this shithead, but that doesn't mean I expect you to work until you drop. I'll rely on your judgment to decide how many hours you guys put in every day." He faced Zack. "Mark said he told you to bring your personal AR in this morning. How's it set up?"

"Sir, it's a piston-operated Stag Arms AR with a sixteen-inch barrel and collapsible stock. It has an EOTECH red dot and a green laser and light combo on the vertical foregrip. I have ten Magpul magazines loaded with 62 grain green-tipped ammo. The mags are attached to my plate carrier. I also have an Armalite AR-10 with a Nikon M-308 scope at home for long-range work."

"How'd you shoot in the Corps?"

"I shot expert with the rifle and pistol."

"Well, you're already better trained and equipped than the rest of the department. Here's a copy of the memo I'm putting in your file authorizing you to use your personal weapons." Blair handed him the paper. "Put this mourning band on your badge. Keep it on there until after the funeral," he instructed.

Zack took the black band of elastic, pulled it over his badge, and pinned it back on.

"Mark, I want you to check in with me at least once a day. Justin's a good trooper, but if you think he's leading the squad down the wrong path, let me know."

"Will do, Boss. C'mon, Zack. Let's go check in with Sergeant Deer." Mark stood up.

Zack stood and stuck out his hand. "Congratulations, Sergeant."

"Thanks. Let's go catch a killer."

Mark and Zack rolled through Burger King, which was becoming their morning routine, before driving up Highway 67 to the Highway Patrol annex in Park Hills in front of the Mineral Area College.

"So, what's the Mineral Area Major Case Squad?" Zack bit into his double sausage, egg, and cheese croissant.

"Most of the rural Missouri Sheriffs' Departments are small and underfunded. Down here, we can't afford to have our own crime labs, medical examiners, and homicide divisions like St. Louis City's Hat Squad. So, the Sheriff made a deal with the sheriffs from Iron, Madison, and Washington Counties, the Highway Patrol, and a lot of the city police departments like Farmington to form the Major Case Squad. When there's a major crime, the Major Case Squad is called out and everybody sends a detective to help. When we get to the annex, there will probably be fifteen to twenty detectives already working the case."

"What's the Hat Squad? I've never heard of it."

Mark smiled. "The old-timers in St. Louis City's Homicide Division used to wear nice fedoras with their fancy suits. They were called the Hat Squad."

"Well, we all have ball caps, maybe we can be the Cap Squad," Zack joked.

Marked rolled into the parking lot of the annex. They walked through the front door and down the hall to the large conference room the Major Case Squad used as their base of operations. Sergeant Justin Deer sat at the conference table with paperwork spread in front of him.

Deer stood up and offered his hand to Mark. "Congratulations. The Sheriff just told me about your promotion."

"Thanks, Justin. This is Zack Goodson. He just started with the department on Monday. He's going to be riding with me until we finish the case."

"Good to meet you, Zack. I guess this is a lot to absorb during your first week."

Zack nodded. "Good to meet you too, Sergeant."

"Please, have a seat. Before we get started, I want to say I'm sorry for your loss. It's always hard to deal with when a LEO goes down. Have any arrangements been made for the services?" Deer asked. LEO stood for law enforcement officer.

"None I'm aware of. The Sheriff didn't say anything this morning. It'll probably take Denny's wife a day or two to get that taken care of. The Sheriff assigned the undersheriff, Captain Baderman, to help her arrange everything. He's excellent at that sort of thing."

"Mark, I'm going to make you the deputy commander of the squad. With your promotion and the fact that the case occurred in your county, it just makes sense. After today, I'd like you to report for duty in the afternoon. That way, one of us will be on duty while both shifts are working. Counting you two, we have ten officers working the case so far, and I'm expecting another eight to ten to roll in at 1400 for the afternoon shift change. I'd like for you to be here for that. For now, though, I left you the task of going out to IMI and talking to Mr. Pagano and his staff about Powers."

"Sounds like a plan, Justin. We'll head over there and be sure to be back before the shift change."

Thirty minutes later, they arrived at the Iron Mountain International training complex in the south end of the county. It sprawled across almost 2,000 acres of densely wooded hills. They climbed out of their cruiser and strolled into the administration building. They stepped up to the counter and were met by an attractive receptionist wearing a tight pink IMI polo shirt. Her name, Kristina, was embroidered above the left breast. "Hi, Kristina, I'm Sergeant Mark Langford, and this is Deputy Zack Goodson. We're investigating what happened to Mr. Pagano's daughter. We need to talk to him as soon as possible."

She picked up the phone to call Pagano's office, but before she could dial, Pagano opened his door. "Good morning, gentlemen. Come in." They walked inside the office and sat down in front of his massive oak desk. "I was sorry to hear about Denny. I hope you have good news. Did you catch Powers yet?"

"No, sir, he took off before we got there. He left his Jeep behind, so we think he hoofed through the woods. We had the Troop C SWAT Team looking for him until sunset, but there was no sign of him. He just vanished. The Sheriff activated the Major Case Squad, so we should be making some progress very soon. We have some questions for you if you're up to it?" Mark asked.

"I'll do anything I can to help you guys. I feel kinda responsible considering Powers worked for me. Denny was a friend of mine for over twenty-five years. Ginny must be going crazy. I'll call the Sheriff and make a donation to help his family."

"Thank you, sir. I'm sure anything you can send will be put to good use." Mark opened his notebook. "Did you know Randall Powers personally?"

"I was introduced to him when he was hired last year, but we didn't socialize. Back then, I did read his résumé and the file our background investigator compiled before we hired him. He was a highly trained and experienced Special Forces operator. He'd been through an ugly divorce right before he came here, but none of us are immune to that."

Mark took notes on his responses. "Did he have any trouble here at work? Did he get along with the other employees?"

"He did have a dustup last week with one of the other instructors. His name's Gilberto Garza. He's a retired gunnery sergeant and Force Reconnaissance Marine. I'll get my chief instructor, Keith Winthrop, in here. He can tell you what happened better than I can." Pagano picked up his phone and told Kristina to call him.

They all heard Kristina yell, "Hey, Keith, Nick wants you."

"Sorry, I didn't know he was in the building," Pagano said.

"Yes, sir, what can I do for you?" Winthrop asked from the doorway. He was wearing the somewhat standardized company uniform: black IMI T-shirt with "Instructor" and the company logo printed on the back, woodland camouflage trousers, IMI ball cap, and dirty boots.

"Come in, Keith. These deputies need to know what happened between Powers and Garza last week."

Keith sat down on the arm of Pagano's leather sofa and spit in his murky, brown liquid-filled bottle. "Randy came to work last Wednesday hungover again wearing yesterday's clothes. We had a platoon-sized element of Marine Raiders here training, and he made an ass of himself in front of them and Gil got pissed. He waited for the Marines to go to their next training event and then confronted Randy. He called him an embarrassment to the other instructors and the company. Randy pushed Gil and told him to fuck off. Gil beat his ass and then came and told me what happened. I already had Randy on a short leash. I told him this was his last chance. The next time, I would fire him."

"Did he always have discipline issues?" Mark asked.

"No, he did a great job for the first nine months or so, then over the last couple of months, he became a problem child."

Mark took more notes. "Keith, what's Gilberto Garza like? Have you had any trouble from him?"

"No, not until he beat the shit out of Randy. Randy fucked up, but he probably didn't deserve the whipping Gil put on him."

Mark turned to Pagano. "Sir, can you call Garza in so we can talk to him?"

Before Pagano could speak, Winthrop said, "Is it alright if I take you to him? He's up in the hills with some Delta boys. They're only here for three days. If we pull him out, it'll fuck up the training plan."

"Sure, that's fine with us. Mr. Pagano, is it alright if we talk to the other instructors while we're out here?" Mark stood up.

"Talk to anyone you like, but please, try not to disrupt the training."

Zack stood up. "Excuse me, Mr. Pagano. Can I ask you if there's any chance Powers and your daughter were seeing each other?"

Pagano's demeanor changed from cooperative to pissed instantly. "No, I don't. Why would you think so? Powers is twice her age."

"When we talked to her roommates, they said she had a secret boyfriend."

"They told me the same thing. She was probably seeing Grant Cunningham again. They dated all through high school before they broke up. Lately, he's fallen on some hard times. She probably didn't want anyone to know she was giving him a second chance. If Powers killed her, I'd be more likely to believe he did it out of some sort of revenge plot to hurt me."

"Why would he want revenge against you?" Zack asked.

"He went through a bad divorce before he came here. He moved here from Fayetteville because I offered him a job, and lately, he was in danger of being fired. So, then he'd be without his family and his job."

"Thank you for your time, Mr. Pagano. Again, we're sorry for your loss. Keith, do you mind taking us to Garza?" Mark said.

The trio climbed into a four-door IMI Jeep Wrangler modified to handle the rough, hilly terrain. Winthrop called Garza and asked for his location. Ten minutes later, they rolled into a clearing on top of a hill. Zack recognized it immediately as a helicopter landing zone cut out of the forest. Garza and the Delta operators were sitting on the edge of the LZ atop a couple of downed trees eating MREs for lunch.

Winthrop waved Garza over to the Jeep. "Do you guys mind if we stay in the Jeep? I'd rather not air our dirty laundry in front of the D-boys," he said.

"Sure, that's not a problem as long as Garza cooperates." Mark set his phone to record and stuck it in his breast pocket.

Garza walked up to the Jeep with a big smile on his face. Winthrop's arm hung down outside the door. Garza punched Winthrop in the arm in a friendly Marine to Marine way, which meant it hurt like a mother. "Hey, Pooh, what's up?" He pulled a red shop towel from his back pocket and wiped his sweaty face.

"Fuck you, dickhead. This is Deputies Langford and Goodson. The Boss would appreciate it if you gave these men your fullest cooperation." Pooh refused to shake out his arm, much less rub it.

Mark waved his hand. "I'm pleased to meet you. Could you hop in the back seat so we can talk for a minute?"

Garza climbed in behind Winthrop. Zack offered his hand. "Zack Goodson, Semper Fi."

Garza shook his hand. "Semper Fi, Devil Dog. So, I assume this is about Powers."

"We understand you had a little tussle with him last week," Mark said.

"It wasn't a tussle. He came to work shitfaced again and made us all look like a bunch of no-talent ass clowns in front of a platoon of Marine Raiders. His performance was getting worse every day. He developed a pattern where he would leave at the end of the day, have dinner at Colton's, then drink himself into a stupor at the VFW in Bonne Terre, and then show up here hungover the next morning. I got tired of covering for his dumb ass, so I put a whuppin' on him to adjust his attitude. I heard about him killing your deputy yesterday. I'm sorry it happened, but I don't think me thumping Randy last week had anything to do with him killing your guy," Garza said.

"Did anyone else witness the fight?" Mark asked.

"Yeah, Jay Sandoval and Zeke Horton were there. They pulled me off him."

"Who are they?"

"They're instructors. Jay came from SEAL Team 4, and Zeke was with SEAL Team 3," Winthrop replied.

Mark nodded as he wrote then looked back at Garza. "Have you ever been to Powers's trailer?"

Garza hesitated as he looked back and forth between the two deputies. "Yeah. Once last year about two weeks after he started at IMI, he invited all the instructors over to his trailer for a cookout. Is that all? I have to get back to training these guys."

"How about Hope Pagano? Did you know her?"

"No!" Garza was clearly pissed now. He climbed out of the Jeep and walked away without looking back.

"I guess we hit a nerve," Mark said.

"He's gone now. You can rub your arm," Zack said with a grin.

Winthrop brought his arm inside and raised the window as he began massaging his quickly swelling bicep. "Fuck you. For the record, I was at the cookout too, along with about twelve other guys," Winthrop said.

"Did you know Hope?"

"No, I never met her," Winthrop replied.

"OK, thanks, Keith. We can head back now. Can we talk to Sandoval and Horton?"

"Yeah, they should be back down at the complex in the kill house." The kill house was a state-of-the-art live fire range contained inside a large building that could be configured to simulate various urban structures.

Silence descended on the Jeep for a few minutes as they drove slowly down the winding dirt trail through the dense forest before Zack asked, "So, why does Gil call you Pooh?"

Winthrop regarded Zack for a moment through the rearview mirror. "Winthrop, Winnie the Pooh, Pooh for short. How about you? What's your callsign?"

"No comment." Zack smiled.

Winthrop smiled back in the mirror. "Pussy. It must really suck."

"You have no idea."

The Jeep emerged from the trees, and Winthrop parked next to the kill house. As they climbed out of the Jeep, they could hear the muffled shooting going on inside the building. "You guys wait out here, and I'll bring them out one at a time so the training can continue. Does it matter who comes out first?" Winthrop asked.

"No, either one is fine, thanks," Mark replied.

The shooting continued as Winthrop went inside. A few minutes later, Winthrop came out with a dark-haired man wearing clear-lensed shooting glasses and hearing protection earmuffs. The man pulled the muffs off his ears and clamped them to his head over his ball cap. He was clad for combat with an armored plate carrier and M4 rifle. The rifle hung at his side on a single-point sling.

"Jay, this is Deputies Langford and Goodson. They're investigating Hope Pagano's and their lieutenant's murders. The Boss told them we would cooperate with their investigation. They have some questions for you."

Sandoval looked at Mark and Zack. "What can I do for you?"

Mark opened his portfolio notebook and set it on the Jeep's hood. As before, he also had his phone recording what was said. "We just have a few questions for you. Did you know Hope Pagano?"

"Well, yeah, I did. Zeke and I eat at Colton's a lot, and we met her there. She waited on us several times. We didn't know who she was until one time I wore my IMI cap in there and she said her dad owned the company."

"Did you ever see Randy Powers with her?"

"No, not with her, but one time Randy was with Zeke and me when she waited on us."

"Did he act like he knew her?"

"No, but after she took our orders, he commented on how hot she was. He and Zeke acted like they wanted to get to know her better."

"How long ago was that?"

"Maybe a couple of months."

"Did Gil Garza every go to Colton's with you?"

"Yeah, he went once with me and Zeke a few weeks ago."

"Did he know Hope Pagano?

"I don't know."

"Was she working there that day?"

"I don't know. I don't remember seeing her."

"Did you know Lieutenant Dennis Close from the Sheriff's Department?"

"No."

"How often did you socialize with Randy?"

"Maybe four or five times since he came to IMI. I'd see him at other instructors' parties."

"How about Zeke? Was he seeing Hope?"

Sandoval smiled. "No way. He would've liked to, but he's shy around women. He's fearless before the enemy, but he has a hard time talking to a girl."

"What happened with the fight between Garza and Powers?"

"Gil got in Randy's face for screwing up again, and Randy pushed him. Then Gil commenced pummeling Randy. We watched it for a while, but Gil didn't act like he was going to stop, so Zeke and I pulled him off."

"Did you think Gil might kill him?"

"Well, for sure there would have been some permanent damage."

"Were any threats made after you pulled them apart?"

"Randy said something about getting even. Then Gil said, 'If you ever come after me, that'll be the last time anyone ever sees your sorry ass.' They were both pretty pissed. Randy was bleeding from his nose and mouth and his left eye was puffing up."

"Was Gil hurt?"

"No, his shirt was ripped, but he wasn't bleeding. Gil's a black belt instructor at that Marine martial arts shit. It really wasn't a fair fight."

"OK, thank you, Jay. Can you send out Zeke?"

A couple of minutes later, Horton came out of the kill house. He was outfitted the same as Sandoval. He looked back and forth at Mark and Zack nervously. "What's going on?"

"Hi, Zeke. I'm Sergeant Langford and he's Deputy Goodson. We're investigating the murders of Hope Pagano and Lieutenant Dennis Close. We'd like to ask you a few questions."

Horton looked at Winthrop, who told him, "Mr. Pagano would like for us to cooperate with the deputies to the fullest extent possible."

"OK, what do you want to know?"

"How well did you know Hope?"

"I met her at Colton's, but we didn't hang out together."

"Did you ever ask her out?"

"No."

"Why not? Didn't you like her?"

"Sure, I liked her. I just never got around to asking her. Besides, she was the boss's daughter."

"Have you ever been to Randy's trailer?"

"I went out there once for a cookout after he got hired."

"How well did you get along with Randy?"

"He was alright. We had dinner a few times after work."

"Do you know if he was seeing Hope?"

"No, I don't."

"Have you ever met Lieutenant Dennis Close?"

"No."

"OK, Zeke, thanks for talking to us. Keith, thank you for helping us out today. We'll get out of your way. C'mon, Zack." They climbed into their cruiser and drove out of the complex and headed north on Highway 221. "What was Sandoval talking about when he said it wasn't a fair fight between Garza and Powers? Do the Marines have their own martial arts program?" Mark asked.

"Yeah, in 2002, the Corps started the Marine Corps Martial Arts Program. It borrowed techniques from about fifteen martial arts like Brazilian Jiu-Jitsu, judo, kickboxing, karate, Muay Thai, taekwondo, aikido, hapkido, and Krav Maga. It gave us options for less-than-lethal force for crowd control and police operations all the way to killing someone with one move. All Marines are trained in it at a basic level. It gave us a lot of confidence in fighting hand to hand, especially if you came from a civilized part of American society where fighting was frowned upon. If Garza's an instructor, he's put a lot of time into practicing the techniques. I wouldn't want to be in a fair fight with him," Zack replied.

"So how good are you at it?"

"When I was in Afghanistan on my last deployment, I advanced to the brown belt level. We had a lot of spare time when we weren't flying. I haven't practiced much in the last year. I'm pretty rusty. I might try a move on somebody and accidentally kill them. I thought about taking up Krav Maga, but the closest school is up in Festus."

"Well, when the fists and feet start flyin', you have my permission to step in front of me. My fragile ego can take a beating much better than my face," Mark said with a smile.

CHAPTER 18

"Central, ten oh five, request 10-44 J4 at Granny Annie's," Zack transmitted as Mark pulled into the parking lot and stopped in front of the diner.

"Ten oh five, cleared J4," Peggy replied.

They walked into the diner and to the reserved table in the back next to the kitchen door. This time, Zack left the menu alone.

"Don't you think it was weird that Pagano didn't ask about his daughter's killer today? And he didn't say anything about Grant Cunningham when we talked to him the first time," Zack said.

"The first time we talked to him, he had just ID'd his dead daughter's body. He wasn't thinking straight, but I have to admit, I was surprised when he didn't ask us if we had any suspects yet. It makes me wonder if he might be having some of his people conducting a parallel investigation for him."

Annie approached the table with two glasses of ice water and kissed Mark. "Zack, what would you like for lunch?"

He smiled. "I'll have whatever Mark has and a Coke." Annie turned for the kitchen. "So, what will the other detectives on the Major Case Squad be investigating today?"

Mark took a drink of water. "Some will be standing by while the pathologist performs Denny's autopsy. Hopefully, they'll recover physical evidence, like bullets to be compared to other cases and possibly identifying the weapon and its owner. Some are going to be doing a deep dive into Powers's cellphone, email, social media, bank account, credit cards, and credit history. Some will be contacting everyone he has called or texted for the last month or so. Some will be following up on the area canvas we conducted. Some will be processing his trailer and Jeep for evidence. After everyone writes up their reports, we'll start comparing them for inconsistencies, then we will conduct another round of interviews to correct the record or catch people lying to us. Right now, everything points to Powers killing Denny, but what if he was set up or our investigation clears him? What if Garza went over there and killed Powers and Denny stumbled on to him and got killed too. As long as we follow the evidence wherever it takes us, we won't be caught looking like a bunch of dumbasses."

Annie emerged from the kitchen with a tray full of food. She balanced it on the edge of the table and placed two bowls of salad and two large plates of lasagna and Italian sausages with garlic bread in front of them. It wasn't your standard chain restaurant version of lasagna. Hers was three inches high and loaded with meat and cheese. Then she gave them another smaller plate with a big piece of Dutch apple pie. "Enjoy your lunch, boys," she said with a grin.

"Thank you, Annie. This looks great," Zack said before she headed back to the kitchen. "How do you eat lunches like this every day without gaining a ton of weight?"

"This is my main meal for the day. We eat something simple for dinner. Besides, the last thing Annie wants to do when she gets home is fix dinner. She usually brings something home from here for the boys. They never go hungry."

"Nick, Mr. Malkowicz is here to see you," his receptionist, Kristina, said over the phone.

"Thanks, send him in."

The office door opened, and a balding man of about sixty-five wearing a conservative dark gray suit entered.

"Howard, thanks for coming over so fast. How's Sally?" Pagano asked as if he were genuinely interested. He stepped around his desk to shake Howard's hand. He motioned for him to sit on the custom-made Italian leather sofa. "Please, have a seat." Pagano sat across the coffee table from him in the matching chair.

"She's fine, Nick. Thanks for asking. Before you start, I'd like to tell you again how sorry Sally and I were to hear about what happened to Hope. She was a wonderful young lady."

"Thank you." Pagano couldn't remember Malkowicz ever meeting her.

"I'd also like to thank you again for bringing me on with IMI. I'm really enjoying the work, and I think you'll be pleased with my findings. I should have the report completed before your deadline in six weeks," Malkowicz added.

"No worries, Howard. You're doing a fine job, and I've been hearing good things from the vice presidents. The reason I asked you to come by is I have another opportunity for you. I know you've only lived in the county for a few years, so you may not be aware of the corruption that's been going on at the Sheriff's Department. Don Blair has been the sheriff for twenty years, and he's running for another term. Over the years, he's developed an organization built on nepotism and cronyism. There's no accountability, and his deputies are so underpaid, many of them are lining their pockets through illegal activity. I've received reports of an active drug ring operating in the jail. The leading citizens of the county are so disturbed, they've asked me to help them unseat the sheriff. Despite his activities, he remains very popular with the voters."

"I can certainly help with that. I worked in Internal Affairs for five years before I got my own precinct. If he's dirty, I'll catch him," Malkowicz said. He was referring to his career with the St. Louis Metropolitan Police Department.

"I have something better in mind. I'd like you to run for sheriff. What do you think?" Pagano asked.

"Nick, I'm flattered, but I don't have the political organization necessary to unseat an entrenched incumbent and, to be honest, even with my police pension, I don't think I could afford to live on the sheriff's salary," Malkowicz said.

"Howard, I understand your reservations, and I know the job doesn't pay much, but I've lived here all my life, and now that I'm in a financial position to give back to the people of the county, I want to help. How's this sound? When you become sheriff, you'll keep your current IMI compensation package in addition to the sheriff's salary. I will finance your campaign completely with an unlimited budget. I have a professional campaign consultant and his team standing by to run your campaign. When you're elected, I'll give your department a grant large enough to replace every deputy with well-paid, highly trained professional lawmen. And I'll also pay to construct a new state-of-the-art station and jail and get the best vehicles and equipment money can buy. With your experience as a lieutenant colonel with the St. Louis department, you're extremely well qualified to run our small Sheriff's Department. After two or three years when you've rehabilitated the Department, you could step aside if you like and appoint your undersheriff to replace you, but if you decide to stay on as sheriff, you'll keep your IMI compensation as long as you're in office."

Malkowicz wiped away the perspiration beading above his upper lip and dried his hand on his trouser leg. "That's very generous. Under the circumstances, you make it hard to say no."

"Howard, on behalf of the people of the county, thank you for stepping up." Pagano stood and shook his hand. "I'll have your campaign manager contact the *Journal* and announce your campaign. He'll be calling you in the next hour or so."

"Oh, what about my report? Should I keep working on it?"

"No. No, I want you to concentrate on your campaign. I'll arrange for another consulting firm to take over your project. Now, go home and tell Sally about your exciting news," Pagano said with a grin.

Mark and Zack arrived back at the Troop C office with fifteen minutes to spare. The conference tables were arranged in a rectangle so the officers could face each other. Justin and Mark sat at the front of the room with a whiteboard behind them. Over the next fifteen minutes, the room filled with men and a few women wearing shades of blue and brown and gray. Some in uniforms, some not.

A bespectacled, gray-haired detective wearing an old blue sports coat that looked cheap enough to throw in the washing machine approached Zack. He reminded Zack of a tall, overweight Mark Twain. Twain stuck out his hand. "You must be Zack. I'm Herman Keller. I'm with Park Hills PD."

Zack stood up and shook his hand. "Yes, I am. Good to meet you, Herman."

Keller pointed over his right shoulder. "This is Detective Cody Gibbs from Farmington. We're partnered up for the investigation."

A much younger, fitter, and better dressed man came forward behind Keller. "Hey, Zack." He presented his hand.

"Good to meet you, Cody." Zack shook his hand.

"I heard you flew Super Stallions in the Corps. I was a Seabee during Iraqi Desert Storm. A flight of four of your helos flew my company and our equipment up to the Kuwaiti Naval Base. That's an incredible helo," Keller said.

"Yeah, I really enjoyed flying them."

"How do you like riding with Mark?" Keller asked.

"Well, it's only my first week, but so far, so good."

Keller looked over at Mark. "You better keep an eye on him. You may have to add him to the suspect list."

"Why's that?" Zack chuckled.

"Ask him about the time Denny almost shot him," Keller said with a huge grin.

Zack eyed him suspiciously and slowly said, "OK." Keller and Gibbs walked away laughing and took their seats opposite Sergeant Deer and Mark. Zack turned to look at Mark and saw him shake his head with a grin.

"Ignore those knuckleheads. They're just jealous," a seductive voice behind Zack said. Zack spun around to find an attractive redhead facing him. She placed her left hand on his shoulder to keep him from standing as she presented her right hand. He shook it. "Mark's one of the best detectives in this room. For sure the best male detective. Hi, I'm Jackie Weber. I'm with Leadwood."

"I'm pleased to meet you, Jackie," Zack replied. "Who are you partnered with?"

"I'm riding with Art Lambert from Bismarck. Hey, Art," she called out. A balding man with a bad comb-over waved from across the room without looking up from his paperwork. "That's him, Mr. Personality. You want to trade?"

"And ride with you? Sure. Ride with him? No thanks."

"Well, don't blame a girl for trying," she said as she left.

Zack watched her walk away.

As she approached Cody Gibbs's seat, he said, "Good afternoon, Jessica," and laughed. As she walked behind him, she flicked the back of his head with her finger hard enough the sound was heard over the conversations in the room. Gibbs continued to laugh as he rubbed his head.

Zack laughed too. She did remind him of Jessica Rabbit except for the blue pantsuit. Over the next few minutes, others entered the room and introduced themselves, but he didn't remember any of their names. He remained distracted by Jackie as his eyes kept drifting over to her. She caught him a few times and smiled back at him. He guessed she was used to it. He thought if he could ever be tempted, it might be by her.

Deer stood up. "Everyone, please, take a seat and we'll get started. I think you all know me; I'm Sergeant Justin Deer from the Highway Patrol. I've been assigned to lead the investigations. Sitting next to me is our second in command, Sergeant Mark Langford from the Sheriff's Department. He will supervise the afternoon shift. One of us should be available at all times. OK, let's go over what we've learned since last night and then the day shift can depart until 0600 tomorrow morning. Herm, tell us what you guys found out today."

Keller opened his notebook. "I'm Detective Herman Keller from Park Hills. My partner is Detective Cody Gibbs from Farmington. We went to the county prosecutor, Missy Gilham, to get a search warrant this morning for Powers's cellphone, bank account, social media, and credit cards. She approved and sent us over to Judge Buchanan. He signed the warrants and let us know he would be eager to help further the investigation. So far, we haven't found any social media accounts for Powers. There's been no activity on any of his accounts since Wednesday morning at 0115 when he paid his tab at the Bonne Terre VFW with his bank card. Either he's using cash for everything or he has accounts we don't know about. It makes me wonder if he established another identity. His iPhone cell carrier is AT&T. They don't store the contents of text messages, but they do record who texted who and when. Seven weeks ago, he began calling and texting Hope Pagano as many as fifteen times a day. Three weeks ago, all contact stopped."

Zack exchanged looks with Mark.

Keller continued, "His bank and credit card accounts indicate he went to Colton's Steak House three or four times a week. We'll be checking to see if Hope was working during his visits to the restaurant."

"Thanks, Herman. Cody, why don't you go next?" Sergeant Deer said.

"I'm Detective Cody Gibbs from Farmington. We attended Lieutenant Close's autopsy, which was performed by Dr. Patel at Parkland Hospital. Patel confirmed the lieutenant was dead before the fire started. He removed three .40-caliber Smith & Wesson rounds from Lieutenant Close's chest and determined they were the cause of death. We won't know for sure until we get the ballistics report back, but they looked like the 180 grain Federal Hydra-Shok rounds we carry at Farmington PD."

"Times like this almost make me wish we had gun registration in this state," Deer said. He received hard looks from the other investigators. "I said 'almost,' dammit!"

Zack had learned in the Academy something every other cop in the room already knew. Missouri was extremely pro–Second Amendment, and under state law, Powers could walk into any gun store and buy as many pistols, rifles, and shotguns as he liked and walk away with them the same day as long as he passed the National Instant Criminal Background Check System (NICS). He could also by a gun from a neighbor or friend without a background check or any paperwork.

"There's no telling how well armed Powers is. Hell, he might be hiding out there in an underground bunker or cave like Rambo for all we know. Colin, tell us what you found at the scene," Deer said.

"I'm Deputy Colin Ward of the Jefferson County Sheriff's Department. My partner and I processed Powers's trailer and Jeep. The fire was definitely arson. Gasoline was poured throughout the trailer and on Lieutenant Close's body to act as an accelerant. The floor under the body wasn't burned. We didn't recover any spent brass in or around the trailer. We did recover some brass from the pistol range he had set up in the woods behind the trailer, but it was all .45 ACP. We printed his Jeep and recovered numerous prints from Powers and Hope Pagano. We also found prints from Zeke Horton and Jay Sandoval. They work with Powers as instructors at IMI."

Mark chimed in, "Zack and I went out to IMI this morning and talked to both Horton and Keith Winthrop. Winthrop is the chief instructor. He said Powers began working there about nine months ago. He started out as a good employee and instructor, but about two months ago, he became erratic. He was coming in hungover, so Winthrop put him on notice to clean up his act or he would fire him. He also told us about a fight that occurred between Powers and another instructor, Gilberto Garza. Last week they were training a group of Marine Raiders, and Powers showed up reeking of alcohol and wearing the same clothes as the day before. He embarrassed himself and Garza in front of the Marines. It especially pissed off Garza because he's a retired Force Recon Marine. Garza took him behind the building and put a first class beatdown on him. Garza's an expert in the Marine Martial Arts Program. Winthrop said it was a little more severe than necessary. Horton and Sandoval had to pull Garza off of Powers. Powers threatened to get even, and Garza told him if he tried, it would be the last time anyone would ever see his sorry ass."

"That sounds like motive to me," Detective Keller said.

The others nodded in agreement.

CHAPTER 19

DAY 8, FRIDAY, JUNE 12

Zack rolled into the Sheriff's Station parking lot at 11:00 a.m. He went to the squad room and checked his mailbox at the back of the room. Being the new guy, his box was in the bottom right-hand corner and was stuffed with all of the unwanted junk mail from everyone else's mailboxes. It was just another part of the harassment package for probationary deputies. It was kid stuff compared to the reindeer games he went through in the Corps and flight school. Here he wasn't cold, he wasn't wet, and no one was shooting at him, so this was a piece of cake. Actually, he kind of missed some of the excitement. Of course, he liked ice cream too, but he didn't want to eat a whole gallon. He grabbed the junk mail with both hands and dropped it in the trash can in the corner.

"Hey, Zack. Thanks for coming in early," Mark said as he entered the room. He glanced in his mailbox on the top row as he walked over to the last table in the back of the room and sat down.

Zack sat down a couple of chairs away. "No problem. So, what's on the agenda for today?"

"Hope Pagano's funeral service is at 1:00 p.m. at Koplin's. We're going to the funeral to see who comes. We'll stay on the edges and try to be discreet, but we want to get photos of the crowd. We'll have a couple of guys in plainclothes at the entrance to the parking lot recording all of the vehicles' license plates and a couple more at the door recording who comes in. We'll have a few more in vehicles cruising the surrounding streets. Maybe Powers will try to watch from a distance and we can bag him. Since Pagano is a billionaire and retired police chief, you'll see a lot of businesspeople, politicians, and LEOs at the funeral. The funeral procession will be extremely long. It'll get a police escort to the cemetery. But first, I figured before we go over there, you might want to get lunch at Granny Annie's."

"Yeah, I was hoping you'd say that."

Twenty minutes later, they were sitting at the reserved cop table waiting for their lunch to arrive.

"Hey, yesterday before shift change, Gibbs called Jackie Jessica, then she thumped him on the head. What was that about?"

"Almost three years ago, the FOP Lodge held a costume party and contest as a fundraiser for BackStoppers. Hundreds of people gathered trying to win the $500 prize for first place. Some of the wives went the extra mile to come up with clever costumes for them and their husbands to wear in hopes of winning the money. Well,

Jackie glided in dressed as Jessica Rabbit. She was the living embodiment of the cartoon character—absolutely stunning. She even had the voice down perfect. Of course, she won the contest by a landslide and, in the process, pissed off a lot of wives."

Zack chuckled. "Why did Herman Keller say you should be on the suspect list?"

"It happened back when I was working for Denny in the Detective Bureau. We were sitting in the office working on reports. It was back when we were carrying the early-generation Glock 17s. They had a smooth grip that could be slippery if your hands were sweaty, so many of us used the Hogue grip. It was a rubber grip kind of like a textured piece of inner tube with finger grooves you could pull over the Glock's grip to give you a better hold on your pistol. Well, Denny got one for his Glock and was trying to get it on his pistol. He removed the magazine and started stretching it over the bottom of the grip. It's hard to do with one hand, so he stuck the pistol between his knees and pulled on it with both hands, but the pistol kept slipping. Then he held the pistol grip with two fingers while he fumbled around with it until he accidentally pulled the trigger. The round the dumbass accidentally left in the chamber fired and flew past my head close enough to tickle my ear. It scared the shit out of me."

Zack laughed.

"Have you ever heard the Winston Churchill quote about being shot at?"

Zack shook his head.

"He said, 'Nothing in life is so exhilarating as to be shot at without result.' It was definitely exhilarating. It was also stressful. Do you know the true definition of stress? It's when your brain denies your body's overwhelming desire the beat the shit out of somebody."

Zack laughed some more.

Mark looked toward the door and saw Lieutenant Ike McLeod and Deputy Kurt Sada enter the diner. They approached the table.

"Do you mind if we join you, gentlemen?" McLeod asked as he and Sada sat down rather than wait for an answer.

Mark looked over his shoulder as if someone more respectable might be there. McLeod and Sada sat with their backs to the door. Apparently, they weren't worried about being shot in the back.

"Hey, Ike, Kurt. Are you guys working the funeral today?" Mark asked.

"Yeah, we're part of the escort over to the cemetery," McLeod replied. "I figured we better eat now. No telling what might happen afterward. Besides, Annie's will be closed by then. By the way, congratulations, Sergeant. We'll be sorry to lose you on the road."

"Thanks, Ike."

"Hey, Zack. How's it goin'?" Sada asked.

"Not bad. I understand I'll be riding with you after this case is over," Zack replied.

"Yeah, that's what they tell me." Sada reached for a menu.

McLeod took the menu from Sada's hand and shook his head as he put it back next to the napkin dispenser. "Just stand by for a minute."

Annie appeared from the kitchen with a platter of food. She set large plates in front of Mark and Zack. They both held two big fried boneless pork chops smothered in gravy, rice, green beans, and corn. Next, she set smaller plates of cornbread muffins and peach cobbler in front of them. "Hello, boys. What would you like for lunch?"

"Hi, Annie, I'll have what they're having," McLeod said with a smile.

Annie looked at Sada. "Same for me, ma'am." She turned and headed for the kitchen. "I don't remember that being on the menu."

"It's not," McLeod said.

"Damn, I've been ordering off the menu for over four years. I didn't know there was a secret lunch club."

McLeod threw his thumb toward Mark. "Haven't you heard of Langford's Laws?"

"No," Sada said.

"Langford's ninth law is 'You don't talk about Lunch Club,'" McLeod said with a grin, "Mark, do you guys have any leads on Powers yet?"

"No, his digital trail ended early Wednesday morning when the VFW closed. He hasn't used his phone, credit cards, or bank account since. We think he did the murders, but we really don't have any evidence. Is there any word on Denny's funeral yet?"

"This morning the Sheriff announced it will be at 1100 on Monday at Koplin's. Les offered Denny's wife a deep discount to help her out. Make sure you wash your car. Uniform is long sleeves with ties, white gloves, and straw hats, no ball caps. We'll meet at the station at 0800 to give everyone their assignments. We're expecting a couple hundred LEOs in addition to his family and friends. The Sheriff said LEOs are coming from as far away as Kansas City. We'll probably have twenty motor officers at the front of the procession. Too bad Denny's dead. He was never this popular when he was alive," McLeod said.

"Maybe they're just coming to make sure they put him in the ground," Sada said.

Zack ate his food without comment. It appeared Mark's warning and his own initial assessment of Close was spot on. Close was, or had been, a dick.

"I wonder if any of the city coppers who hooked him up for soliciting will come to the funeral." Sada said with a snort.

Zack choked on his food. He cleared his throat. "What was that?"

McLeod laughed. "Back when he was running the Detective Bureau as a sergeant, he went to St. Louis to question a guy being held in the city jail. Afterward, he stopped by Cherokee Street to visit with the ladies. He offered the first girl to approach his car twenty bucks to polish his knob. She said for twenty he could have a handy. He agreed, and she told him to pull into the alley. As soon as he did, a couple of unmarked city cars boxed him in. It turned out she was a police officer. They yanked him out at gunpoint. Then they searched him, cuffed him, and stuffed him in the back seat of one of the unmarked cars while his car was moved out of the way. They continued with their operation while Denny was cuffed up in their back seat. He was telling them he was a deputy and begging them to look in his car. He told them his badge, gun, and ID were under the rear floor mat, but they weren't buying it. After he started crying, they agreed to go look just to shut him up.

"As a professional courtesy, they let him go without putting anything on paper, but you can't keep something that good a secret for long. One of the detectives told a patrol cop who happened to know one of our deputies. Since there was no report written, Denny got away with it. Of course, soon thereafter, Denny conducted an internal affairs investigation on Clint Nickmeier for falling asleep in his car. Denny tried to shame him while he was questioning him. Clint said, 'C'mon, Lieutenant, it's not like I was propositioning the hoes up on Cherokee Street.'"

After the laughter died down, McLeod said, "Hey, Kurt, tell these guys about your fit for confinement yesterday at Parkland."

Sada smiled. "I arrested a drunk shitbird who beat up his wife and then took off in his truck. I stopped him out at the intersection of Highway K and D. When I got him out of the truck, he took a swing at me. I blocked it with my baton and accidentally split his right eyebrow open. He started bleeding like a stuck pig, so I called an ambulance for him. The EMTs put a turban on his head, but he cussed them a blue streak the whole time they were treating him.

He continued threatening me and cussing me all the way to the hospital. He tried to spit on me through the cage, so I stopped and pulled his T-shirt up over his head. That really freaked him out. I guess his one good eye could still see a little bit through his shirt because after I got him into the emergency room, he started yelling and screaming at everybody in the waiting room, so they moved us to the front of the line and put us in a treatment room. I cuffed his hands to the bed so he couldn't hurt anybody.

"When the nurse came in to treat him, she pulled his shirt off his head and began removing the turban. He began MF'ing her, so she turned right around and left. A few minutes later, the doctor came in to stitch him up and he did the same thing to the doctor. The doctor's this muscle-bound Army Reserve surgeon who did a couple of tours in Iraq. He's used to dealin' with pissed-off jihadis. So, the doc says, 'OK, I'm going to have to numb up your eyebrow so we can stitch it closed.' The guy keeps on acting like an ass as the doctor sticks the needle through his eyebrow and squirts the lidocaine out onto the floor in the corner. The doc looks at me and I shrug. I mean, he's the doctor, right? So, then the doc looks at the wall clock and says, 'OK, we need to wait five minutes for the anesthesia to start working.' He made small talk with me, asked me how I like being a deputy, and talked about the weather and the Cardinals. He seemed like a really nice guy. After five minutes of the guy yelling like a jerk, the doc pinches his eyebrow closed with his thumb and finger, and the guy starts screaming and jerking his head around. So, the doc gets the guy in kind of a headlock with his left arm as he pinches the eyebrow closed and he starts putting in the sutures. The guy's screaming and jerking his head with every stitch as the doc is calmly saying 'Hold still. Hold still.' I think he put in three or four extra stitches just to make sure it would stay closed. He was very thorough."

Mark and Zack stopped eating to keep from choking. "There's another lesson, Zack. Don't piss off the doctors and nurses. You never know when you're going to open your eyes and see one of them standing over you."

Zack laughed again. "I learned that six years ago when I married one."

"Mark, do you remember the time we took that wife beater to Parkland for a fit for confinement back when we were young deputies?" McLeod asked.

Mark smiled and shook his head with a mouthful of food.

"We had a domestic one night about two in the morning. This fella came home shitfaced and woke his wife up to fix him something to eat. She mouthed off at him for waking her up, so he punched her in the face. She agreed to get out of bed and fix him some food. When he sat down at the kitchen table, she walked behind him and grabbed the cast-iron frying pan off the stove. She smacked him on the back of the head with it and called 911. She said the sound surprised her. She said it was like banging a gong. When we arrived, he was still lying on the kitchen floor moanin'. We quickly determined he was the primary aggressor and cuffed him up. After the cuffs went on, he got belligerent so we decided we should both take him to the Parkland ER for a fit for confinement physical.

"They had this black lady admitting nurse back then, Miss Nadine. She was probably mid-forties, about 5'10", 250 pounds. She was the sweetest woman in the world, but look out if you got on her bad side. She didn't take no shit from nobody. We sat the guy down in front of her desk and told her what he had done and where he was injured. When she heard he was a wife beater, you could tell it pissed her off.

"Her computer was on the right side of her desk, and she swiveled in her chair to start typing. She placed her fingers above the keyboard and peered at the guy over her red cat-eye reading glasses and said, 'Name?' The guy said, 'Fuck you.' She frowned at him and said, 'I'm only going to ask you one more time. Name?' He said, 'Fuck you, Jemima,' and then he laughed. She slowly swiveled around to face him and opened the center drawer of her desk, and then she whipped out this big lead-filled leather sap like we used to carry and swung it across the desk. The sap hit him on the side of his head and knocked him out of his chair. It surprised the shit out of us. After a few seconds, we picked him up and put him back in his seat. We had to hold him up after that because he was wobbling back and forth. She calmly placed the slapper back in the drawer and closed it with her thumbs. She swiveled around to the right and placed her fingers above the keyboard. She turned to look at him over her glasses and said, "Name?" He was very cooperative after that... Damn, I miss the old days," McLeod said wistfully.

After another good laugh, everyone went back to eating their meals as the other meals had been delivered by Annie during Ike's story. Zack's phone was sitting on the table, and it lit up with a message. He picked it up to read a message from his buddy Bruce Anders, callsign Gumby: "Hey, Turd Blossom. I sent you an email you need to read ASAP." He clicked on his email account and opened the email. It got right to the point. It said, "One of our pilots just got permanently grounded with a heart condition. I told Keebler you were trapped out there in Mayberry, and he's throwing you a rope. He's inviting you to apply to come to HMX-1. He only invited three guys to compete for the slot. I know you're the best qualified, and we both know Keebler's sweet on you. He'll make his decision in two weeks. Also, headquarters just sent out the bonus message. You're eligible for $25,000 a year for six years if you come back. By then, you'll be a lieutenant colonel and be four years from retirement. Get your package together ASAP and send it in. The attachment has the instructions." The attachment was a letter on official letterhead from the Commanding Officer of HMX-1, Colonel Michael J. Harrington, USMC. It told him about the vacancy and short suspense and gave him directions on what information to submit with his selection package. Above the official signature block it was signed "Keebler." He had commanded the Flying Tigers when Zack and Gumby were there. Keebler was a good shit. Zack could already imagine himself sitting inside the cockpit of one of the white tops on the White House lawn while he waited for the president to finish talking to the reporters being held back by the rope line. He was both instantly excited about the prospect of flying for HMX-1 and depressed with the realization that it would never happen. His future was right here in St. Francois County.

Mark and Zack roamed around inside the funeral home and tried to be inconspicuous as they took photos of the mourners with their cellphones. Zack stopped in the back of the room and watched. Nick Pagano sat in the first row on the left side with his elderly parents sitting next to him. His ex-wife sat across the aisle from him on the right with a gray-haired and well-tanned man who looked like he spent a lot of time on Florida golf courses. They refused to acknowledge each other. They were two warring camps brought together by a shared tragedy.

Mark walked over to Zack and quietly asked, "Have you seen anything yet?"

"No, nothing suspicious. It's pretty much your standard funeral, except for the ice storm in the front row. I've been watching Pagano and his ex-wife. People approach one of them with their condolences and then the other, but they act like the other doesn't exist."

"I guess that's not too surprising. I'd bet they both feel guilty for not protecting their daughter, and they probably blame each other for causing the divorce. I took pictures of the guest book. We can check the names later," Mark said. His cellphone vibrated. "C'mon." They walked outside and Mark answered the call, "Hello."

"Hey, Mark. It's Herman. I'm over on the south end of the lot. Gilberto Garza just arrived in his truck. He's heading your way."

"OK, thanks, Herm. We'll keep an eye on him." After hanging up, Mark said to Zack, "Herm said Garza is on his way to us."

A moment later, Garza walked up wearing a dark gray suit. "Gentlemen," was all he said as he passed them and entered the building. After a few seconds, they followed him inside. They watched as he approached the front of the room and leaned over in front of Pagano. He said something and shook his hand. He then found a seat in the back of the room with Sandoval and Horton.

CHAPTER 20

Zack and Mark sat in the unoccupied corner of Colton's Steak House on the far side of the bar. It was between the lunch and dinner rushes so that side of the restaurant wasn't being used.

The attractive young bartender came over. "Hi, my name is Sarah. Can I get you anything?"

"Yes, ma'am. I'd like a sweet iced tea with lemon," Mark said.

She looked at Zack. "Just a Coke and some peanuts, please." She smiled at him and headed back to the bar. A few minutes later, she returned with their drinks and peanuts.

She put her hand on Zack's shoulder and stared directly into his eyes. "If you want anything at all, just let me know." She smiled and walked back to the bar.

Mark smiled too. "Is it getting hot in here?"

Zack ignored him.

A man with a pot belly wearing a white short-sleeved shirt and a red tie approached the table. "I'm the manager. The hostess said you wanted to talk to me. I hope the service was alright?"

"Yes, it was. Please, sit down, sir. I'm Sergeant Mark Langford, and this is Deputy Zack Goodson. We're investigating the murders of Hope Pagano and Lieutenant Dennis Close. Is it alright if we ask you a few questions?"

"Of course. I was sorry to hear about what happened. Hope was a wonderful young lady. I'm sorry, but I didn't know your lieutenant. I'll do anything I can to help."

Mark opened his portfolio to take notes. "Thank you, sir. What is your name?"

He pushed his glasses up on the bridge of his nose. "Norman Carlson."

"How long have you worked here?"

"I moved to this location to become the manager about five years ago."

"When did Hope start working here?"

"It was last summer. July, I think." He ran his fingers through his thinning hair.

"And her roommates, Lindsay and Krista?"

"All three of them started around the same time, probably within a week or so of each other."

"Have any of them been in trouble at work?"

"No, I haven't had any trouble at all from any of them."

"Did you notice anyone paying too much attention to Hope. Flirting with her or touching her?"

"No. I wouldn't have allowed that to go on." Carlson combed his mustache with his thumb and forefinger.

"Is Grant Cunningham here today?"

"Yes, he's in the kitchen."

"Is it alright if we talk to him for a few minutes?"

"Sure, I'll send him out." Carlson got up.

"Thank you for your help, Mr. Carlson." Mark stood up and shook his hand.

"You're welcome. No trouble at all." He headed for the kitchen.

A couple of minutes later, Grant Cunningham approached the table. "Mr. Carlson said you wanted to see me."

"Yes, Grant. Have a seat. We're investigating Hope Pagano's death. We need to ask you a few questions. I understand you and Hope dated all through high school. Had you been seeing her socially before her death?"

"No. We split up after high school. I saw her here at work, but we didn't hang out anymore." Cunningham squirmed and rubbed his arms constantly.

"Did you notice her hanging out with a new boyfriend recently?"

"No. I work in the kitchen, and she was a server, so I didn't see her much except when she came back to pick up her orders. We didn't run around with the same people anymore."

"OK, thanks, Grant. Oh! One more thing. Where were you on the afternoon of Friday, June 5, through the morning of Saturday, June 6?"

"I worked here on Friday until around eight and then I went home. I stayed there until I came back to work the next morning at eleven."

"Can anyone confirm you were home?"

"No, I was alone."

"OK, thanks again, Grant," Mark said. Grant stood up and returned to the kitchen.

After Cunningham was out of sight, Zack asked, "What do you think of that character?"

"I think he's a kid who's already reached the top and is on the way down. He was the Big Man on campus at the high school for his junior and senior years, and he was dating the most popular girl. They were the power couple on their way to great lives. He was the quarterback on the football team, captain of the basketball team, and a starting pitcher on the baseball team with a full ride to Mizzou. After he threw his arm out, he lost his scholarship and his girlfriend. Now he's smoking, drinking, using drugs, living in a crappy little apartment, and has a dead-end job with no hope of bettering his life," Mark replied.

"I saw the cigarette pack in his shirt pocket, but how do you know about the drugs and alcohol?"

"He has the look. A year ago, he was about 200 pounds of muscle. Now he's probably around 170. He has blemishes all over his face, and he has that gaunt, wasting-away look. His teeth are going bad. All meth users end up with that look, but he's getting there faster than most. Eventually, he'll get fired from here, and when he can't find another job, he'll start committing petty thefts and burglaries. It's an all too common occurrence," Mark said solemnly.

CHAPTER 21

DAY 9, SATURDAY, JUNE 13

Just after noon, Zack sat next to Mark at the table at the front of the squad room. They were in civilian clothes. Mark had called him and said the sheriff had called a meeting at the station for all of his deputies. Over the last fifteen minutes, deputies had arrived and filled every seat. Some were leaning against the walls. Most were in their street clothes. The room was buzzing. Everyone wondered what the meeting was about.

Sheriff Blair walked to the front of the room and stood behind the lectern. He surveyed the room and all his deputies like he was trying to firmly implant the memory in his mind. "Thank you for coming in, ladies and gentlemen. I'm sorry if it's your day off, but I wanted to talk to all of you before you heard this information somewhere else. A friend has alerted me that I will not be running unopposed for reelection this year. A retired lieutenant colonel from the St. Louis Metropolitan Police Department has filed to run against me. His name is Howard Malkowicz, and he's an executive working for IMI. His campaign is being financed by Nick Pagano." Groans and slurs were murmured around the room. He put his hand up to quiet the crowd. "I received an advanced copy of an article that will appear in the *Journal* tomorrow. Malkowicz accuses me and this department of incompetence, corruption, cronyism, racism, and everything else except kidnapping the Lindbergh baby. He said as soon as he takes office, he will clean house and replace my entire staff."

"Screw him, Boss," Deputy Wainwright said from the back of the room to the approval of the crowd.

Blair continued, "Look, I don't know if y'all have noticed, but Nick's worth over a billion dollars now, so if he wants to, he can throw a ton of money at getting his boy elected. I'm old enough I can retire, but you'll have to do what you think is best for you and your families. I wouldn't blame you if you started looking for other jobs right now, but for those of us who are staying till the end, we are going to have to up our game. I know you're all good deputies, but any missteps between now and the election could hurt our chances. The opposition could even attempt to set up situations where they get us on video doing or saying something that appears improper to embarrass us publicly. So, do your jobs, but stay aware of the political climate we are working in. Thank you all for coming in, and make sure you log an hour of OT for the meeting." The sheriff left the lectern. He stopped in front of Mark and Zack, leaned over on the table. "I know you guys don't need any more pressure, but it could really help our chances if you can catch Powers before the election."

"Boss, you know we'll do everything possible," Mark replied.

Blair slapped him on the shoulder and nodded before heading for the door.

"Zack, have you got an hour or so? I'd like to show you something."

"Sure, what is it?"

"Just follow me over and I'll show you."

They got in their vehicles, and Zack followed Mark into Farmington's business district down near the County Courthouse. They drove around to the back of a mom-and-pop hardware store with a single unmarked steel door leading into its basement. There were no windows in the concrete wall. A handful of cars and trucks were parked along the wall. They parked, and Mark waited at the door for Zack. As he approached, Mark stuck his key in the lock and opened the door. He stepped aside and held it for Zack. Zack stepped into the room and waited for a second to let his eyes adjust to the dim interior. He surveyed the large room. It was part man cave, part party room. It smelled of beer, popcorn, and nachos. They walked across the room to the bar. It was obviously homemade, but much better than the plywood bars he and his fellow pilots had built in Asscrackistan. Several tables with chairs were scattered across the area near the bar. Two deputies were using the pool table in one corner. Several pinball machines and video games stood against the wall. Another wall had what Zack estimated was an eighty-inch flat screen TV attached to it. Three deputies sat in recliners watching the Cardinals game. Zack smiled and looked at Mark.

"Welcome to the St. Francois County Deputy Sheriff's Association Lodge," Mark said. He pointed at a red neon sign behind the bar. "We call it the Squad Room. C'mon, I'll get you something to drink." Mark walked around the bar. "There's a list of what we have and how much it costs on the wall next to the fridge." He opened the door. "What'll you have?"

Zack studied the list. "I'll have a Coke and a bag of pretzels." He pulled a dollar out of his pocket and laid it on the bar. "I don't see an oven or stove. Do you guys have bar food?"

Mark retrieved a Coke and Budweiser from the fridge and two bags of pretzels from the shelf behind the bar. He pushed Zack's dollar back to him. "This one's on me." He dropped his payment into an open cigar box on the shelf. "That's our cash register." Mark handed the Coke and pretzels to Zack. "We have a small kitchenette over there with a microwave, a toaster oven, and an electric pizza oven. Guys bring in Crockpots full of chili or stew for parties like the Super Bowl. When the weather's nice, we set up grills or smokers in the parking lot. Some guys play nickel poker on Wednesday nights. Sometimes the night shift crew comes in here after their shift and cooks up biscuits and gravy before they go home. I've seen guys crash here overnight when they've gotten kicked out of the house.

"If you want to become a member, the dues are $10 a month. The hardware store above us is owned by Kurt Sada's uncle. He rents us his basement for $100 a month. We've been renting it since before the Sheriff was first elected. This gives us a place we can socialize without running into the knuckleheads we arrest every day."

"So, the Sheriff is OK with this?"

"Sure, he was a member when he was a deputy. Now he has an open invitation to come by, but he doesn't abuse the privilege."

"How many members do you have?"

"Right now, everyone but you and Baderman. He was a member for a while, but he just didn't fit in."

Zack pulled a ten-dollar bill from his wallet and put it on the bar. "OK, I'm in."

Mark put the money in the cash register and handed Zack a key to the door.

"Thanks. I need to take a leak. Where's the head?"

Mark pointed toward the corner. "There's just one. It's behind the door marked Deputies."

Zack walked through the garage door into the kitchen. Patty was at the stove mashing potatoes to go with her famous fried chicken. Approaching her from behind, he wrapped his arms around her as he buried his face in her hair below her ear. She rolled her head back and leaned into him. After a moment, he let go and she turned around and kissed him. They broke their embrace as he eyed the stove suspiciously. "What's going on?"

"What do you mean?"

"You like fried chicken, but you hate cooking it. You only make it for special occasions. So, what's the occasion?"

She studied him for a moment. She was smiling, but she also seemed apprehensive. "You're getting good at this cop stuff…" She hesitated before adding, "I'm pregnant," and waited for his reaction.

He smiled and excitedly wrapped her up in another hug. "That's great, babe! How far along are you?"

"About eight weeks. Are you sure you're OK with it?"

"Well, the timing might not be ideal, but we'll make it work."

"What's wrong with the timing?"

Zack released her and searched her eyes. "That meeting the Sheriff called us all in for today was to tell us Nick Pagano is financing one of his boys to run for sheriff against Blair. This guy, Malkowicz, says when he becomes sheriff, he'll fire the whole department and replace us. Don't worry about it. You know me. If it happens, I'll improvise, adapt, and overcome. Where's Danny?"

"He's staying at Mom's tonight." She smiled.

"Wow! Date night and fried chicken. Then what? Popcorn and a movie or ice cream and a movie?"

"We can splurge and have it all," she said and then leaned in and kissed him passionately.

"Give me ten minutes to take a shower." He headed for the bedroom.

CHAPTER 22

When Pagano's private cellphone rang, he answered, "Hello."

"Hi, Mr. Pagano. This is Lindsay Miller. I'm sorry to disturb you, but I need my laptop back. Can I come over and get it?" she asked nervously.

"What? I don't understand." He tried to remain calm.

"The laptop you took from our house wasn't Hope's, it's mine, and I need it for school."

Pagano tried to quickly think his way out of this complication. "I'm sorry. It was in her room and I thought it was hers. I went a little crazy; I was so desperate to find her."

"I understand, really. Can I come and get it?"

"No! No, I'll bring it back. This is really embarrassing. Please, don't tell anyone. I'll be right over, and please, call me Nick."

"OK, we'll be here." She hung up.

Twenty minutes later, Pagano's old truck pulled onto the gravel driveway, and he it drove around to the back of the house with its headlights off. He noticed the windows were closed and the air conditioner was running. He walked around the house to the front door and rang the bell.

Lindsay opened the door. "Hi, Mr. Pagano. Come in."

Pagano stepped inside with a big smile on his face. He hugged her with his free arm and then handed her the laptop. "Here you go. For the record, I couldn't figure out your password, so I didn't see anything." He saw Krista sitting on the sofa. "Hi, Krista."

"Hi, Mr. Pagano."

Lindsay took the laptop and set it on the coffee table. "Thank you for bringing it over. Can I get you anything?"

"No, thanks. I don't want to ruin your night. I'll get out of your way. Again, I'm sorry for taking your laptop. I'd be mortified if word got out that I came in here and took it. How did you know I had it?"

Lindsay glanced over at Krista, who nodded. "I have tracking software on my laptop to help me find it if it's lost or stolen. I knew as soon as I got home and saw it was missing that you had it, but I didn't want to bother you with all that was going on. I called tonight because I have homework due on Monday."

"And you're both sure you didn't tell anyone I had it?"

They both immediately shook their heads, and Lindsay added, "No, Mr. Pagano."

Pagano smiled. "OK, thanks, girls." He pulled Denny's Glock from under his shirt and quickly double-tapped Lindsay twice in the chest. The impact knocked her off her feet. She fell backward to the floor, her head landing at Krista's feet. Krista screamed in terror at the top of her lungs. She brought her hands up to cover her mouth right before two bullets ripped jagged tears in her forearms before they plunged into her chest. Pagano stepped forward and looked down on Lindsay. His face was devoid of sympathy as he robotically shot her in the face. Her nose exploded as the bullet mushroomed on its journey through her skull. Krista's chin was resting against her chest as if she was looking at the blood on her arms. Pagano fired a round into her forehead that rocked her head back. Bone, blood, and brain tissue splattered the wall and slowly slid down to the floor.

This time he left the brass on the rug where it fell. He would blame this on Powers too. He picked up the laptop and left. His fingerprints were all over it. He could explain his prints being in the house, but not on Lindsay's laptop. He got in his truck and slowly rolled toward the road with his lights out. The automaton quickly faded away, and he became human again. He stopped the truck as the tears began to flow. They ran down his cheeks and made it even harder to see in the darkness. He cried so hard his nose started to run. He wiped his eyes, and when he didn't see any traffic coming down the road, he flipped his headlights on and drove away. He cried all the way to the back gate. Along the way, he thought of Hope and her two best friends and how loyal they had always been to one another over the years and of their big plans to be nurses and help the people of Farmington. He thought of all the soccer games and dance recitals and concerts he had watched them perform in. Then he thought of their parents and knew exactly how devastated they would be when they found out their girls were dead. And he knew they would not be able to fathom why anyone would hurt them but would still blame themselves for not protecting them.

He regretted shooting them in the head. He thought a normal person wouldn't have done that. It was unnecessary. Then he realized how crazy that thought was. As if it was normal and acceptable to shoot two innocent girls in the chest, but somehow shooting them in the head was out of bounds. Like that was where he crossed the line. If he wasn't so selfish, he would have just killed himself rather than take these innocent lives, but the truth was, Hope was the only person in the world he loved more than himself and she was gone forever.

CHAPTER 23

DAY 10, SUNDAY, JUNE 14

It was just before midnight local time at Camp Dwyer, Afghanistan, and Captain Zack Goodson was walking across the expansive concrete ramp where his squadron's aircraft were parked to begin the preflight inspection on his massive CH-53E Super Stallion helicopter. The rest of the crew was still enjoying their midrats, but he had decided to get an early start. He was an experienced aircraft commander, but tonight he was acting as copilot for his squadron commander, Lieutenant Colonel Mike Harrington, callsign Keebler. He wanted to make sure everything was squared away for the colonel.

It was a black moonless night, and Zack was relying on the night vision goggles attached to his flight helmet to navigate across the ramp without tripping over a tiedown chain or walking face-first into a blade rope or the side of a helo. He was carrying a heavy load. In addition to his helmet and goggles, he wore his aviation armor, which included two ceramic plates, survival vest, M9 pistol, M4 rifle, combat pack, CamelBak, flight bag, and gas mask. His load weighed in at just under 120 pounds. Even this time of night, it was over 90°F. If he hadn't already known what spot his helo was parked on, he never would have found it. He opened the bottom half of the crew door on the right side of the helo aft of the pilot's seat and climbed into the cargo compartment. He folded down the first troop seat and started shedding his gear. He switched on his blue-lensed flashlight and pushed the top half of the door up out of the way and secured it to the overhead. Next, he stepped up into the cockpit and staged his helmet, rifle, and flight bag next to the left seat.

He stepped down out of the cockpit and was about to go outside through the crew door when his blue-lensed flashlight shone on a large Afghan National policeman standing on the ramp in front of the exit. That was odd because the ANP weren't allowed on the flight line. The policeman's eyes went wide, and he yelled something Zack didn't understand. He had a canvas backpack in his hands and an AK-47 slung over his shoulder. Instantly, Zack realized the man might actually be an ANP, but he was definitely a saboteur. The man dropped the backpack at his feet and grabbed for the AK to bring it to bear. Zack jumped from the doorway onto him, and they both fell together to the concrete ramp. The angry ANP moaned as the back of his head smacked the pavement. Zack's flashlight also fell to the ramp with the blue beam pointed at their faces. They wrestled nose to nose for control of the rifle, with Zack on top. He could feel the man's beard brushing against his chin and smell the stale tobacco the man smoked.

Zack was still on top about to gain the upper hand when the ANP headbutted him, breaking his nose. Zack winced with the intense pain; when he opened his eyes, he saw stars. Blood ran profusely out of his nose and down his throat, making him gag. "Motherfucker!" Zack yelled angrily.

"No! You fuck your mother!" the ANP replied in broken English as Zack's blood flowed onto his face. Seconds later, the ANP pushed Zack's body away from his own about four inches and shifted his body to the right. He rolled Zack off of him and quickly traded places with him. The man was inches away from bringing his rifle barrel under Zack's chin when Zack drew his Kabar from the sheath on his belt with his right hand and plunged the knife deeply into the man's groin. The man howled in agony and screamed something Zack didn't understand, but he maintained his pressure on the rifle. Zack twisted the blade and wrenched it back and forth. He could feel the warm blood soaking his hand and stomach. The man's strength faltered enough for Zack to withdraw his knife and then drive it repeatedly into the man's neck. Blood sprayed onto Zack's face. Finally, the resistance ended and the man stopped moving. Zack pushed the body off and took control of the AK. He stabbed the motionless body in the stomach once more to make certain it was dead. It lay motionless. Zack laid there on his side next to the body, gasping for air through his open mouth. The blood continued to flow from his nose and mouth. Soon a puddle formed under his head on the ramp. He was shaking uncontrollably. The fight lasted less than a minute, but he was physically and emotionally drained.

Rifle fire erupted in the distance. Zack quickly rolled to his stomach and aimed the AK-47 into the darkness under the next helicopter in the row. In the distance, he could see muzzle flashes and tracer rounds zipping back and forth. Marines from the Quick

Reaction Force (QRF) were following their training: shooting, moving, and communicating. Zack could see the red tracers the young Devil Dogs fired as they pursued an unseen enemy down the row of helicopters toward him. Sporadically, green tracers from the saboteurs' AKs were returned toward the Marines. Their fight was coming to him. Zack realized if he used the AK-47, the Marines would think he was one of the enemy and light him up without hesitation. He really didn't want to be killed by another Marine. He grabbed his flashlight and scrambled back inside his helicopter. He dropped the magazine on the AK and pulled the bolt back to eject the round in the chamber. He threw the AK on the troop seat and turned for the cockpit.

He retrieved his M4 and flight helmet from the cockpit. He lowered the night vision goggles and immediately saw three ANPs running down the ramp in his direction through the right-side cockpit window. He jumped to the ramp and ran to the nose of the helicopter. He hopped over the refueling probe and proned out behind the nose landing gear. He flipped on the infrared (IR) laser attached to his rifle, thumbed the safety switch to burst, and waited. Seconds later, as the terrorists closed to within twenty yards, he began firing bursts at them until they all fell to the ramp. The goggles and laser made him very efficient. One of the ANPs moaned and started crawling toward a pack on the back of one of the dead terrorists. Zack fired two more bursts into him and stopped him in his tracks. The firing from down the ramp slowed to a trickle and then stopped. Zack could hear Marines yelling back and forth as they maneuvered from helo to helo toward him. He knew he needed to identify himself quickly, so he pulled his IR strobe light from his flight suit pocket. He turned it on and stuck it to the Velcro on top of his helmet. He yelled, "Hey, Marines! Don't shoot! I'm Captain Goodson."

A voice with a New York accent said, "Hey, Captain, are the New York Yankees the best baseball team ever?"

"Hell no! The Cardinals are!" Zack replied.

He heard a voice from behind him say, "Damn straight! Fuck the Yankees."

He turned and through his goggles saw three Marines from the QRF approaching him from behind the helo parked next to his. Zack stood up on his shaky legs. "How many of these assholes are out here?" he asked and then spit a ridiculous amount of blood onto the ramp.

"As near as we can tell, six, Captain. We got two of them further down the line," one of the Marines replied as he watched the dark liquid splatter between them.

"The first ANP I killed was carrying a backpack," Zack said and thought for a moment. "One of the other three I shot also had one. Shit!" Zack ran back around to the other side of the helo, followed by the Marines.

Another Marine was standing over the dead ANP as Zack approached, and he said, "Damn, sir, you really fucked this guy up. Chesty ain't got shit on you."

Zack went to one knee next to the backpack. "Here, hold my light." The Marine held the light over the pack as Zack opened the flap and looked inside. He saw a cheap cellphone connected to a tightly wrapped package of explosives. The phone lit up brightly as a call came in.

Zack jerked awake and sat up gasping for air. He was soaked in sweat. His cellphone rang again, and he grabbed for it on the bedside table and missed. It fell between the table and bed. He pulled it up by its charging cord. "Hello," he said, half-asleep as he checked the time. It was 0803 on Sunday morning. Patty had taken pity on him and let him sleep in while she made breakfast for Danny. Her mom had brought him back home on her way to church.

"Zack, it's Mark. I'm sorry to call you on Sunday morning, but Dispatch just called me. Hope's roommates, Lindsay and Krista, were murdered in their house last night. They both took two to the chest and one to the head. The brass left behind was .40 S&W, just like we carry. Meet me at their house ASAP. Do you remember where it is?"

"No, I don't."

"It's in Desloge. I'll text you the address. Desloge PD is waiting for us to get there before they let Les take the bodies, so hustle."

"Roger that." Zack hung up. He threw on a clean uniform and ran down the steps. Patty was helping Danny eat breakfast as he came into the kitchen. He kissed Patty and Danny. "I have to go to work."

"I thought you were off. What's going on?"

Zack grabbed an apple from the bowl on the counter and a bottle of water from the fridge. "Desloge PD found Hope Pagano's roommates murdered in their house. Keep that to yourself. I gotta go."

"Wait!" She placed a fried egg and three strips of bacon between two pieces of toast and wrapped it in a paper towel. "Take this and don't forget we have dinner at four with my family."

He grabbed the sandwich. "OK. Thanks, babe." He hurried out to the garage.

Fifteen minutes later, Zack drove past a line of five police cars parked on the grass shoulder in front of 811 West Walnut Street on the far western edge of Desloge. The old farmhouse was hidden a couple hundred feet off the road in the trees. Over time, the city had grown around it. A Desloge police officer was standing at the end of the gravel driveway waving curious drivers down the road. He stopped next to the officer. "I'm Zack Goodson. Sergeant Langford called me in."

"Good to meet you, Zack. I'm Paul Barnes. You'll have to park out here on the road. They don't want any more vehicles up by the house."

"OK, no problem." Zack pulled forward off the road onto the grassy slope. He hopped out of the truck cab and jogged to the house along the tree-lined driveway. He saw a man and woman in the large front yard being held back from the house by four Desloge police officers. He was stopped by another one at the bottom of the porch steps who asked for his name and department service number for the crime scene log. Zack told him and then he walked through the open front door. He was shocked to see Lindsay's body splayed out on the carpeted floor. Her dead eyes were wide open and clouded over. A pool of dry blood ran from her mangled nose and down her cheeks to the carpet. It surrounded her head and upper torso. Krista's head was back against the sofa as if she was looking at the ceiling. Blood and brain matter splattered on the wall behind her head formed a halo. A Desloge detective wearing a black polo shirt was photographing the scene.

"Zack, put your gloves on and don't touch anything until after they're done processing the scene," Mark said from across the room.

Zack pulled a pair of black nitrile gloves from the pouch on his belt and put them on.

"Look for things that should be here that aren't and things that shouldn't be here that are," Mark said. "So far, I see two cellphones, two purses, and two cars. The TV is still on the wall. There's a laptop in its case in, I believe, Krista's bedroom. There's a laptop case in Lindsay's bedroom but no laptop. See if you can find another laptop sitting around somewhere."

"Who found the bodies?" Zack asked as he scanned the room.

"Two of their friends named Debbie Quinn and Jenna Hall. They all planned to go hiking in St. Joe Park today. They came by this morning to pick them up, and when no one answered the door, they looked through the window on the porch and saw their bodies," Mark replied.

A commotion could be heard coming from outside. "Let me see her! Lindsay!" her father yelled as he crossed the porch and entered the living room. The Desloge chief, Jimbo Blair, and another officer were right behind him. Miller saw his daughter's bloody body on the floor and bent over, covering his mouth like he was going to throw up. Mark grabbed him by the shoulders and directed him back out the door. He leaned him over the porch rail as Miller threw up into the bushes.

Mark kept him on the porch and called to Zack, "Check the kitchen for a bottle of water for Mr. Miller."

Zack returned with a cold bottle of spring water and gave it to him.

Miller tried to gargle as he cried. He spit into the bushes and wiped his mouth with the back of his hand. "Who would do this? Why would anyone hurt my girl?"

"I'm really sorry about your daughter, Mr. Miller. We don't have any answers yet, but the best way you can help us is to take your wife home and let us investigate. I'm sure you don't want her to see what you just saw. Let her remember Lindsay the way she was before this happened."

"C'mon, Larry, let me take you and Holly home. We'll call you when we have more information." Chief Blair put his arm on Miller's back and directed him to the steps. They walked back to Holly and the officers holding her back. Larry put his arms around her, and they cried together as they walked back to their car. Chief Blair drove them home in their car with one of his officers following them.

Lester Koplin's van rolled up the driveway and stopped next to the porch. He and Timmy went to the back of the van and pulled out two stretchers with body bags strapped to them and headed for the stairs.

"Hold up a minute, Les. Let me make sure they're done photographing the scene," Mark said from the porch railing.

A voice from inside said, "I'm done. Let him in."

Les and Timmy mounted the stairs and went inside followed by Mark and Zack. Les took in the scene. He shook his head. "The whole darn county's gone mad. Who would shoot two pretty young girls in the head like this? Two more closed caskets."

"Les, can you roll Lindsay's body over? I want to see if the chest shots exited her back," Mark said.

Les and Timmy rolled her on her side so Mark could see there were no exit wounds.

Mark turned to Zack. "The casings we recovered are .40 S&W Federal nickel-plated brass. I think the shooter used expanding bullets like the Hydra-Shok rounds we carry. Patel will find out one way or the other. We may be able to lift a good print off the brass."

"Did you check the cellphones?" Zack asked.

"Yeah, but they're locked. So is Krista's laptop."

"Can't they be unlocked?"

"I don't know. Remember that Arab terrorist shooter at Pensacola Naval Air Station? It took the FBI over four months to get into his phones."

"This has to be connected to the other murders, but why would Powers want to hurt these girls? It doesn't make sense," Zack said, perplexed.

"Maybe he thought they could connect him to Hope. Maybe before Hope died, she said Lindsay and Krista knew about their relationship. Maybe Hope was holding something for him in this house. Who knows. Maybe he's just an evil bastard," Mark said.

"Does the Sheriff know we have two more victims?"

"Yeah, I called him before Jimbo got here. He's really pissed off."

"What should we do now?"

"Debbie and Jenna are sitting outside in their car. Let's go talk to them," Mark said. They walked outside to Jenna's old Subaru Outback. When they approached the driver's side, Jenna lowered the window. "I'm Sergeant Mark Langford, and this is Deputy Zack Goodson. I know this is a bad time, but it could really help us catch whoever did this if we could talk to you for a few minutes. Can I see your drivers' licenses? That way I can cut down on the number of questions I need to ask." The girls produced their licenses. Mark looked at them and then handed them to Zack. "10-98 and 99." Zack walked far enough away that they couldn't hear him call the station.

"We're not wanted, and we don't have records," Jenna said.

"What?" Mark asked, surprised.

"10-99 and 98 are the codes for wanted person and arrest record. We're clean," Jenna said.

Mark smiled. "And why would you know that?"

"We're in the Academy at MAC," Jenna replied.

"Good, then you understand why I have to ask what I'm going to ask."

They both nodded.

"Why did you come here this morning?" Mark asked.

"We were supposed to meet Krista and Lindsay at St. Joe Park and go on a hike," Jenna said.

"I thought you came over here to pick them up for the hike."

"No, sir. After they didn't show up at the park, Debbie called Krista, but she didn't answer. So, she called Lindsay, who didn't answer either. We thought that was weird because we were over here yesterday afternoon and made the plans to go hiking today. We thought it would be good to get them out of the house and get their minds off what happened to Hope," Jenna said. "When they didn't answer, we decided to come over here and check on them. Debbie rang the doorbell while I waited in the car."

"What happened next, Debbie?"

Debbie leaned forward to look around Jenna. "I knocked a few more times, but nobody answered. I figured they had to be home because their cars were here." She pointed at the cars. "I saw the blinds on the front window were up about a foot, so I peeked under it. I saw Krista on the couch with blood all over the wall behind her. I screamed and ran back to the car. I told Jenna what I saw, and we went to the police station. We figured it was safer over there. We followed the Desloge officers back over here. They told us Lindsay was dead too."

Zack walked back over. "No record."

Mark nodded. "Did you see anyone or any vehicles around the property when you came over?"

"No, sir," they both said.

"Do you know if anyone had threatened either of them?"

They both shook their heads.

"Did you know Hope very well?"

"Yes, we all went to high schoo_ together. We've been friends since we were freshmen," Jenna said.

"Do you know if Hope had a new boyfriend?"

They both nodded. "She was seeing someone but wouldn't tell us who he was. It was like a game she was playing with us," Debbie said.

"I think she wouldn't say because she knew we wouldn't approve of whoever he was," Jenna said.

"OK, girls, here's my card. If you think of anything that might help us, give me a call, anytime night or day," Mark said as he handed them two of his cards. "Look, we don't know who did this.

We don't have a motive for anyone to hurt Lindsay or Krista. We know they were very good friends with Hope, and it sounds like so are you. You need to be careful until we catch this guy. Do you understand?"

They both nodded again.

"OK, you can go now. Take care." Mark patted the roof of the car and stepped back. The car pulled away.

"Don't you think Powers did this?" Zack asked.

"He's the only person who comes to mind, but we still don't have any evidence. We can't prove he killed any one of these people," Mark said.

"We must have missed something. Why don't we go back to the trailer?" Zack asked.

"What for? Everything was destroyed in the fire," Mark replied.

"We never did get a dog out there to sniff around. Let's ask Mrs. Cantwell if we can borrow Bruno for a couple of hours," Zack suggested.

"I guess it wouldn't hurt. We gave Powers an electronic anal exam and we didn't come up with…well, shit. We don't have anything else to follow up on right now."

CHAPTER 24

Mark and Zack drove to the station to pick up their cruiser and then headed for the place where this calamity started for them, 401 King School Road. They crossed the grass, and Zack stopped at the old Camaro peeking out from under the tarp. He raised the tarp to take a look at the car. "There's an old FOP Lodge 68 sticker in the corner of the rear window."

"That's the St. Louis City Police Officers' lodge. The car probably belonged to Mrs. Cantwell's son," Mark said. They stepped up on the porch, and Mark rang the bell.

Mrs. Cantwell answered the door with a cigarette in one hand and a cup of coffee in the other. "What can I do for you boys?" She held the screen door open against the spring.

"Ma'am, we have a favor to ask. We'd like to borrow Bruno from you for a couple of hours," Mark said.

"What the hell for?"

"Well, we've had two more young women murdered last night, and we think the same man who killed Hope Pagano and Lieutenant Close did it. We were hoping Bruno could help us track him down."

She turned to look at Bruno. He was on his back with his legs in the air trying to scratch an itch against the rug. He farted loudly. She turned back to Mark and smiled. "I suppose you can have him for a while if you think he can help. I'll get his leash." Seconds later, she returned with the dog. She held out the leash to Mark. "Here you go."

Mark passed the leash to Zack. "Thank you, ma'am. We'll take good care of him."

"Uh-huh," she said as the screen door slammed shut.

"C'mon, Bruno, it's time to go to work, boy." Zack patted him on the side. He opened the back car door and Bruno jumped right in. Zack unhooked the leash. Bruno sat down on his haunches right in the middle of the seat facing forward. He was panting and slobbering all over the seat.

Mark pulled out onto King School Road and headed for the north end of the county over thirty miles away.

"I have a good feeling about this. I bet he finds something," Zack said.

They heard a loud fart erupt from behind them before a God-awful odor assaulted them.

Zack looked at Bruno. "Jesus, that's fucking disgusting. What is she feeding you?" Bruno gifted him with a contented doggie smile.

"It smells like he ate the ass out of a dead rhinoceros," Mark said as he lowered his window. "Damn, I can taste it."

The next thirty miles were marked by a series of farts followed by curses and desperate stabs for the window button. Finally, a half hour later, they arrived at the trailer.

"I guess it goes without saying, if he gets loose and tears ass off into the woods, you're going after him." Mark shut off the engine and opened his door.

"He won't run, will you, boy?' Zack opened the back door, but before he could get the leash on Bruno's collar, he bolted past him and disappeared around the corner of the burnt-out shell of the trailer.

"Get him, Rabbit!" Mark yelled to Zack as he ran off in pursuit.

Zack rounded the corner of the trailer and saw Bruno barking and frantically scratching at a concrete septic tank lid partially obscured by a downed burnt tree. Zack put the leash on Bruno. "Good boy! Good boy, Bruno!" He petted him vigorously. Bruno sat down on his haunches with his tail wagging. Zack held the leash out to Mark. "Hold this." Then Zack snapped off the dead branches over the lid and threw them aside. He lifted the heavy concrete lid off the tank and immediately stepped back, dropped the lid, and turned away to hurl.

The stench was a mixture of human waste and human decomposition. He violently retched until his stomach was empty. He spit in an unsuccessful attempt to cleanse his mouth. He held his breath and leaned over the opening with his flashlight. He saw a bloated black hand sticking out of the muck. "There's a body in there." He gagged. "I gotta get something to drink." He hurried past Mark. He returned a minute later with two bottles of water from the cruiser and an old hubcap.

Mark held his hand out for a bottle, but Zack walked right past him. He poured water for Bruno in the hubcap and watched him lap it up. Then Zack gargled with his bottle until he got the taste out of his mouth.

Mark was on his cellphone and put it on speaker. "Hey, Justin, it's Mark. Zack and I just found a body in the septic tank behind Powers's trailer."

"No shit! Can you tell who it is?"

"No, all we can see is a decaying hand, but Powers is the only one missing. If it's him, we still have a killer running around. Can you get the Patrol to send out a CSI team to get him out of there?"

"Yeah, I'll ask. Damn, this is going to piss off a lot of people, calling them out on a Sunday to pull a decomposing body out of a septic tank full of shit."

"That's why you get the big bucks, Sergeant." Mark smiled at Zack.

"Yeah, right. Have you called Sheriff Blair yet?"

"No, I'll call him after we hang up."

"OK, stand by. Helps coming. Oh, wait. Do you have any ideas on how to empty that tank so we can get the body out?"

"Yeah, I might know a guy. Talk to you later." Mark hung up.

Mark dialed again and put it on speaker. "Hey, Boss, it's Mark. Sorry to bother you again on a Sunday. Zack and I just found a body at Powers's trailer in the septic tank."

"Dammit, that's five bodies in a week! What the fuck is going on? Do you think it's Powers?"

"We can't tell. All we can see is a hand sticking up out of the shit."

"What made you think to go back up there?"

"It was the kid's idea. We went and borrowed Mrs. Cantwell's retired police dog. As soon as we got here, he beelined right for the septic tank. That dog, Bruno, is something else."

"Damn! If we had a dog that first day, Denny and those girls would still be alive."

"We don't know that, Boss. If it's Powers in the tank, then it means we have another killer running around. Denny might have stumbled right into a murder being committed."

"Alright, I'm on my way. I don't know what good I'll do, but I can't sit at home with my thumb up my ass. I never thought my last days as sheriff would be like this," he said before hanging up.

Mark made a third call. "Hey, Ike. Sorry to bother you on your day off, but Zack and I just found a body in the septic tank behind Powers's trailer."

"Is it Powers?"

"We can't tell. Can you get your brother to come up here with a clean truck to empty the tank? All that shit will be evidence until the Patrol's CSIs go through it, so the holding tank needs to be clean. We gotta get this septic tank emptied out before we can send any of them in to recover the body. It's going to be nasty enough even if we empty it. If I was them, I don't know if I'd go in there," Mark said.

"Aw, those gung-ho young troopers will jump right in there just so they can tell the story later. Besides, you got a jarhead with you. He's used to being up to his neck in shit. Strip him down to his skivvies, give him a flashlight and a 1911, and tell him he's clearing a tunnel." McLeod laughed. Even though he was an Army vet, he had great respect for the Marine Corps.

"I think he's smarter than your average crayon eater," Mark replied as he looked at Zack.

"OK, I'll call Asa. You know, he's going to charge us out the ass for coming up there on a Sunday for an emergency service call." McLeod hung up.

"The Lieutenant's brother cleans out septic tanks?" Zack asked.

"Yeah, he installs them, repairs them, and cleans them. His company's in Bonne Terre. He's got a big crew and a fleet of trucks.

Hey, I'm starving. I didn't eat yet today. Do me a favor and go over to the gas station at Highway V next to the Valles Mines Post Office. They have a small deli counter. Get me a big sub sandwich and a large iced tea and whatever you want. I'm buying. I'll stay here with Bruno."

The red, white, and blue truck had McLeod Plumbing & Septic painted on its tank, but today's service call had nothing to do with plumbing. It was just about sucking the disgusting sludge out of the tank. Asa McLeod stood talking to Mark and Zack as they ate their sandwiches. They made sure they were far enough away from the hole to avoid the aromas wafting from the tank. Asa watched closely as his son slowly moved the vacuum hose back and forth in the tank to make sure he was not damaging the body.

"I've been making a good living from this business for over twenty years, but this is the first time I've ever been called out because there was a body in a tank. My boy just started a few months ago, and he's already had one. What's he got to look forward to for the next twenty years?"

The sheriff rolled up and climbed down from his truck. He sniffed the air. "I don't know how you boys can eat with that God-awful stink in the air. You must've been starving."

"I guess we've gone kinda nose blind. I can't smell it from over here. It was really bad when Zack pulled the lid off," Mark replied.

"Have you heard from Les yet?" Blair asked.

"He's on his way. I told him about the septic tank, so he's probably trying to figure out a way to seal off the cab of his van from the cargo area," Mark answered.

"Excuse me," Zack said as he wandered over to where Sergeant Deer was talking to his two Highway Patrol troopers that were preparing to go into the septic tank. They were at the back of their Ford Explorers changing out of their uniforms and putting on white disposable hooded coveralls.

"Hey, guys, this is Zack Goodson," Deer said.

"Hi, Zack, I'm Corporal Doug Butler. He's Trooper Adam Wilson. So, you're the guy who found the body. That's pretty good police work," Butler said as he traded looks with Deer and Wilson.

"Yeah, well, the dog, Bruno, actually found it. He's a great dog. Hey, thanks for coming out here to give us a hand. As soon as I opened the lid, I lost my breakfast. Do you guys do this sort of thing often?" Zack took another bite from his sandwich.

As Les Koplin came around the gravel driveway in his van, Deer said, "Excuse me," and walked off to join Mark and the sheriff.

Butler and Wilson both pulled on a second pair of coveralls over the first pair. "We handle some pretty disgusting crime scenes once in a while, but I've never had to go down into a septic tank to recover a body," Butler replied as he held out a small stack of personal protective equipment to Zack. "Here's your gear."

"Wait! What?" Zack said with a mouthful of roast beef and Swiss.

"Sergeant Langford said you would help us out in the tank," Butler replied.

"He did?" Zack said as more of a comment than a question as he shot a weary look at Mark. He felt like someone had just taken away his birthday. Mark smiled back as he ate the last bite of his sandwich. Zack stuck his sandwich in his mouth, accepted the stack in both hands, and turned toward his cruiser to gear up.

"Hey, Zack!" Butler yelled, "take your uniform off before you put the coveralls on or that smell will ruin it."

Zack nodded as he started changing. He watched as Butler and Wilson pulled on rubber boots and taped their coverall legs to the boots to form a seal. They opened a jar of Vicks VapoRub and rubbed it on under their noses. They each put on a pair of thick rubber gloves and taped their sleeves closed. Then they went over to Zack and helped him get sealed up in his suit. Butler offered Zack some Vicks, which he eagerly accepted. Next, they all added respirator masks and safety goggles to their ensembles. Last, they pulled their hoods up over their heads.

"C'mon, boys. Let's get this over with," Butler said.

They walked over to the hole, and Wilson climbed down inside the cramped concrete box followed by Zack.

Butler stood over the hole, looked down, and hesitated. Wilson and Zack already had shit smeared all over them and they hadn't done anything yet. Butler said, "It looks pretty tight in there. I'll support you guys from up here. Here's the body bag."

Even though his respirator hid his face, they could tell he was wearing a huge grin.

As the bag dropped through the hole, Zack and Wilson knew they had been outfoxed. They started wrangling the decomposed body into the bag. It was like trying to catch a greased pig, but worse.

"Hey, guys, before you bag him, check his pockets for ID!" Mark yelled behind them.

"Fuck this…shit!" Zack said so lowly only Wilson could hear him. A couple of minutes later, Zack flung a nylon wallet out of the hole, which Butler caught. He handed it back to Mark's gloved hand.

"Jesus, this thing stinks!" Mark said as he held the wallet at arm's length. "Powers's driver's license is in here. It would be pretty clever of him to plant his DL on a body and dump it in the tank, but I'm betting this is him."

"Lower the backboard!" Wilson yelled from the tank.

Butler slid the yellow plastic backboard down to him. Ten minutes later, the bag was strapped to the board and they started pulling it up through the hole. Six men pulled the rope back from the hole as Zack and Wilson guided the board out of the opening. As soon as the board was clear, they popped out of the hole and ran straight for the hose on the other side of the trailer. They hosed each other down and then cut their suits away.

Zack walked back over to his cruiser wearing nothing but his tighty-whities and rubber boots. He sat on the bumper and started getting dressed.

Asa McLeod yelled, "Hey, Deputy. If you get tired of the Sheriff's Department, I got a job for you." He laughed at his own joke as he handed the sheriff a bill for the service call. "C'mon, son, let's go. Mom's got dinner waiting."

"Thanks for coming out, Asa," Blair said as he folded the invoice and put it in his shirt pocket.

Zack saw Mark approaching and prepared for the hazing to come.

"The Sheriff was really impressed when he saw you go down that hole. Thanks for stepping up."

"Yeah right, very funny. Butler told me you volunteered me to go in the hole."

Mark started laughing. "He played you, son. I didn't give you up, but I guess that's why he's a corporal."

Zack looked over at the troopers getting dressed and saw Butler laughing while Wilson shook his head. "Asshole," Zack said as he pulled his trousers on.

Blair approached and slapped Zack on the back. "Thanks for going in there, Zack. We don't want the Patrol thinking we're a bunch of pussies."

"No sweat, Boss," Zack replied begrudgingly.

"Do you like Snickers, Baby Ruths, or Tootsie Rolls?" Mark asked.

OK, here it comes. "Sure, why?" Zack asked.

"Because after the rest of the department hears about this, your mailbox will be full of them," Mark said as he and Blair started laughing.

"If I get the munchies, can I come by for a snack?" Blair guffawed at his own joke.

"After you finish getting dressed, I think it's time for us to go talk to Mr. Garza again," Mark said.

CHAPTER 25

P agano sat alone in his den with a half-empty crystal tumbler of Pappy Van Winkle in his hand surrounded by oak-covered walls, leather furniture, and silence. He had refilled the tumbler five times. In his other hand, he held a framed photo of his smiling daughter. She was wearing her cheerleading uniform. It was taken during her senior year at a football game. A trail of tears streaked his face. His cellphone rang, so he put his drink down. He fumbled around with the phone and squinted to read the blurry caller ID. He cleared his throat. "Hello."

"Sir, is this Mr. Pagano?"

"Yes, who is this?" he replied as he rubbed his eyes and tried to focus on the screen.

"Sir, this is Captain James Baderman with the Sheriff's Department."

"Oh, of course. What can I do for you, Jim?" Pagano asked.

"Sir, we have some news on your daughter's case. Please, keep this to yourself, but I thought you would want to know that we found a body in the septic tank behind Randall Powers's trailer. It's not confirmed yet, but we think the body is Mr. Powers. We have a suspect named Gilberto Garza who we believe is responsible for the deaths of your daughter, Lieutenant Close, and Powers. We'll be bringing him in for questioning soon," Baderman said.

Pagano's heart began to pound. "Uhhh, thank you for calling, Jim. This is good news. Hopefully you guys will get a confession soon and the people of the county can feel safe again. Please, feel free to call me anytime. If you ever get tired of the Sheriff's Department, give me a call," Pagano said.

"Well, thank you, sir, but, if possible, I'd really like to stay on the department in my current position," Baderman replied.

Even in his drunken stupor, Pagano realized Baderman was giving him information in exchange for the possibility of keeping his job after Blair lost the election. "No worries, Jim. We'll need a man like you who knows the inner workings of the department to help us reform and rebuild after the election. Thank you again for calling," he said before he hung up. He took several deep breaths to calm himself. He had prepared himself for the possibility of Powers's body being found. Hopefully, the investigators on the Major Case Squad were smart enough to find Denny's Glock where he had hidden it last night. He picked up the half-finished bottle of twenty-three-year-old bourbon with his trembling hand and poured himself another glass.

Zack and Mark parked a couple of houses down from Gilberto Garza's house at 339 Boyce Street in Farmington. They cautiously approached his front door. Detectives Herman Keller and Cody Gibbs were parked behind the house on Montgomery Avenue in case he decided to rabbit out the back door. Zack rang the doorbell and stood to the left of the doorway. Mark stood to the right. They already had their Glocks in their hands held down at the side of their legs.

Garza opened the door and stepped out on the porch in his bare feet. He suspiciously eyed them up and down. Both wore level-three armor inside plate carriers covered with magazine pouches. "What?"

"Mr. Garza, we would like to ask you to voluntarily come down to the station and answer some questions. Will you come voluntarily?" Mark asked.

"Why should I come with you? What's changed since you saw me at the funeral?"

"We found a body we believe to be Randall Powers. You are the only person we know of who had a problem with him recently."

"Am I under arrest?"

"No. At this point, we're just gathering information. By cooperating with our investigation, you could help us eliminate you as a suspect."

"I'll call my lawyer and see what he says." Garza raised his cellphone to see the screen. He selected the contact and dialed. "Hello, Chester, this is Gil Garza. The cops are here, and they want me to go to the station voluntarily to answer some questions. They say they found a body they think is Randy." Garza listened and nodded. "I understand that, but I'd really like to get this behind me so they can go look for someone else. Can you meet me at the Sheriff's Department?" He listened again. "OK, thanks." He hung up. "He'll meet us at the station. He said not to answer any questions until he gets there. I'll follow you over there."

"It would be better if we ride together."

"For you maybe. Look, I'll drive myself or we can just forget the talk."

"OK, we'll lead the way. C'mon, Zack." They walked back to their cruiser and pulled it up in front of his house. Mark called Herman on his cellphone. "Hey, Herm, Garza's going to follow us to the station. His lawyer's going to meet us there. Hang back a little but follow him to make sure he gets there."

Less than five minutes later, they pulled into the parking lot at the station with Garza's Black Ram truck right behind them. When Garza joined them at the side door, Mark said, "We need to pat you down before we go inside." Garza held his arms out from his sides. He was only wearing a polo shirt, khaki shorts, and sandals. Zack circled behind him and searched him. He found a wallet, keys, cellphone, and a pair of Oakley's. Mark opened the door. "Follow me." They went directly to the gun lockers mounted to the wall outside the interview room.

HOPE IS DEAD - *A Zack Goodson Novel*

"Step inside the interview room while we lock up our weapons," Mark said to Garza. Zack put his Glock in a small locker and put the key in his pocket. Mark removed his Glock model 27 from his ankle holster and put it in a locker before putting his Glock model 22 in with it. Zack stepped into the interview room. Instead of a large one-way mirror, the room was wired for video and audio. Mark stopped in the doorway. "Excuse me for minute." He left the room to go next door and turn on the recording equipment. Mark came back into the room and removed his plate carrier. He leaned it against the wall behind him. His shirt was soaked through with sweat, and he tugged at it to try to get some cool air underneath. He sat down next to Zack. He opened his brown leather padfolio to access his notes. It had a large gold St. Francois County Deputy Sheriff's badge embossed on the front above his name. It was a gift from his wife years ago when he first became a detective.

Garza was on his phone. "OK, thanks. My lawyer, Chester Greer, is in the lobby."

"Zack, do you mind bringing him back?" Mark asked.

"Sure." Zack went to get him. In a minute, he came back with Greer, who sat down next to his client.

"Hello, Mark. Sorry to hear about Denny. Who's your partner?"

"Hey, Chet. Thanks. This is Zack Goodson."

Greer nodded to Zack, then he sniffed the air as if he smelled something not quite right. He scanned the room for the source.

"Gil, like I told you on the phone, I strongly advise you to remain silent."

"I just want to get this over with. Let them ask their questions and then we can decide if I should talk to them. What do you want to know?"

"Let's start with the easy questions. You told us that you 'put a whupping on Powers' for screwing up in front of the Marine Raiders. Is that the only time you attacked him?" Mark asked.

"Yeah, I beat his ass, and to be clear, he pushed me before I hit him, and yeah, that's the only time."

Mark took notes even though everything was being recorded. "Where were you last Tuesday night through Wednesday morning?"

Garza thought for a moment. "I was with my girlfriend at her house all night."

"What's her name and address?"

"Sheri Tucker. She lives at 448 Redwood Drive in Farmington."

Mark took more notes. "You know we're going to talk to her. Is she going to verify your story?"

"Sure she will."

"Did you go to work on Wednesday morning?"

"Yes."

"Straight from Sheri's house?"

"No, I went home first to shower and get dressed."

Mark wrote it down. "Have you ever met Hope Pagano?"

"No."

"Have you ever met Lindsay Miller or Krista Snyder?"

"No."

"Have you ever met Lieutenant Dennis Close?"

"No."

"Have you ever eaten at Colton's Steak House?"

"Yes."

"How many times do you think?"

"A lot. Maybe, two or three times a month. I like steak."

"Hope, Lindsay, and Krista all worked at Colton's, but you never met them?"

"Well, I don't pay attention to who the servers are. They could've waited on me. I don't know."

Mark placed photos of Hope, Lindsay, and Krista on the table in front of Garza. "How about now?"

"Yeah, I think I saw them working at Colton's, but I don't know their names."

"You went to Hope's funeral, but you didn't recognize her?"

"The casket was closed, so I didn't see her. Which one is she?"

Mark pointed at Hope's photo.

"Where were you from yesterday afternoon through this morning?"

"At my house with Sheri. We ordered pizza and watched the Cardinals game. They went into extra innings, so we went to bed around midnight."

Mark scribbled more notes. "Did she stay all night?"

"Yeah, she left around noon to go home and do her laundry."

"Do you own any pistols in .40 S&W?"

"No, I have several in .45 ACP and one .380 Ruger LCP."

"Do you mind if we search your car and house?"

"Hold it, Gil," Greer said. "Do not let them search. That's the worst possible mistake you could ever mistake."

"I'm innocent. I don't care if they look." Garza slid his keys across the table.

"Please, sign this consent to search waiver form," Mark said as he slid the form across the table.

Garza signed it and slid it back to Mark. Mark keyed his walkie, "Herm, would you come in here please?" Seconds later, Keller entered the room. Mark handed the keys to him. "Take Cody with you and check Mr. Garza's truck." Keller left the room. "Can you think of anyone who would want to kill Randy Powers?" Mark asked Garza.

"No, but he's retired Special Forces. I don't know what kind of secret squirrel shit he might've been involved in before he came to IMI last year. He knows or, at least, knew his shit. He was a good soldier before his drinking got out of control. We were fine until he started making us look bad.' Garza was quiet for a minute. "I do remember something odd that happened at Colton's about three weeks ago. Zeke Horton and I had eaten dinner there, and we left the restaurant about nine o'clock. It was cloudy, so it was already dark. We got in my truck, and I drove around the back of the building to head for the exit. We saw Randy's Jeep parked behind the restaurant kind of hidden next to an old white piece-of-shit F-250. When I drove by, we saw he was in there making out with a girl, so I stopped behind his Jeep and honked. He pushed her down so we couldn't see her and gave us the finger. I laughed and drove off. Zeke seemed kind of jealous. I asked him if he knew her, but he said no."

Mark wrote as fast as he could and was about to ask another question when Keller reentered the room with a white cardboard gun evidence box.

Keller opened the lid with his nitrile-gloved hand and showed everyone in the room a Glock model 23. The slide was locked back, and the magazine was removed. "The serial numbers match. It's Lieutenant Close's pistol. I found it in the storage compartment under the rear passenger's side seat wrapped in a red shop towel."

Mark looked at the pistol for a moment and then at Garza. "Would you like to explain how you came into possession of Lieutenant Close's weapon?"

Garza's eyes grew wide and darted back and forth between Keller and Mark. He went wild as he sprang to his feet. His chair skidded into the wall and fell over. Zack quickly stepped around the table and put his hands on Garza's chest. Garza exploded, "That's bullshit! I didn't have that gun! I've never met Close! You fuckers are settin' me up!" Garza yelled at his lawyer, "Dammit, Chester, do something!"

"Gil, calm down and sit. I've been trying to help you. I warned you not to talk to them, and I told you not to let them search your truck. Now, I strongly recommend you withdraw permission for them to search your house. There's no telling what they'll find."

Garza turned to Mark. "You can't search my house!" He shook his head as he looked at the pistol Keller was holding. "Fuck me!"

"Yeah, well, you pretty much fucked yourself." Mark smiled. "You're under arrest."

"What are you charging my client with?"

"Well, we'll start with possession of the stolen firearm." Mark pulled a Miranda rights card from his folder and read it to Garza.

Mark showed Zack how to book Garza into the jail and then they met in the squad room with Detectives Keller and Gibbs.

"Congratulations, gentlemen. It looks like you caught Denny's killer. Hopefully, Garza used Denny's pistol to kill the girls from this morning too," Keller said.

"Thanks. Did you record the search of the truck?" Mark asked.

"Yeah. I had Cody hold my phone as I went through the truck. This would be a lot simpler if we had body cams."

"I don't know about your departments, but we're lucky if we have enough money to put gas in our cruisers. Zack and I will stay here and write up the warrant affidavits for the arrest and the search of Garza's house. Then we'll take them to the prosecutor's office. Wait…it's Sunday. The office is closed. We'll have to track her down. Hopefully, she's at home. Good job finding the pistol. You guys can knock off for the day."

"Thanks. C'mon, Cody, let's head for the barn," Keller said as he and Gibbs walked out of the room.

Zack watched them leave. "Doesn't it bother you how easy it was for us to find the gun?"

"This isn't like on TV where the killers are all criminal masterminds. Remember number seven? Most of the time the obvious answer is the answer. Tomorrow while we're at the funeral, Justin will have the other guys on the Squad digging deep into Garza's recent activities. Hopefully, Sheri Tucker will have a different story than him."

CHAPTER 26

Mark and Zack pulled into the driveway of Missy Gilham's home in a new subdivision on Farmington's north side. She was waiting at her front door as they approached.

"Good afternoon, Ms. Gilham. I'm Mark Langford and this is Zack Goodson."

"Yes, I remember you, Mark. It's good to meet you, Zack. Please, come in." She led them to her kitchen table.

"I hope we haven't disrupted your Sunday afternoon plans."

"No, nothing planned. I understand you made a breakthrough today."

Mark passed the warrant package to her. "The only charge we have today is possession of the stolen firearm. We hope to keep Garza in jail on this charge while we get a warrant to search his house."

She sniffed the air and detected something foul. "I'm going to read this in my office. There's juice and sodas in the fridge, and the

TV remote is on the counter. Please, help yourselves. I'll come back out when I'm done."

"Thank you," Mark said as she left the room.

"What's next?" Zack asked.

"Assuming she approves, she'll send us to Judge Otis Buchanan to get the warrants signed. You'll like him. He's a modern-day hanging judge. He doesn't mess around. He has a very low bullshit tolerance, and he loves cops."

Thirty minutes later, Gilham came back to the kitchen and sat down at the counter on the other side of the kitchen. "How high of a bond do you want me to ask for?"

"How about $200,000?"

"I'll try, but O. B. will probably bring it down to around a hundred. What's your plan going forward?"

"We're going to interview his girlfriend to see if she confirms his alibi. And we'll do a deep dive into his financial and phone records and email and social media accounts. We should be able to bury him or clear him pretty quickly."

"Do you think he committed all of these murders?" she asked.

"We know he had a motive for Randall Powers because of their fight at IMI. If Denny stumbled onto him at Powers's trailer, he may have killed him too. As far as the three girls, it's just wild speculation, but what if Garza had a thing for Hope Pagano and she rebuffed him in favor of Powers? Garza kills her and Powers and then Denny because he sees Garza at the trailer. Then maybe he kills Hope's roommates, Lindsay Miller and Krista Snyder, because he's afraid Hope may have told them about his unwanted advances. We know she waited on him at Colton's, so they had at least met. Like I said, this is all speculation."

Gilham signed the warrant application and handed it to Mark. "Good luck. I'm looking forward to applying for the death penalty in this case."

"Thank you, ma'am. C'mon, Zack, let's go talk to O. B. He only lives a couple of miles north of here off of Highway D." They headed for the door.

"Is O. B. the judge?" Zack asked after they climbed back into the cruiser.

"Yeah, for most of us, O. B. is short for Otis Buchanan, but the defense attorneys and shitbirds say it means Ornery Bastard. He's given a handful of people the death penalty over the years, and he makes it a habit to attend their executions."

Mark and Zack pulled off the road on to the judge's asphalt driveway. It ran a good 400 feet through the trees before it ended at his house.

"How big is the judge's spread?" Zack asked as he took in his surroundings.

"It's probably a hundred or so acres. Most of it's wooded. There's a pasture behind the house that's maybe twenty acres."

"How can a state judge afford a place like this?"

"Before he was a judge, he made a ton of money representing victims of mesothelioma."

"What's that?"

"It's a form of aggressive cancer caused by asbestos exposure. Once you develop symptoms, you'll die within a year or two. It's incurable—a horrible way to die."

As they climbed out of their cruiser, they could hear sporadic gunshots coming from a distance behind the house.

"That's probably O. B. He likes to shoot."

They stepped up onto the porch and rang the bell. Seconds later, the judge's wife answered the door.

"Good afternoon, Mrs. Buchanan. I'm Sergeant Mark Langford and this is Deputy Zack Goodson. Ms. Gilham sent us over here with a warrant application for the judge. Is he home?"

"Hello, Mark, it's good to see you again, and it's nice to meet you, Zack. Come in, please. Missy called and told us you were coming. O. B. is out back in the field shooting some of his guns. He's expecting you. Can I get you boys a bottle of water or soda?"

"No thank you, we're fine."

"Alright, you can go out through the kitchen."

They followed her through the house and went outside through the French doors in the kitchen. They trekked across the backyard and over the galvanized steel cattle guard onto the gravel road running along the edge of the field. They could see about thirty head of Black Angus cattle gathered under the trees on the far side of the field. After about 300 feet, they arrived at the judge's gun range. He was standing in front of a white picnic table. His green camouflage-covered UTV was backed up to the table with its bed loaded with guns and shooting gear. The judge was shooting his AR-15 into a man-sized paper target attached to a wooden frame about fifty yards away. Behind the target, an eight-foot-high stack of logs served as his backstop in front of the woods. He was wearing a dark blue T-shirt, faded blue jeans, and scuffed brown work boots. When he emptied the magazine, he removed it from the rifle and stuck it in his back pocket. He cleared the rifle and removed his earplugs. When he turned to walk back to the table, the front of his shirt became visible. It depicted President Ronald Reagan with an RPG launcher slung across his back while riding a velociraptor and shooting a machine gun.

He saw Mark and Zack. "Hey, Mark, who's your partner?"

"Sir, this is Zack Goodson. He just started working with us a week ago."

Buchanan put his rifle on the table and held out his hand. "Good to meet you, Zack. How are you liking it so far?" For a man in his late sixties, he had a viselike grip. His hands were rough and calloused like a farmer's.

"It's good to meet you too, sir. So far, it's been just fine."

"Are you the Marine everyone's been talking about?"

"Well, I don't know. I am a Marine."

"Someday, I want to talk to you about flying those giant helicopters. That just impresses the hell out of me." Buchanan raised his boots one at a time. "It smells like one of us stepped in a fresh cow patty."

Mark and Zack innocently raised their boots to look. Zack was afraid he knew where the smell was coming from.

"I was sorry to hear about what happened to Denny. Do you think this guy is responsible for the murders?" Buchanan asked as he pointed at the warrant package.

"It's too soon to tell, Judge, but we found Denny's Glock in Garza's truck. He says it was planted and we're trying to frame him. We'd like a warrant for the stolen pistol to keep him in custody long enough for us to search his house and check his alibi. Here's the warrant package." Mark offered it to Buchanan.

The judge put up his hand to stop Mark. "That's OK. Do you have the videos of the vehicle search and interview that Missy was telling me about?"

"Yes, sir." Mark brought up the vehicle search on his cellphone and handed it to the judge.

Buchanan watched the video and chuckled as he handed the phone back to Mark. "And he actually signed the waiver form after Chet told him not to?"

"Yes, sir."

Buchanan shook his head. "Let me see the part of the interview where you show him the pistol," Buchanan said with a big grin on his face.

Mark brought it up on his phone and handed it back to Buchanan. Mark and Zack watched, and as the video progressed, the judge's grin gradually changed to open laughter.

The judge composed himself. "I can't believe this guy. He's either an idiot or the most naive man on the planet. Why did he hire Chet if he was just going to ignore all of his advice? What a moron. Give me the warrants." Mark pulled them from the folder and a pen from his pocket. He watched as Buchanan signed them. "I'll see you boys tomorrow at the funeral. Enjoy the rest of your day." He handed them back to Mark.

"Thank you, Judge. C'mon, Zack, let's go give Garza the good news." They turned and began walking back to their cruiser. As they reached the cattle guard at the backyard, they heard several strings of automatic weapon fire behind them.

Zack looked back. "Does the judge have a machine gun?"

Mark continued walking straight ahead without looking back. "I don't want to know."

Mark pulled the cruiser into the employee lot, and he and Zack entered the station through the side door. They secured their weapons in the small gun lockers attached to the wall outside the holding cells. Before Mark could press the intercom button, the jailer buzzed them in.

"Thanks, Barry. Do you remember Zack?" Mark said as they entered the holding area.

"You bet. Hi, Zack."

"Hey, Barry."

"We're here to serve the arrest warrant on Garza," Mark said as he handed it to Barry. Barry made a copy for their records and handed it back to Mark. "Garza's in cell number 3."

Mark and Zack strolled over to cell number 3, and Mark tapped on the large window next to the steel door. He pressed the warrant up against the glass. "Hey, Garza, do you want to see your arrest warrant?" He was sitting on the worn-out vinyl-covered mattress on the steel bunk in his newly issued orange jail scrubs. He got up and shuffled over to the glass in his plastic slippers to look at the warrant.

"The judge set your bail at $200,000. You've been read your rights. If you have any information that might help us clear you, speak up and we'll see if the judge will release you without bail."

"Fuck you," was all Garza said as he shuffled back to his bunk.

"OK, don't say I didn't offer." Mark placed a copy of the warrant in the document tray attached to the wall next to the door. Mark turned to the jailer. "Hey, Barry, is it bologna or cheese sandwich night?"

"Bologna."

"Do me a favor, will you? Throw on an extra slice for Mr. Garza." Mark snorted.

"The cuffs are too tight, motherfucker!" a muffled voice said from just outside the jail entrance. Barry buzzed open the steel door, and Kurt Sada escorted a prisoner into the booking area.

"Sorry, they're not made for comfort," Kurt said. "Howdy, gentlemen."

Mark looked up at the lanky prisoner with dirt and grass stuck to the side of his head. He had some road rash on his left cheek. "Whatcha got there, Kurt?" Mark asked.

"He had a little too much to drink and launched his car off the highway into a cow pasture. Somehow, he thinks it's my fault."

"Hey, do you mind if Zack watches you book him? He hasn't handled a DWI yet."

"Sure, no problem."

"I'll be out in the squad room when you guys are done," Mark said as Barry buzzed him out.

Kurt stared up at his prisoner. "If you promise to behave, I'll take the cuffs off." The guy only weighed around 170 pounds but had to be at least 6'9". Kurt waited for a response.

"Yeah, I promise."

Kurt went behind him and removed the handcuffs. "Stand on those red footprints in front of the counter." The man stepped forward rubbing his wrists. Kurt walked around the counter. He pulled a Missouri Alcohol Influence Report form from the stack on the shelf. "Zack, this is an A.I.R. form like they had at the Academy. It's all fill-in-the-blanks until you get to the questions on page three." Kurt removed his black aluminum tactical police pen from his breast pocket and filled out the information quietly and efficiently. When he got to page three, he read the prisoner his Miranda rights off the form and asked him the first question. "Were you involved in a motor vehicle accident today?"

"I ain't answerin' any of your fuckin' questions," the prisoner said.

Kurt wrote down his answer verbatim: *I ain't answerin' any of your fuckin' questions.* He asked the second question, "Were you operating the vehicle at the time of the crash?"

"Fuck you."

Kurt wrote down his answer on the form: *Fuck you.*

The prisoner squinted down at the form. "Are you writin' down every fuckin' thing I say?"

Kurt wrote down, *Are you writin' down every fuckin' thing I say?*

With smooth, lightning-fast moves that defied his current condition, the prisoner snatched Kurt's pen from his hand. He stood tall holding the pen up between them with a big shit-eating grin on his face, celebrating his tiny victory as he swayed back and forth.

Kurt said, "Oh, no. We don't do that," as he pulled his pepper spray from his belt and sprayed it in the man's face.

The prisoner immediately dropped the pen and screamed in pain as he doubled over holding his hands to his burning eyes. "Aughh! You motherfucker!"

Zack stepped back to escape the cloud of oleoresin capsicum.

Barry picked up his oscillating fan from the floor. He put it on his end of the counter and pointed it at the offending cloud.

Kurt winked at Zack. He stepped around the counter and placed his left hand on the man's shoulder. He leaned over and asked, "Hey, man, are you alright?"

The prisoner, with great difficulty, managed to open his right eye to look up at Kurt. Kurt quickly brought up the spray can and gave him another squirt.

"Dammit! Motherfucker!" The prisoner held his face in his hands to shield it from another blast and stomped his feet.

Kurt gently shoved the man aside so he wouldn't stomp on his favorite pen. "Do you want to go wash your face?"

The prisoner nodded his head repeatedly.

"Are you going to behave?"

The man nodded his head even harder.

"Use your words," Kurt said.

"Yes, dammit, I'll behave."

Kurt put his hands on the man's hunched-over back and pushed him toward the shower room like a shopping cart.

He stood in the doorway watching the man fumble around the wall until he found the shower controls. "Cold water works better. Hot water will just irritate it more," Kurt said.

"Fuck you!" the man yelled as he turned both knobs on full blast.

Kurt shrugged. "Suit yourself."

The man screamed again as the warm water sprayed his face. "Fuck!"

CHAPTER 27

Zack left the station and climbed behind the wheel of his truck. Before he could pull out of the parking lot, his phone rang. He saw it was Patty calling. "Hi, babe."

"Where are you? We're supposed to have dinner at my parents, remember? Everyone is already here," she said in the way a perturbed wife can that sounds perfectly sweet to everyone but her husband.

Zack noticed the time on the dashboard: 4:30. He was already a half hour late. "I'm sorry. We've been scrambling all day, and we just got done. We made an arrest in the case. Tell them to go ahead and eat. I'll run home, take a quick shower, and be there in forty minutes." He pulled out onto the road.

"Can't you just come straight over here?"

"Trust me. You want me to take a shower. I'll make it quick. Love you." She hung up without answering. "It's not like I was out playing golf all day," he said to himself. Sunday dinners were a big deal in Patty's family. Now that they were living in Farmington, they were expected to attend just like Patty's sisters and their husbands and children. Her sisters were good people, but between the three of them, they were competitive about everything. Fortunately, Patty had the best husband and kid hands down.

Five minutes later, he pulled into his driveway, and thirty minutes after that, he was pulling into his in-laws' driveway at their farm on Highway F, east of Farmington. He walked around the side of the house to the rear where the grown-ups were gathered at the table under the roof of the outdoor kitchen next to the pool. The older kids were splashing around in the water, and the little ones were playing in the portable kiddie jail that had been erected next to the table. Patty's dad, Dan, was telling a story to those gathered around the table. He was a retired tax attorney. In his glory days during the late 60s, when many of his college classmates were protesting the Vietnam War, he was slogging through its jungles and rice paddies as a recently commissioned second lieutenant and Army Ranger.

"Hey, there he is. Pull up a chair, Zack," Dan said as he motioned from the head of the table. Zack already had a leg up on the other sons-in-law because he was a Marine officer and aviator. The others were slimy civilians.

"Sit down, Hon. I'll get you a plate," Patty's mom, Patsy, said as she got up and headed to the kitchen. He had learned early on not to argue with her.

Zack looked around the table at Patty's sisters and their husbands and said, "I'm sorry I'm late, everyone. I was supposed to be off today, but I got called in to work this morning." He sat down next to Patty and kissed her on the cheek. She wrinkled her nose at him.

"I thought you were going to take a shower."

"I did. You still smell it?"

Patty nodded.

Patsy returned with a clean plate and utensils and patted Zack on the shoulder before she returned to her chair next to Dan.

Zack faced Dan. "I'm sorry, Dan, don't let me interrupt. Finish your story."

"I was just telling everyone about the time my grandma took her .38 out of her dresser and walked three miles to a tavern in Doe Run to retrieve Grandpa at gunpoint after he didn't come home on time, but," he sniffed the air and said with a smile, "it smells like you have a more interesting story."

Zack loaded his plate with brats, baked beans, and potato chips. He squirted mustard on the brats. "Well, if you all really want to know, I spent part of my Sunday in a septic tank recovering a decomposing corpse. I thought I scrubbed it all off, but I guess it's lingering." Zack bit off a mouthful of bratwurst.

"Oh, my Lord!" Patsy said as she placed her hand on top of Dan's.

Dan chuckled. "That sounds a lot more interesting. Who was he, and why was he in the septic tank?"

"He was a retired Green Beret and instructor at Iron Mountain named Randy Powers. He was having a secret tryst with

Hope Pagano. We thought he had killed Lieutenant Close, but now it looks like another IMI instructor who is a retired Force Recon Marine named Gilberto Garza killed him and stuffed him in the septic tank to hide his body."

Dan laughed again and said, "Wait...so, you're saying you found your primary suspect in the tank swimmin' with the feces?"

Pagano sat in the state-of-the-art reinforced concrete safe room in his basement surrounded by gun safes and commercial-grade shelves loaded with ammo, water, and long-term storage food. He had it built into the foundation of the house when he still had a wife and daughter to take care of. Now he knew his days were numbered. It was just a matter of time before the Major Case Squad connected the dots and zeroed in on him. He was surprised Langford hadn't questioned him yet. He picked up the revolver off the shelf next to his chair. It was the six-inch .357 magnum Smith & Wesson model 686 he carried as a young patrolman on the Farmington Police Department. His parents had given it to him when he graduated from the Academy. It would do the job. He unscrewed the top on the Pappy Van Winkle and took another long draw of liquid courage. He thought about praying, but he didn't believe. Now that Hope was gone, he was the center of his universe. He stuck the blue steel barrel in his mouth and closed his eyes tight. His hand quivered as he began applying pressure to the trigger with his thumb. As he took one last breath through his nose before making the final squeeze, his cellphone rang. His eyes popped open, and he let out a shaky breath as he removed the barrel from his mouth. He wiped his eyes with the back of his gun hand and answered the phone. "Hello."

"Mr. Pagano, this is Jim Baderman again. I just thought you would want to know we got a warrant on Garza. He's sitting in the county jail. Bond was set at $200,000."

"Thank you, Jim. That's definitely good news. Did he confess?" Pagano asked. Maybe Garza would, hoping it would pay for prior unpunished sins by taking the blame for this one.

"No, sir, but we'll take a real hard look at him. We'll know one way or the other in a day or two."

"Thank you for calling me, Jim," Pagano said before hanging up. He gazed at the revolver for a minute before putting it back on the shelf. Maybe he would give it another day or two.

Chapter 28

Mark and Zack stood outside the main viewing room at Koplin's Funeral Home with Sheriff Blair. They were wearing their most formal uniform: brown straw hats, white gloves, long sleeves, and a tie. Sheriffs from over thirty Missouri counties had come to honor Lieutenant Close and pay their respects to his family and the St. Francois County Sheriff's Department. The small funeral home had over 300 mourners inside the building. All the people were overwhelming the air conditioning system, with the temperature passing 80°F and steadily rising. Out on Taylor Avenue in front of the parking lot, ladder trucks from the Farmington and Bonne Terre Fire Departments formed an arch with their ladders and hung a massive American flag over the street.

Nick Pagano approached the group, followed closely by three of his men. "Excuse me, gentlemen. Sheriff, I have a donation for Mrs. Close. Would you please give it to her? I don't think she would accept it from me. Maybe funnel it through the BackStoppers." He handed a cashier's check to Blair.

The sheriff's eyes opened wide. "$500,000! That's very generous, Nick," he said quietly.

"Well, I feel partly responsible for bringing Powers and Garza to the county in the first place. If I hadn't, Denny would still be alive. Please, keep this to yourselves. I'd like the donation to remain anonymous." Pagano stepped away.

Blair folded the check and put it in his breast pocket as he watched Pagano walk away. "Just when I was convinced Nick was a selfish asshole, he goes and does something like this."

"Are you going to give it to her today?" Mark asked.

"I don't know. It'd probably be better to wait until tomorrow or at least until after the ceremony."

"Excuse me, I'm going outside for minute," Zack said. He was getting claustrophobic. He hurried out of the crowded building to the parking lot. Two funerals in less than a week reminded him of all the military funerals he had been to. Even outside of combat, it was hard for a squadron to fly 25,000 hours without having a Class A mishap. A Class A was usually a crash involving a fatality, a person totally disabled, or $2 million in damage to the aircraft. In his ten years in the Corps, he had been to over twenty funerals.

The funeral he remembered most vividly was for John, his next-door neighbor in base housing at Miramar. Captain John Berman was a Super Stallion pilot with the Wolfpack of HMH-466. Zack's squadron was a couple of weeks away from replacing John's on a six-month deployment to Okinawa. Zack and his new bride, Patty, were in their front yard working on their flower bed when they saw a sedan pull up in front of Berman's house. The commander of Marine Air Group 16, a Navy chaplain, and a Marine captain exited the car. The Marines were wearing their green Class A uniforms, and the chaplain was wearing his Navy dress blues. Zack knew that could mean only one thing: John had bought the farm. Patty had never met John, but she had become good friends with his wife. Patty looked across the cul-de-sac and asked him what was going on.

He said, "C'mon. Let's go in the house." Patty stood there dumbfounded holding a garden trowel in her gloved hand. Zack took her other hand and led her to the house. "I'll explain inside."

An hour later, the colonel and chaplain departed, leaving the captain behind. He was a casualty assistance officer. Zack never told Patty the details, but he found out later that John's copilot had flown them into a mountaintop in southern Japan while trying to fly under a low overcast. The crew and three passengers were killed instantly. The accident investigators determined the copilot was at the controls because both of his wrists were broken from feedback through the rotor blades to the cyclic and collective when the rotor blades struck the mountain about thirty feet below the summit. The impact was so severe the copilot's armored seat separated from the cockpit and was found on the other side of the summit hanging upside down from a tree. The funeral occurred a week later at Miramar, and Zack deployed to Okinawa a week after that, leaving behind a very nervous newlywed. He rubbed his face in an attempt to clear the memory from his thoughts.

He scanned the area outside the funeral home for anything that looked suspicious but came up empty. He saw two columns of police motorcycles lined up in front of the hearse. Thirty motor officers from departments all over Missouri and Illinois were waiting in the sun, but none were from his poor department. They didn't have a motorcycle. Zack saw a familiar uniform and approached the officer. "Excuse me, I just wanted to introduce myself. I'm Zack Goodson. I saw you're from Ballwin; I grew up there and went to Marquette High School."

"Pleased to meet you, Zack. My name's Dino Castillo. You're sure a long way from Ballwin."

"Tell me about it. My wife grew up down the road in Farmington, and I promised her we'd move back to her hometown after I got out of the Marines. So, how's West County doing?"

"It's booming. It's more crowded than ever. Manslaughter Road is a mess every morning and evening, and on weekends, it's bumper to bumper all day," Dino replied. Manslaughter Road was actually Manchester Road. It ran east and west across St. Louis City and County and was famous for its horrible traffic jams.

"That's one of the few things I don't miss about living there. Is Ed Robertson still around?"

"Yeah. He has close to forty-five years on the department. He just made sergeant again. Hey, the word's going around that your sheriff is taking us to a place called Granny Annie's after the service. They're saying the food is terrific."

Zack nodded. "Don't tell my wife, but it's the best food I've ever had. Everything on Annie's menu is great, but if you want a special treat, ask for whatever Mark's having. It was nice meeting you, Dino, but I better get back to work."

"OK, Zack. Catch you later."

Zack decided to take a walk around the lot.

The rest of the parking lot was reserved for family and friends. Over a hundred police vehicles lined both sides of Taylor Avenue in front of the lot. He heard the familiar roar of a jet engine and the whir of rotor blades. Shielding his eyes from the sun, he tilted his head up and saw a helicopter from the FOX News affiliate in St. Louis slowly orbiting the funeral home. It reminded him of the TH-57 Sea Ranger helicopter he flew during flight school.

Zack saw Pagano come out of the building followed by his security detail. When he motioned for them to hang back, they stopped abruptly. "Excuse me, Deputy Goodson, can I speak to you for a moment?"

"Yes, sir. What can I do for you?"

"I'm buying a MH-6 Little Bird and a UH-1H Huey for my training facility here at Iron Mountain and I need another pilot. I was told you flew Super Stallions in the Corps, so I had my background investigators check you out. They tell me you had an impressive career in the Corps and were on the short list for HMX-1. If you're interested, I'd like to talk to you about it after the funeral. I know what the county pays new deputies, and my pilots start at four times that and our benefits package is the best around. Please, just think about it, and we can talk later."

"I'm surprised you would want to hire me after our previous conversations," he said.

"Zack, I was a cop for over twenty years. I understand why you had to ask the questions you asked. I'll admit, I haven't dealt with my daughter's murder very well, and I was annoyed by having a rookie cop asking me troubling questions, but I know you were doing your job. Please, give me a call later. Excuse me." Pagano walked away to talk to the mayor of Farmington.

Zack made his way through the throng milling about outside the entrance and back into the building. He took his place standing along the wall next to Mark and the other deputies. Two deputies stood watch at the head and foot of the casket. Behind them, a slideshow of photos and videos was being run on the large wall-mounted screen showing all assembled what a wonderful person Denny had been and the impactful life he had lived. Zack watched Mrs. Close and her boys. They were sitting in the front row nearest the casket with Lieutenant Close's mother and father. Captain Baderman sat directly behind them scanning the room like a stage mother at her six-year-old daughter's first beauty pageant. Mrs. Close still wore the same vacant, stunned expression the sheriff had described seeing when he gave her the bad news on Wednesday. He figured she must still be in shock. The boys were wearing what looked like new suits, probably bought yesterday at the Farmington JCPenneys. They sat quietly and appeared more bored than sad. Due to the horrific damage to the body, the lid would remain closed. Just the smell alone would have been enough to clear the building. The funeral director, Les Koplin, had arranged to have an American flag provided by the Department of Veterans Affairs, due to Denny's veteran status, draped on the closed casket. Denny had served as a truck driver in the Missouri National Guard during Operation Desert Shield in Kuwait.

At the appointed time, Koplin approached the lectern. "Would everyone please stand?"

A voice from the back of the room bellowed, "Attention! Present arms!" Those law enforcement officers present and in uniform came to attention and saluted. The Sheriff's Color Guard marched up the center aisle to post the colors next to the casket. They placed the United States and Missouri flags in their stands and marched back down the aisle. The same voice as before bellowed, "Order arms! At easy!" The officers lowered their arms as directed.

"Ladies and gentlemen, please be seated. On behalf of the Close family, I welcome you and thank you for coming today to honor the life of Lieutenant Dennis Close. I would like to invite the Sheriff's Department chaplain, Pastor Glen Watts, to offer the opening prayer." Koplin stepped away to the edge of the room.

Pastor Watts approached the lectern and opened his Bible. He read aloud, "The Lord is my shepherd; I shall not want. He maketh me to lie down in green pastures: he leadeth me beside the still waters. He restoreth my soul: he leadeth me in the paths of righteousness for his name's sake. Yea, though I walk through the valley of the shadow of death, I will fear no evil: for thou art with me; thy rod and thy staff they comfort me. Thou preparest a table before me in the presence of mine enemies: thou anointest my head with oil; my cup runneth over. Surely goodness and mercy shall follow me all the days of my life: and I will dwell in the house of the Lord for ever." The pastor closed his Bible and returned to his seat.

Koplin returned to the lectern. "Thank you, Pastor Watts."

Next, a series of spiritually uplifting musical selections were played followed by speeches from the local state senator, state representative, presiding county commissioner, and several local mayors, many of whom had never met Lieutenant Close.

Koplin returned to the lectern. "Sheriff Donald Blair will deliver the eulogy." He walked back to his position.

Blair first approached the widow, Virginia Close, with his hat in his hand. His uniform was a little more formal than his deputies. He wore an Eisenhower jacket. He and the undersheriff, Captain Baderman, were the only people on the department who rated the extra expense. He leaned over and took her hand in his and whispered something comforting to her and her boys. She came out of her stupor for a moment and smiled at him. He walked over to the lectern and removed some folded paper from the leather band inside his hat. He hung his hat by its chin strap over his holstered pistol. He smoothed the papers on the lectern and set his gaze on the widow and her family.

"To Ginny and the boys; to Denny's parents, Dave and Maggie; and to all the members of Denny's family and his friends, on behalf of the Saint Francois County Sheriff's Department, I extend our deepest condolences to you. As we honor Denny's memory today, I ask you to think about the sentiment inscribed in the granite at the National Law Enforcement Memorial. It says, 'It was not how these officers died that made them heroes; it is how they lived.'

"Dennis Cornelius Close was born just down the road in Farmington on March 15, 1970. He grew up in Farmington, and after he graduated from high school, he married his long-time sweetheart, Virginia McGuire. He worked construction, building houses, to provide for his small family, but money was always tight, so he joined the Missouri National Guard to help make ends meets. Shortly after completing his initial training, he deployed for seven months to Kuwait and later Iraq for Operation Desert Storm as a member of the 35th Infantry Division.

"After he returned home, my predecessor hired him as a deputy sheriff. A year later, the Highway Patrol tried to recruit him away from our department, but he declined because St. Francois County was his home and he wanted to continue serving our community. He had no desire to live anywhere else. Two years later, he made the papers when he arrested a couple of bank robbers single-handedly as they fled Farmington down Highway 67. That same year, he rescued a four-year-old boy from a house during a domestic dispute. The boy's deranged father was barricaded in the house with a shotgun. Denny saw the little boy standing alone inside the screen door. When the father was distracted by something he heard at the back of house, Denny ran across the front yard and ripped the screen out of the locked door. He grabbed the boy and ran back across the yard, shielding the boy with his body as he ran. He was, subsequently, awarded the Missouri Department of Public Safety's Medal of Merit.

"In 2003, their son Dean was born, and their son David followed two years later. After ten years on the department, I promoted Denny to sergeant and put him in charge of our Detective Bureau. Five years later, I promoted him again, this time to Lieutenant. All total, Denny served the citizens of our county for over twenty-eight years.

"He lived his life full of love and enthusiasm for his family, friends, and fellow deputies. He was brave to a fault, always ready to defend the weak and fight for what was right no matter the cost. He believed in justice and our Judeo-Christian values. He believed justice had to be impartial. He also served as our department's internal affairs investigator. The position was often underappreciated but vital to the health of the department. After all, someone must be available to police the police, especially when accusations of malfeasance are lodged against them. Denny was always happier to clear good deputies than he was to uncover a bad one. The other deputies felt safer knowing where Denny was.

"Denny was a devoted family man. Back at the station, his desk was covered in photos of his beloved, Ginny, and the boys, Dean and David. They meant everything to him. Even though overtime hours were rare and extra money was always needed at home, he would turn it down to spend more time with his family, especially during baseball and football seasons when the boys were playing.

"He downplayed the dangers of his job so Ginny and the boys wouldn't worry about him. Due to his position, he often worked alone. Despite my instructions to take backup with him when it was available, he preferred to leave them available to answer calls for help from the county's citizens. The day his life was taken, he was searching for one of his brothers, an Army veteran, who had been reported missing.

"Denny wasn't one to seek recognition. He didn't feel the need for praise. But let there be no mistake: Denny led the way in fighting crime in this county. He was a hero for the way he lived and for what he helped to accomplish. He left an everlasting impression on those of us who had the privilege of working with him. His hard work and dedication are greatly appreciated. He will be sorely missed. He helped make sure our little corner of the world was a better place." Blair gathered his papers and walked back to the widow. He bent over and put his hand on her shoulder. He whispered something in her ear again and then returned to his seat.

The room was called to attention, and the Color Guard marched up the aisle to retrieve the flags. They removed the flags from their stands as the order to present arms was given. The Color Guard marched to the front row and stopped. The Honor Guard of eight deputies took their positions around the flag-draped casket as a bagpiper marched up the center aisle to the first row playing "Amazing Grace." A second bagpiper played from the lobby, creating a stereo effect. The first bagpiper stopped in front of the Color Guard and turned about-face. The Honor Guard lifted the casket off its support and began slowly following the bagpiper and the Color Guard down the aisle past the mourners and saluting deputies, police officers, and troopers. The mourners fell in behind the casket and followed it outside to get to their vehicles.

As the casket was being loaded into the hearse, Denny's oldest son, Dean, approached Blair.

"Sheriff, I'll be going to MAC next year for a law enforcement degree. I would appreciate it if you'd hold a spot for me."

Blair wrapped his arms around the kid. "Dean, as long as I'm sheriff, you'll be welcome on the department."

CHAPTER 29

After the funeral, Mark and Zack got into their freshly washed cruiser.

"It sounded like Lieutenant Close started out as a good deputy. What happened to him?" Zack stuck his finger between his sweat-stained collar and neck. He hated wearing a tie, even the cheap clip-on variety cops always wore. Of course, he knew they wore the clip-on for a very good reason. If someone grabbed it, it would just come off instead of being used to strangle him or drag him around.

"The Sheriff tried to put as good a spin on Denny's career as he could. He was hired by the previous sheriff because his dad was a political supporter and big campaign donor. Those bank robbers he caught were a sixteen-year-old couple running away from home who robbed the bank because they needed gas money. The girl strolled into the bank and said she had a bomb in her purse. They gave her around 300 bucks. Denny didn't even know about the bank robbery. He stopped them out on the highway for a broken taillight. As soon as he approached the car, they both started crying and confessed to robbing the bank."

When the motorcycles at the front of the procession roared to life, they and the other marked cruisers flipped on their emergency light bars. The procession slowly pulled out onto Taylor Avenue and headed south. They drove under the enormous flag hanging from the ladder trucks.

"When he saved the little boy, that happened under the old sheriff too. Blair was a sergeant back then. Everything he said about the call was true. What he didn't say was the suspect was falling-down drunk and Denny's partner was at the back of the house talking to him through the kitchen window while the guy sat on the floor with a shotgun in one hand and a bottle of peppermint schnapps in the other. He alternated putting them in his mouth. His partner talked to the guy until he finished the bottle and passed out. If anybody deserved a medal, it was his partner, but it happened under the old sheriff, and he owed Denny's dad more favors, so he put his kid in for the medal." Mark turned left with the procession onto Main Street. A Park Hills police officer blocked oncoming traffic with his cruiser and stood at attention in the intersection. He saluted as the procession passed.

"Once he was sheriff, Blair promoted Denny to sergeant because none of the other sergeants wanted to come off the road and run the Detective Bureau. The rest of us hadn't been with the Department long enough to earn the promotion. I had only been here two and a half years, but Blair made me a detective to work under Denny. Five years later, there was a reorg, and all the sergeants were promoted to lieutenant and given a little bump in pay. Then three road deputies were promoted to sergeant. When Denny fucked me over and sent me back to patrol, it kept me from being promoted. So, no, he didn't change. He was always the same miserable asshole."

"Which cemetery are we heading to?"

"Parkview. That's the one on Flat River Road north of Farmington."

Zack nodded.

Both sides of Main Street were lined with people holding signs and flags who came out with their children to show their support. Entire Boy Scout troops were lined up saluting as they passed. It reminded Zack of the support he had seen for fallen Marines brought back from Afghanistan. "It has to be 95° today, and there must be over 500 people out here."

"Yeah, it's a pretty good turnout. Hopefully it'll help Denny's family cope with what happened."

Minutes later, the procession drove through the archway into the cemetery and followed the path through the well-manicured grass as it wrapped around the headstones before coming to a stop at the grave site. The Honor Guard formed up at the rear of the hearse and carried the casket to the open grave as the bagpipers stood off at a distance playing "Amazing Grace."

Pastor Watts stood at the head of the casket waiting for the mourners to assemble. When they were ready, he addressed them: "Friends and loved ones, we have gathered here to praise the Lord Almighty and show our faith as we celebrate the life and sacrifices of his servant, Denny Close. We come together in grief to mourn the loss of our beloved brother." He lowered his head and said, "Lord, may you grant us grace, that in our pain we may find comfort, in our sorrow we may find hope, and in death we may find resurrection."

He raised his head and opened his Bible. "From the book of Matthew, chapter 5, verses 3 through 12, I quote the blessings of Jesus: 'Blessed are the poor in spirit: for theirs is the kingdom of heaven. Blessed are they that mourn: for they shall be comforted. Blessed are the meek: for they shall inherit the earth. Blessed are they which do hunger and thirst after righteousness: for they shall be filled. Blessed are the merciful: for they shall obtain mercy. Blessed are the pure in heart: for they shall see God. Blessed are the peacemakers: for they shall be called the children of God. Blessed are they which are persecuted for righteousness' sake: for theirs is the kingdom of heaven. Blessed are ye, when men shall revile you, and persecute you, and shall say all manner of evil against you falsely, for my sake. Rejoice, and be exceeding glad: for great is your reward in heaven.'" The pastor closed his Bible and walked over to Mrs. Close. He went to one knee and placed his hand on her shoulder. He bowed his head and said a quiet prayer for her. He rose to his feet and took his place at the end of the line of mourners.

The Honor Guard marched forward in unison to the casket and began meticulously folding the flag.

The commander of the rifle detail of seven deputies, Lieutenant McLeod, ordered, "Detail, attention! Present arms! Ready, aim, fire!"

The detail fired one volley in unison and readied their rifles for the next volley. The less initiated in the assembly flinched as the deafening crack ripped the air.

McLeod ordered again, "Aim! Fire!"

Another volley was fired.

And again, "Aim! Fire!"

The final volley was fired.

McLeod ordered, "Order arms. Parade rest!"

The bugler was standing off at a distance and immediately began playing "Taps."

The sheriff approached the Honor Guard and accepted the flag. He turned and approached the widow. He went down to one knee in front of her. "Please accept this flag as a symbol of the heartfelt appreciation and gratitude the citizens of St. Francois County have for your husband's service and sacrifice. I cannot express how sorry we are for your loss." He stood, saluted, and stepped away as Central Dispatch transmitted the End of Watch call over the radio for all to hear.

"Central calling nine eighty-three." A momentary pause of silence filled the air. "Central calling nine eighty-three, Lieutenant Close." Another momentary pause. "Lieutenant Dennis Close is 10-42, end of watch on the tenth of June, 2020. We thank him for his dedication, loyalty, and service to the citizens of St. Francois County. Yea, thou I walk through the valley of the shadow of death, I will fear no evil; for thou art with me; thy rod and thy staff they comfort me. Blessed are the peacemakers: for they shall be called the children of God. Last call for Lieutenant Dennis Close, serial number nine eighty-three. Rest easy, Brother, we have the watch."

Koplin stepped in front of the assembly. "Ladies and gentlemen, this concludes our service. On behalf of the Close family, I would like to thank you for the outpouring of kindness and support you have graciously given them during these difficult days. There will be a reception immediately following at the Farmington Baptist Church. All are welcome and invited to attend."

As the group began to disperse, the bagpipers played "Eternal Father, Strong to Save."

CHAPTER 30

Zack and Mark walked into the conference room at the Troop C Annex. Herman Keller and Cody Gibbs were sitting at the table behind several stacks of paperwork. Evidence photos and key details were posted on the whiteboard in front of them.

"Hey, gentlemen, how was the service?" Keller asked.

"Good. The turnout was huge. Several hundred LEOs from all over Missouri and Illinois came, including over thirty Missouri sheriffs. Citizens lined the route all the way to the cemetery. His wife and boys are still in shock, but I'm sure they'll look back on it and appreciate the respect everyone showed for Denny," Mark said.

"Clearly, they didn't know him," Gibbs said.

"Thanks for working today while we were on funeral detail. What did you find out?" Mark asked.

"Well, I'm sorry to say, it's not looking too good. We executed the search warrants for Garza's house, phones, email, and social media. Colin Ward took four guys over to Garza's house three hours ago, and so far, they haven't found shit. He has a huge gun safe and a man cave full of Marine shit. His girlfriend came in and gave a statement verifying he was at her place from Tuesday evening to Wednesday morning, and she was with him at his place all day Saturday through Sunday morning until she left to do her laundry. We even tracked down the kid who delivered the pizza to them. Garza paid cash for the pizza and gave him a good tip. His cellphone never left the house. There's nothing on his phone, email, or social media that connects him to Hope Pagano, Lieutenant Close, Lindsay Miller, or Krista Snyder. So far, the only thing that connects him to Denny is him being in possession of his Glock," Keller replied.

"What about the autopsy on Powers?" Zack asked.

"Patel just emailed it to us. Can you bring it up, Cody?" Keller asked.

Gibbs spun his laptop around so Mark and Zack could see it. "The doc says the body is definitely Powers, and he was shot multiple times by a .22 LR caliber firearm. He was shot in the left thigh, both forearms, twice in the chest, and finally, the coup de gras, three times in the back of the head."

"Whoever killed him sure wanted to make it hurt before he finished him," Mark said. "OK, it's been a long day. Let's knock off and hit it again tomorrow. We'll go back to working the afternoon shift at 1400. I'll call Justin and let him know. C'mon, Zack, let's head back to the barn. We'll see you guys tomorrow." They emerged from the building. "Hey, wait a minute. Granny

Annie's is open for another hour. They might still be serving all those motor officers. Do you want to go?" Mark offered.

"Sure. Patty won't be home with Danny until five. Let's go."

They drove the short distance to the restaurant in five minutes and saw two rows of shiny police motorcycles lined up in front of Annie's. Inside, they were surprised at how crowded it was. Clearly many of the deputies had skipped the free food at the reception and came to Annie's instead.

"I see two chairs at your normal table. Do you want to horn in over there or wait for something to open up?" Zack asked.

"Let's go." Mark made his way between the tables and headed for the far corner. "Do you boys mind if we join you?"

Dino Castillo said, "Hell no, it's your party. Have a seat. How's it going, Zack?"

After they sat down, Zack said, "Hey, Dino. This is Sergeant Mark Langford. Do you want to introduce everybody?"

"I would, but we really don't know each other. He's Troop C, he's St. Charles, he's Sunset Hills, and he's St. Louis. St. Louis was about to tell a story. Go ahead," Dino said.

"I helped Clayton PD reconstruct an accident, and I was called to testify. The case was delayed for a couple of hours, so I sat in on a preliminary hearing. This Clayton copper was on the stand in uniform. He said, 'I took my wife to a late movie at the Esquire, and after it ended, we stayed and watched the credits in case there were any extra scenes at the end. It was after midnight, and we were the last people out of the theater. We walked around the building to the parking lot in the rear. Our car was parked out in the middle of the lot all by itself. I walked around the car with my wife to open her door and this man stands up. He was hiding behind my car with a knife in his hand. I stepped in front of my wife, and the suspect tells me to give him my wallet or he'll kill us both. I reached into my back pocket and brought out my wallet and tossed it far enough away that he couldn't catch it. He turned and bent over to pick it up, and that's when I pulled my off-duty weapon and badge and told him I was a police officer and to drop the knife. Instead of complying, he spun around and tried to stab me. I stepped back out of the way and fired one round, which struck the suspect in the buttocks. He fell to the ground and stopped resisting my attempt to arrest him.' So, this was cut-and-dried, right?

"Well, then the suspect agrees to get on the stand, and he says, 'I admit I tried to rob him and his wife, but he didn't pull out his badge and identify himself as Five-O. He just tossed his wallet on the ground, and when I bent over to pick it up, he yelled, "Guess who, motherfucker!" and shot me in the ass.' I'll let you guys decide who told the truth." The officers laughed.

"There's another lesson. Don't bring a knife to a gunfight," Mark said.

Annie approached the table and kissed Mark. "What would you and Zack like?"

"Is my lunch still available?"

"Yes, sweetie. I held back a couple of servings in case you and Zack came by. Is that what you want, Zack?"

"Yes, ma'am. Thank you."

Annie turned and headed for the kitchen.

"So, you're that Mark?" Dino asked.

"What do you mean?"

"The 'I'll have what Mark's having' Mark."

Mark shot Zack a look. "Do we have to go over number nine again?"

"Sorry."

Mark turned to the St. Louis officer. "Have any of the old-timers in the city told you about the rabbit the Hat Squad had back in the old days to help them with interrogations?"

"That's a new one to me," St. Louis replied.

"Back in the days before the Miranda decision, some police departments came up with some inventive ways to solicit confessions out of uncooperative suspects. When the Hat Squad brought a suspect back to the old headquarters building on Tucker, they'd take him to the interrogation room and handcuff him to the table. They'd let him sit there and sweat for an hour or so and then a detective would come in and sit down across from him. He'd start asking questions, and when he thought the suspect wasn't being truthful, he'd say, 'I'm going to go get a cup of coffee and give you a few minutes to think about your situation.' He'd get up and leave the room. A couple of minutes later, this seven-foot-tall white rabbit wearing a black bow tie and top hat would hop into the room carrying a three-foot-long wooden carrot. He'd hop around the room a couple of times and then stop next to the suspect. He'd sniff the suspect for a few seconds and then whack him with the carrot. Then the rabbit would hop out of the room, and a couple of minutes later, the detective would come back and sit down. The suspect would say something like, 'What the fuck was that?' The detective would say, 'What are you talking about?' The suspect would say, 'That giant fucking rabbit came in here and hit me with his carrot!' The detective would say, 'C'mon, man. That's crazy.' Then he'd go back to asking his questions. When the suspect became uncooperative again, the dick would say, 'OK, I'm going to go have a smoke and give you some time to think about your situation.' A couple of minutes later, the rabbit would hop in again and hop around the room a few times and then smack the guy a couple more times with the carrot. The rabbit would hop out, and a few minutes later, the detective would come back. The suspect would say, 'This is bullshit, man, letting that rabbit come in here and beat me!' The cycle would continue until the suspect confessed. This technique worked for a while until enough people complained to the FBI that they felt compelled to send over a couple of agents to investigate. They came down and talked to the Chief and told him they had received several complaints about the department using a giant rabbit to beat confessions out of suspects. The chief laughed and said that was ridiculous. The lead agent replied, 'Well, we're not saying it's happening, we're just saying it better not happen anymore.'"

CHAPTER 31

Pagano sat in his home office behind his desk staring at the expensive leather-bound books in his custom-built bookcases. The wood was something exotic from Africa—bubinga, or something like that. The books simply served as decoration in the room. He had never intended to actually read them. He wondered if he had a book on how to get away with murder. He looked at the wall clock. Denny's funeral must be over by now. He couldn't bring himself to go to the graveside service and watch the flag presentation and gun volley knowing he had caused it all. His cellphone rang.

"Hello?"

"Hello, sir. This is Jim Baderman again. I thought you would want to know that we've determined Garza's alibi checks out. We can't connect him to any of the murders. We're still holding him on the weapon charge, but it's looking more and more like someone framed him. We'll be broadening the investigation."

"I see. That's too bad. I was hoping you guys had put an end to all of this madness. At any rate, thank you for keeping me updated. The uncertainty is driving me crazy." Pagano finally said something truthful.

"You're welcome, sir. I can't imagine how difficult this has been for you."

Pagano ended the call and rubbed his forehead. He could feel the walls closing in on him. Sitting around waiting for the axe to fall was infuriating. He decided enough was enough. Since they were coming after him anyway, he would start fighting back. He wasn't going out with a whimper. He would start with Langford and that fucking irritating rookie.

Chapter 32

Pagano tried to make himself comfortable beneath the trees at the edge of the pasture behind 3707 Hazel Run Road. He estimated the range to the teardrop-shaped driveway in front of the house at 200 yards. He was armed with the Remington 700 he had stolen from Randy Powers the night he brutally murdered him. The Leupold scope on the rifle should make the shots he planned easy, even for an amateur like him. He knew he wouldn't be disturbed. This farm had been for sale for three months, and the owners had already moved to Arizona. He pulled out his new burner phone. It was one of hundreds his company bought for cash over the years at various locations. It could not be traced back to him or IMI. He sent a message to Mark Langford's cellphone. The message said, "I know who killed Deputy Close. I will only talk to you and Goodson. Meet me at 3707 Hazel Run Road in fifteen minutes. If you're late, I won't be here. Don't bother trying to call me back. I will have already destroyed this phone."

Mark and Zack were on their way to the Troop C Annex to start their shift. They were driving northbound on Highway 67 approaching the Leadington exit when Mark's phone chirped with a message. Mark pulled it out of his pocket and took a quick look at the screen. "Shit, we may have gotten a break." He handed the phone to Zack as he accelerated past the exit and continued northbound. He flipped on the light bar and siren.

Zack read the message. "Can we get there in fifteen minutes?"

"It'll be tight. Call Justin and tell him where we're going and have Keller handle the shift change for us and have them send two more guys our way." Mark raced up the divided highway at 95 MPH. The posted limit was 60 MPH. He took the exit at Bonne Terre and headed east on Highway K. He had to slow down considerably to maintain control on the undulating, curvy two-lane road as he blew past the state prison. He killed the siren as he turned northbound on Hillsboro Road. "Zack, remember what I told you about big game hunting? Put your armor on before we get there."

Zack took off his seatbelt and reached behind the seat to grab his plate carrier. He pulled it over his head and secured the Velcro side straps. Then he lifted his rifle over the seat and threw the single-point sling over his head. "What about your armor?"

"I'll throw it on as soon as we get there. We're getting close. The T intersection up there is Hazel Run. We'll be turning right. Put us 23."

Zack grabbed the mic. "Central, ten oh five, 10-23 at 3707 Hazel Run Road for an investigation."

"Ten oh five, 10-23, at 1357," Peggy replied.

Mark switched the light bar off and slowed to turn onto the long gravel driveway next to the massive, manicured lawn. He pointed at the realtor's sign. "This place is for sale. It's probably vacant. When we get out, bring your rifle, just in case." Mark continued slowly up the driveway. He stopped about fifty feet from the house. They sat for a moment and surveyed the area.

"No cars in the driveway. If it's vacant, you think this could be an ambush?" Zack asked.

"I don't know. I've never been ambushed. Keep your rifle ready. Cover me while I get my vest on." Mark opened his door and got out.

Zack stepped out of the cruiser and rested his rifle muzzle between the door and doorframe. As he scanned the area, he could hear Mark open the rear hatch to retrieve his armor and rifle. Mark had a Colt AR-15A2 with a 20-inch barrel and fixed stock. It was a semiautomatic version of the military M-16A2. It was an excellent rifle but lacked the red dot optic and light and laser vertical foregrip Zack installed on his own. "Do you want me to go knock on the door?" Zack asked.

"No. Stay where you are. I'll go to the door." Mark approached the door with his rifle muzzle pointed toward the ground.

Zack continued to scan the area. As Mark got halfway to the front door, Zack heard a loud smack and, out of the corner of his eye, saw Mark spin around to the left and go down on his face. A fraction of a second later, he heard a rifle shot come from the distant trees. He was scanning for a target when the windshield next to him spidered, followed again by the sound of the shot. He instinctively ducked behind the door and retreated to the rear of the cruiser. The explosions and chaos and blood from Afghanistan flashed through his thoughts. Once again, an unseen enemy was trying to kill him. He looked around the left side of the cruiser and saw Mark trying to crawl to cover behind the corner of the house. He looked toward the trees and saw a muzzle flash. Then he saw and then heard a round hit the gravel driveway in front of Mark and zip by above him. The driveway was crowned in a way that provided Mark with some cover as long as he stayed down on the ground. If he so much as raised his head, he would be visible to the shooter. Zack fired off a rapid string of rounds toward the trees about 200 yards away where he thought the rounds were coming from. "Mark! Stay down! He doesn't have a good shot at you as long as you stay down!"

The firing was slow enough, he figured the shooter must have a bolt-action rifle. When another round skipped off the gravel, Zack hurried into the driver's seat and pulled the cruiser forward to place it between the shooter and Mark. He got out and grabbed Mark by his vest's handle and pulled him toward the rear driver-side door. The shooter adjusted his aim and began methodically putting holes in the passenger-side doors. Zack realized his plan wouldn't work and instead dragged Mark toward the corner of the house. There was a gap of about five feet from the front bumper and the corner of the house where the shooter would have a clear shot. Zack threw his muzzle up over the hood and sprayed the tree line with about fifteen rounds until he ran dry. He dropped down to reload and repositioned himself at the rear of the cruiser and emptied another full magazine into the trees. He grabbed Mark by his vest's pull handle and quickly dragged him behind the house. He reloaded again and then yelled into his walkie, "Central, ten oh five, 10-33, shots fired! Nine eighty-seven is down! There's a sniper in the tree line with a rifle! Send help ASAP!" Zack turned his attention to Mark. He was holding his bloody left bicep with his right hand. "Are you hit anywhere else besides your arm?" Zack heard deputies and troopers on the radio putting themselves en route, their sirens wailing in the background.

Mark grimaced against the pain and said through gritted teeth, "The round hit my plate first and then hit my arm. It hurts to breathe. I think some ribs are broken."

Zack removed a six-inch Israeli bandage from the pouch on his plate carrier and quickly wrapped up Mark's arm as he talked. "I don't know where the sniper is. He could be maneuvering on us right now. I can kick the front door in and drag you into the house or get you in the cruiser and take you to the emergency room. It's your call. What do you want to do?"

"I can't hardly breathe. Let's get the fuck out of here," Mark replied as tears ran down his cheeks.

"Suck it up, Sergeant! I'm going to pull the cruiser behind the house!" Zack stood up. He advanced to the corner of the car and put another twenty rounds into the tree line. He jumped behind the wheel and quickly pulled behind the house next to Mark. He grabbed Mark under the arms from behind. "C'mon, use your legs to help me get your fat ass in the back seat."

Mark pushed up with his legs as he leaned back into Zack to get to his feet. "I'm not fat, kid. Wait twenty years and see what shape you're in." Mark half sat, half fell into the back seat.

Zack ran around to the other door and pulled him the rest of the way inside. He closed both rear doors and jumped behind the wheel. He spun the cruiser around, leaving two neatly plowed furrows in the pristine turf as he headed straight for the road. He flipped on the lights and siren and transmitted, "Central, ten oh five, I have nine eighty-seven in the cruiser. He's been shot in the left bicep and says he's having a hard time breathing. He thinks he may have broken ribs from a round hitting his armor. I'm taking him to the Parkland Emergency Room in Bonne Terre. Get them ready to receive him."

The sheriff came up on the frequency and talked to Zack directly, "Zack, should I send the Air Evac helicopter to the ER to pick him up?"

"He says he's having a hard time breathing. Yeah, go ahead and send them. We'll be at the ER in about five minutes," Zack replied. "How are you doing, Mark?" He could hear Mark pulling Velcro straps loose.

Mark dropped his front plate in the floorboard. "That's a little better, but fuck, my arm is killing me. I thought it was supposed to go numb after you got shot."

"Hey, Mark?"

"Yeah."

"That's what an ambush is like."

"No shit, asshole."

"We're coming up on 67; hang on." Zack could feel the cruiser get light on its wheels as it came over the rise on Highway K and then bottomed out as it started downhill to the Highway 67 underpass. A Highway Patrol trooper and Bonne Terre police officer passed him going the other way toward Hazel Run. Zack saw that two other officers from Bonne Terre PD had already stopped traffic at the Highway 67 underpass to give him a clear path to the entrance ramp. Zack made a hard left turn and shot up the ramp onto 67. Within a minute, he was approaching the small Parkland satellite emergency room that sat just off the west side of the highway. There was no exit from the highway in front of the ER, so Zack made his own. He slowed enough to drive off the right side of the shoulder into the grass-covered drainage ditch and up on to the outer road leading to the entrance to the ER. He turned into the parking lot and came to a stop under the portico in front of the entrance. The cruiser was immediately surrounded by men and women in surgical scrubs moving like a NASCAR pit crew. In seconds, Mark was on a gurney being rolled into the ER while the doctor shouted orders to his staff.

Zack pulled the cruiser away from the entrance into a parking spot. He looked down at the dried blood on his trembling hands. He keyed his mic. "Central, ten oh five, 10-23 at the Bonne Terre ER. Nine eighty-seven is being treated." He dropped the mic on the passenger seat and went inside to check on Mark. He went to the front counter, and before he could ask, the receptionist told him the doctor was with Mark and would give him an update as soon as he could. He handed her his cellphone. "Can you take a couple of photos of me and the blood on my armor and hands?" She looked confused but did as he requested and gave him back his phone. He looked down and realized his rifle was still dangling at his side on its single-point sling. He went back outside onto the grass to clear it and make it safe. He dropped the magazine and pulled the charging handle back to eject the live round from the chamber. He picked up the round from the grass and put it back into the magazine. He stuck it back in the pouch on his plate carrier. He shuffled over to the cruiser and considered putting his rifle in the rear storage area. He stopped when he saw the windows on the right side and the rear had all been shot out. The passenger half of the windshield had been shattered. He counted five holes in the right-side doors.

Deputy Kurt Sada pulled into the spot next to him. He hopped out and hurried over to Zack and saw the blood. "How're you doing, brother?"

"I'm OK. The blood's Mark's. Can you take some pictures of the cruiser and secure Mark's rifle? It's in the back floorboard. I need to wash this blood off."

"Sure thing. Do you want me to take your rifle too?"

Zack stared down at the rifle he held. "No...I think I'll keep it." He turned and walked into the building to find a sink. He entered the empty men's room. He stepped up to the sink and washed his hands with soap and water. The blood washed away quickly, but his hands didn't feel clean, so he washed them some more. After ten minutes of washing, he still didn't feel clean, but his hands were getting raw so he stopped. He pushed the door open to a stall and sat down. He dialed Patty's cellphone.

She answered the phone with a cheery, "Hi, honey, what's up?"

He wasn't sure what to say. The words just wouldn't come.

"Zack, are you there?"

"Uh, yeah, I'm here. Uh, look something bad happened today. I'm OK, but Mark got shot. I'm at the Bonne Terre Parkland ER waiting to hear how he's doing." Zack tried not to cry.

"Oh my God! Are you sure you're alright? I'll be there in twenty minutes."

"No! No, really, I'm OK. You don't need to come. I just wanted to talk to you and tell you what happened before you heard it on the news or something. I'll give you the details when I get home tonight."

"How bad is Mark hurt?"

"The bullet hit his armor plate and then went into his left bicep. He was having trouble breathing, so he may have some broken ribs, and I think the bullet broke his arm. I'll call you later when I know more. I better get back out there. I love you." Zack hung up. He walked into the lobby and heard the Air Evac helicopter approaching the asphalt landing pad. The building began to vibrate as the helicopter came down and settled onto the pad. Zack stared out through the glass doors of the emergency entrance at the red, white, and blue Bell LongRanger. *What am I doing here?* He knew he could easily get a good job flying. He could even go to the major airlines, thanks to the 1,200 fixed wing flight hours he racked up as an instructor teaching new naval flight officer students at VT-10 in Pensacola.

Two hours later, Zack sat slumped in the waiting room with Ike McLeod and Kurt Sada. He had his armor and rifle propped up on the floor in front of him. He was still hesitant to go too far from his rifle. It was like a security blanket.

McLeod was on his phone. "OK, thanks, Herm," McLeod said before he hung up. "Herman Keller and the Major Case Squad are still out there on Hazel Run processing the scene. He says they found the spot where the sniper was hiding on the edge of the trees about 200 yards from the house. The tree trunks around it are riddled with your bullets. They found twelve Remington .308 casings left behind by the shooter. They didn't see any visible prints on the brass. They followed his trail through the field and woods back to Rustic Acres Drive. They found some good boot prints and took a cast. They estimate he wears a men's size 10."

"Is Garza still in jail?" Zack asked.

"Yeah, I think he's having a hard time coming up with his bond. His little house probably isn't worth a hundred grand, much less two," McLeod replied. "His girlfriend rents her house, so she can't help him out."

"I wonder if he's tight enough with any of the other IMI instructors that they'd be willing to kill for him?" Sada asked.

"Garza and the chief instructor, Keith Winthrop, are both retired Force Recon Marines. They're buddies, but I don't think Winthrop would kill for him. Besides, if a Force Recon Marine wanted to ambush Mark and me, we'd be dead right now," Zack stated.

Sheriff Blair and Mark's wife, Annie, emerged from the ICU down the hall with the doctor. Zack, McLeod, and Sada observed from the waiting room. She nodded her head as the doctor talked. Blair and Annie walked down the hall to the waiting room. The men stood up to greet her. She walked directly over to Zack and threw her arms around his neck and squeezed as hard as she could. Through her tears, she said, "Thank you for bringing him back to me."

Zack didn't know what to say so he just returned her hug. He had been afraid she would hate him just because he was there when her husband got shot. He felt uncomfortable with the extra attention. "How's he doing?" he asked through tear-filled eyes.

Annie released him, and they all sat down. She dabbed her eyes with a tissue. "He's sleeping now. His left arm was broken by the bullet, and he'll need more surgery to repair his bicep. He has two fractured ribs that will heal on their own. The doctor said you saved his life by putting that special military bandage on his arm and getting him here so fast. I can't thank you enough for what you did."

"I'm just glad he's going to be OK," Zack replied.

"Annie, are you going to stay here for a while, or would you like us to take you home?" Blair asked.

"The doctor said Mark will be sleeping for hours. I better go home and talk to the boys before they hear about what happened to their father."

"Ike, do you mind taking Annie home?" Blair asked. "I need to talk to these boys for a minute."

"Sure thing. Come on, Annie. Let's get you home to your boys," Ike said as he led her to the exit.

"We got the autopsy results back on Lindsay Miller and Krista Snyder. They died from multiple gunshots fired from Denny's Glock. So, we have Garza locked up for possession of the gun, but he has a solid alibi for the time of their murders," Blair said.

"Maybe we have more than one killer. One commits the murder while the other makes sure to establish a good alibi," Zack said.

"Maybe so. Normally, I'd give you three days off to decompress from the shootout, but right now, I can't spare you. I'll try to make it up to you after we catch whoever is doing this. I'm going to team you up with Kurt starting tomorrow. You'll continue to work with the Major Case Squad. Both of you meet me for lunch tomorrow at Annie's around noon.

Give me the keys to your cruiser. I'll have it towed back to the garage to be processed. Kurt, take Zack back to the station."

CHAPTER 33

Kurt parked in the station lot next to Zack's truck. Zack hopped out and started walking toward the station. "Hey, brother, what are you doing? You should go home and get cleaned up before your wife sees you."

"I'm going to talk to Garza first."

"No, that's a bad idea. You can't talk to him without his lawyer. Anything he says will be thrown out."

They walked down the hall and stopped in front of the wall-mounted gun lockers outside the jail door. Zack put his Glock in the locker and took the key out. He watched Kurt put his Glock in the locker. Then he took a smaller Glock from his ankle holster and put it in the locker. Then he removed a nasty-looking five-inch-long folding knife from his pocket and put it in the locker before finally removing the key.

"Sure you don't still have a Tommy gun or machete on you?"

"I ain't going to get killed for lack of fighting back. We're not all big, tough Marines," Kurt said with a smile.

Zack aimed his face at the camera, and they were buzzed into the jail. "Barry, we're going to take Garza to the interview room and talk to him for a while." Zack approached the cell, and as he grabbed the handle, the lock opened.

Garza looked up from his bunk and saw the dried blood on Zack's shirt and trousers. He sat up. "What the fuck happened to you?"

"Get up and put your hands behind your back." Garza complied, and Zack cuffed him and led him out of the cell to the jail door. Kurt followed. They entered the interview room, and Zack moved Garza's cuffs to the front and then fastened them to the eyebolt in the table. "Kurt, would you turn on the recorder?" Kurt did so and returned to the room.

Garza looked back and forth at them. "You guys can't question me without my lawyer."

"For now, you can just listen. Sergeant Langford and I received a message today telling us to meet someone who knew who killed Lieutenant Close at a vacant farmhouse east of Bonne Terre. When we got there, someone sniped us from the trees a couple of hundred yards away. Sergeant Langford was shot in the chest by a .308-caliber rifle. The round deflected off his plate carrier and broke his arm. He almost bled to death," Zack said.

"Well, I have an alibi," Garza replied glibly.

"Look, we've already cleared you for the murders. Your alibi checked out. Only an idiot would let us search his truck if he had hidden a murder weapon in it. What we don't know is how and why you wound up with Lieutenant Close's Glock. I think the killer framed you, but I don't know who that is. Help me find out who framed you, and we can get you out of here. Now, do you want to call Chet, or will you talk to us?" Zack asked as he stared down Garza.

Garza stared back but soon dropped his gaze to his handcuffed hands. He nodded and said, "Alright, I'll talk to you. If I call Chet, he'll just tell me to shut up and then I'll be stuck in here even longer. What do you need from me?"

"You need to sign another waiver form first." Zack slid the paper and pen across the table.

Garza hesitated, weighing his risks as he skimmed the form. Finally, he picked up the pen. "Fuck it." He signed and slid the pen and form back to Zack.

"Who do you know that are good long-range shots that knew Powers and Garza?"

"Well, shit, that's all of the instructors at IMI. Two hundred yards is nothing. We could all do that offhand. Even Mr. Pagano could make that shot if he was prone, and he's an amateur. Most hunters could do it prone."

"Have you seen Pagano shooting recently?"

"Yeah, Zeke was giving him some personal instruction last week."

"Is that Zeke Horton? Isn't he a SEAL sniper?"

"Yeah, but he's really good. You and Langford would be dead if Zeke was shooting at you."

"Do you know if Zeke knew Hope Pagano?"

"Yeah, he knew her from Colton's. Jay used to tease Zeke about asking her out because he knew Zeke liked her but was afraid to ask."

"That night you and Zeke ate at Colton's, you said both of you saw Powers making out with a girl behind the restaurant when you left. You said Zeke seemed jealous. Could the girl have been Hope Pagano?"

"She was working that night, so yeah, I guess it's possible," he said with a shrug.

"I have a question. How tight are you guys at IMI? Would you kill for each other?" Kurt asked.

Garza looked at him. "Over in the sandbox, against jihadis, sure, in a fuckin' heartbeat, but here, kill civilians? No fuckin' way. You guys watch too much TV. We're not all ate up with PTSD. Powers was an exception. I guess being forced to retire from the Army after twenty years and getting divorced fucked him up. We're highly trained, disciplined professionals. And we're patriots. We believe in good fighting evil. Hell, a lot of us become cops.

"I guess I fucked up by leaving my truck unlocked. I figured in a small town like this, there would be less crime, and as long as I didn't leave anything worth stealing in my truck, it would be left alone. I never imagined someone would plant a fucking murder weapon in it. I know you guys didn't plant the gun. Chet told me

Close was your internal affairs investigator, so one of your guys might've had a reason to cap him, but that doesn't explain the other victims. I think you should be looking for someone at IMI," Garza suggested.

"Someone like Zeke?" Zack asked.

"I guess he's where I'd start."

Kurt and Zack sat in the squad room. "We need to tell the Sheriff and Herm what we found out. You call Herm and I'll call the Boss," Kurt said.

Zack dialed his phone. "Hey, Herm, it's Zack. Kurt Sada and I took another run at Garza. He gave us some insight into who may be a viable suspect. He reminded me that Zeke Horton had the hots for Hope Pagano but was afraid to ask her out. Then Garza and Horton saw Powers behind Colton's making out with a girl. Garza couldn't tell who she was, but Horton got jealous over what he saw. If Horton saw Powers making out with Hope, he could've had a motive for killing him. He also witnessed the fight between Powers and Garza, so he could have planted Denny's Glock in Garza's truck to frame him."

"It's pretty thin, but you might as well talk to him. Why don't you take Jackie with you? If he's afraid of girls, maybe she'll shake him up. Besides, Art's driving her crazy. Where's he live?" Herm asked.

"He rents a little house in Bonne Terre over by the park."

"OK, pick Jackie up at the annex on your way. I'll tell her to be ready. Talk to you later."

When they arrived at the annex to pick up Jackie, she ran up to the cruiser with concern all over her face and put her hands on the open window frame. She asked Zack, "How's Mark doing?"

"The bullet ricocheted off his armor and hit him in the arm. He has a couple of cracked ribs, a broken humerus, and torn bicep. He'll need some surgeries and rehab, but he'll be fine."

"How are you doing?" she asked.

"It scared the shit out of me, but firefights always do. I'll be fine. Hop in."

While asking about Mark and Zack, Jackie was warm and caring. Then when she was sure they were alright, she calmed down and became the confident, tough Jackie he had met almost a week earlier. "OK, so this guy, Zeke, is a SEAL sniper, but he's afraid to talk to girls," Jackie said as she sat in the center of the back seat of Kurt's cruiser with her face up against the cage. "That's precious. I can't wait to talk to him," she said with a grin.

Zack didn't see the humor. He still kept his rifle with him in the front seat just in case. Mark was right—this was big game hunting, except the game had rifles too. "Remember, he's a murder suspect. Don't drop your guard around him."

"When we get there, I want you guys to wait in the car," Jackie said.

"What? No way!" Zack said.

"That's a really bad idea, sis," Kurt said.

Jackie was about to get offended at being called "sis" when she remembered Kurt called the guys "brother." Then she decided it was sweet. "I'll be fine. I'll call you guys and put it on speaker so you can hear what goes on. Just mute your microphone."

"Shouldn't we have a signal to know if you get in trouble and need our help?" Kurt asked.

Jackie studied the side of his head through the wire mesh. "Yeah, OK. If I scream and start shooting, you should come in and help," she replied sarcastically.

Zack hadn't laughed all day, but he did now.

"I guess that was kinda stupid," Kurt said. He parked a couple of houses down the street from Horton's house.

Jackie got out and leaned into Zack's window. "If you guys need me for something, just disconnect the call and call me back." She turned and headed for the house.

They admired her in her tight pantsuit as she walked away.

"Damn! She's hot!" Kurt said.

"Mute your mic, dumbass," Jackie said without looking back as she walked down the sidewalk.

Kurt's face reddened, and Zack had his second laugh of the day.

"Smooth," Zack said.

Jackie rang the bell, and when Horton opened the door, she turned on her big, beautiful smile. She held her badge out for him to see. "Excuse me, I'm Detective Jackie Weber of the Mineral Area Major Case Squad. Woo, that's a mouthful, isn't it? I'm sorry to disturb you, but I'm investigating the recent series of homicides that have occurred over the last week or so. Are you Zeke Horton?"

"Ahhh, yes, ma'am."

"Please, call me Jackie. Can I call you Zeke?"

"Uhhh, yes, ma'am...ummm, Jackie."

"Is it all right if I come in and talk to you for a while?"

"Sure." He held open the screen door for her. "Have a seat. Can I get you anything?"

"Do you have bottled water?"

"Sure." He took a couple of steps into the kitchen and came back with a cold bottle of Ice Mountain. "Here you go." He sat down across from her in his recliner and muted the ball game he was watching.

She opened the bottle and took a drink. "Thank you." She patted the sofa next to her. "Why don't you sit over here so we can talk?" Horton got up and moved to the sofa next to her. "I know you've already been interviewed, but we're following up with everyone to fill in some missing information. How old are you, Zeke?"

"Twenty-eight."

"And you served eight years in the Navy and seven of that was as a SEAL sniper?"

"Yes, that's right."

She looked up from her notepad. "That's very impressive," she said flatteringly. "And you've worked for IMI for about a year and a half?"

"Yes."

"You said previously that you knew Hope Pagano."

"Yes," he said as he shifted uncomfortably in his seat.

"We were told that you had an attraction to Hope but never pursued it. Why not? You're both young and attractive. You would've been a good fit."

"Well, like I told them last week, Hope was my boss's daughter, and I need my job. And she was only nineteen years old. That's a little too young for me. Actually, I like women a little older than me," he said as he looked into her eyes.

She looked up at him again and smiled then consulted her notepad. "Gil Garza said you and he saw Randy Powers behind Colton's making out with a girl, and he thought you recognized her and it bothered you to see her with Powers. Was Hope the girl?"

"I don't know."

"Zeke, this is really important. Could the girl have been Hope?"

"Yeah, I guess so."

"Is that why you were upset, because you thought the girl was Hope?"

"Maybe."

"Why specifically did it bother you?" He didn't answer immediately, so she sat there silently until he talked.

"Randy was old enough to be her father. He was just using her. I guess she was too immature to see it for herself," he said with a hint of sadness.

"Did you confront him and tell him to stop?"

"No. I thought about it, but they were both adults, and it really wasn't any of my business."

"Zeke, I know this is really personal, but are you a virgin?"

He smiled sadly. "No. I was married and had a little girl until two years ago. My wife and daughter died in a car accident while I was deployed."

Jackie put her hand on his thigh. "Oh, Zeke, I'm terribly sorry... I guess that's enough questions for today. Is it alright if I come back if I need anything else?"

"Sure. I'll see you then." He got up and opened the door for her.

Kurt and Zack closely watched Jackie walk back up the sidewalk. "I don't care if she hears me, she's smokin' hot," Kurt said.

Jackie hopped in the back seat. "Did you hear all that?"

"Yeah, I recorded it on my phone," Zack said.

"I hope he didn't do it," she said.

"Why not?" Kurt asked as he peeked at her through the rearview mirror.

"Because, if he's in the clear, I'm going to take him for a ride."

"Well, it sure sounded like he had a reason to kill Powers. If he thought Powers was taking advantage of Hope and then thought Powers killed her, he might have sought revenge for her," Zack said as Kurt pulled away from the curb.

Chapter 34

Zack knocked on the door before entering Mark's hospital room. He had about an hour and a half before he and Kurt were supposed to meet the sheriff for lunch. "Good morning, sunshine," Zack said, with a big grin on his face. "How are you feeling?"

Mark was sitting up in bed trying to eat a cup of chocolate pudding with his one good arm. An IV ran out of the back of his right hand to a clear bag hanging from the stand next to his bed. "Good morning, yourself. I feel pretty good as long as they keep the pain meds coming."

"What are they giving you?"

"I'm not sure. Morphine, I think, is my favorite, and oxycodone and some other shit. Every time they come in and offer me something, I say yes." He dipped his spoon in the pudding and the cup came up with it. He wiggled the spoon, but the cup hung on. "Any chance you went back out to the farm and found the asshole who shot me lying dead and riddled with your AR rounds?" he asked hopefully.

Zack grabbed the cup and held it still for Mark. "No, all I killed was a bunch of trees and fence posts, but the Major Case Squad searched the area and got a good cast on a boot. They estimate the boot to be a men's size 10."

"Well, that narrows it down to millions of people. Maybe we'll get lucky and he'll hang on to the boots. I hope I get a shot at this motherfucker." Mark put a spoonful of pudding in his mouth. "Who's running the evening shift?"

"Justin gave it to Herm Keller."

Mark nodded. "That's good. He has his shit together. What about you?"

"The Sheriff assigned me to ride with Kurt Sada. We're supposed to keep working with the Major Case Squad. He also told us yesterday that Dr. Patel recovered the bullets during the autopsies on Lindsay and Krista. They all came from Lieutenant Close's Glock. We took Jackie over to Zeke Horton's house to interview him again. She got him to admit he saw Powers making out with Hope behind Colton's. Horton said Powers was taking advantage of her. The squad is looking into him now." Zack stood awkwardly next to the bed for a minute. He could tell Mark felt useless lying in bed. He didn't know how to make him feel better. "I should head out. I'm glad you're feeling better." He turned for the door.

"Hey, Zack?"

He turned around. "Yeah."

"Thanks for getting me out of there."

"No sweat. I'll see you soon," Zack said as he headed for the door again.

"We missed something somewhere," Zack said from the passenger seat of Kurt Sada's cruiser. They had met at the station to pick up the vehicle and were en route to meet the Sheriff for lunch.

"Like what?" Kurt asked and then spit in his bottle and screwed the cap back on.

"I don't know, but something happened along the way that caused an escalation. Somebody thinks we're closing in on him. We found Hope Pagano's body, but we were stymied because we didn't have a suspect. We didn't know who her new boyfriend was. Then the lieutenant gets killed, and we assumed Powers did it. We dug into him and found out he had something going on with Hope. So, we concentrated our efforts on finding him. We looked for him for days not knowing he was already dead in the septic tank. Then somebody killed Lindsay and Krista with Close's Glock." Zack thought for a moment.

"So, whoever killed Powers and Close likely also killed the roommates and then tried to pin it on Garza but didn't know he would have a solid alibi. Maybe we have more than one killer running around. Maybe a couple of guys have teamed up."

Kurt spit in his bottle again. "I would say, go back to the beginning, but that would be Middlebrook Creek. I don't think we'd find anything out there, and Powers's trailer is burnt to shit."

"Maybe we should take another look at the girls' house," Zack said.

Kurt shrugged as he palmed a three- by five-inch piece of quarter-inch steel in his left hand and lightly punched it with his right hand as he drove.

"What are you doing?" Zack asked, confused.

"Building up my hands for punching."

"Won't that damage your knuckles?"

"No, it will protect them. You harden them over time. You start with light strikes to create micro-traumas and build up to harder strikes. It takes years to complete the process," Kurt explained.

"Good luck with that. Let me know how your hands feel in thirty years."

Undeterred, Kurt looked at Zack and punched the plate again. "Have you heard anything new about Mark?"

"They transferred him over to the main hospital in Farmington this morning. I saw him before coming to the station. He's really pissed off over being shot. He wants some payback, but with reconstructive surgery on his arm and the rehab, he'll be out for months. The doctor told him he would have full function of his left arm eventually, but he would never pitch in the big leagues.

Mark told him he threw right-handed, and the doctor said, 'Yeah, I know.'"

Kurt and Zack entered Granny Annie's and took seats at the reserved table in the back of the room. The sheriff hadn't arrived yet. Annie came out of the kitchen and approached them. "What are you doing here? You should be with Mark or home or anywhere but here," Zack said.

She put her arm on his shoulder. "I've already been to the hospital today. After an hour, Mark told me to quit hovering over him. He gets cranky when he doesn't feel good. I want to thank you again for what you did for him yesterday. You saved his life." Her eyes started to tear up.

"I'm just glad we were able to get out of there."

Annie wiped her eyes with her apron. "What would you boys like today?"

"I'll have whatever Mark would be having today and a Coke," Zack said.

"The same for me, Annie, thanks," Kurt agreed.

"Coming right up." She headed for the kitchen.

Sheriff Blair entered the diner and took a seat between Zack and Kurt. "Good afternoon, boys."

"Hey, boss," Kurt said.

"Good afternoon, sir," Zack said.

"What's good today?"

"We're having Mark's lunch," Zack said.

"Yeah, that's always a good choice. I asked you to meet me here so we could talk. First, Zack, I want to thank you again for what you did yesterday. In fact, you've done an outstanding job since you started last week. Normally, as a new deputy, you'd be on probation for a year, but based on your actions and background, you have proven to me you have what it takes to be a professional lawman. So, your probation is over. Having said that, there's still a lot you don't know about the day-to-day duties of a road deputy, so you will continue your field training with Kurt. He's the most squared-away young deputy I have. Even though he has six years on the department, he's still a couple of years younger than you. I want you boys to continue to work with the Major Case Squad. Herman Keller from Park Hills has taken over leading the evening shift. Neither of you are detectives, but you are both sharp, level-headed men. I know you're up to it."

Annie came out of the kitchen with a large tray of food. One of the other ladies followed her with another. "I saw you come in, Don, so I brought yours out too with a strawberry shake." She served them all Swiss steak and mashed potatoes smothered in brown gravy with sides of corn, green bean casserole, and fresh French bread. Dessert was a large slice of caramel-drizzled Dutch apple pie.

"Thank you very much, Annie. Everything looks wonderful," Blair said. She smiled and left to attend to her other customers.

Blair centered his plate and picked up his fork. "So, what's your next step?"

"Sir, Kurt and I were talking on the way over here, and we think we should take another look at the girls' house. All three of them have been killed now. All five of these murders and the ambush have to be connected. Somehow, Hope Pagano's murder became a catalyst for the other murders. This may sound crazy, but I think we should take a hard look at Nick Pagano," Zack said.

Blair choked on a mouthful of mashed potatoes. He took a drink of water and cleared his throat. "I'll be the first to say Nick's a world-class arrogant asshole, but that's a long way from being a murderer. Besides, he has around-the-clock security watching him. He doesn't move without his security detail."

"What if after he identified Hope's body, he went home and called one of his investigators to dig into Hope's cellphone, laptop, and social media? We never found her cellphone or laptop. His investigator finds the connection between Hope and Powers before we even get a warrant. Then, Nick calls in one of his wet-work guys to kill Powers. While the guy is at Powers's trailer putting him in the septic tank, Denny shows up, so he has to kill him too," Zack said.

"Then why does the guy kill Lindsay and Krista?" Sada asked.

"Hell, I don't know. Maybe they found something that indicated the girls were culpable in some way for Hope hooking up with Powers. Maybe they made a bet with her or dared Hope to go out with Powers. Maybe Nick hired Zeke Horton to do it. Somehow, all of these murders come back to IMI. Another thing, when Mark and I went out to talk to Pagano after Lieutenant Close was killed, he didn't even ask us about our progress on finding Hope's killer. Wouldn't you ask us if one of your children had been murdered? But if he already knew Powers killed her and one of his men killed Powers and Close, he might decide to stay silent," Zack explained.

"Well, it won't hurt to take another look in the house or talk to Nick, for that matter, but clear it through Justin or Herman first. I want to respect the chain of command," Blair said.

After arriving at the Troop C annex, Zack and Kurt talked to Sergeant Deer and Detective Keller and received the key to the house and permission to take another look. Now they stood just inside the front door to the girls' house. They could smell death in the air. The blood-stained rug was still on the floor. Kurt had never been there before and was mesmerized by the macabre scene. Finally, he said, "So, what are we looking for?"

"When I was here with Mark, he said to look for things that are here that shouldn't be here and things that aren't here that should be here. We never found a laptop for Lindsay. All we found was an empty laptop bag. So, the shooter probably took it with him. You take the bedroom on the right, and I'll take the one on the left. We can meet in the middle bedroom. I think it was Hope Pagano's."

Zack entered the bedroom and began going through the drawers on the dresser. He pulled the drawers out and looked behind and underneath them. All he found was clothing, makeup, and brushes. He saw a framed family photo on top and determined this must have been Lindsay's room. Next, he moved to the closet. He checked the pockets of every piece of clothing hanging on the rod. He went through every shoebox on the shelf but didn't find anything unusual. The bed had been neatly made before the murders. Zack pulled the covers back and then raised the mattress to look under it, but nothing was there. He went to the AC vent in the floor and pulled the cover off and stuck his hand in the duct. He pulled out a very dirty empty hand. He wiped it on his trouser leg. He dragged her vanity chair under the return vent. The cover was screwed into the wall. He stood on the chair and shined his new flashlight past the louvered slats and saw a dusty but otherwise empty duct. He sat down on the edge of the bed. He slowly scanned the small bedroom. There was nowhere else to look.

From the other bedroom, Kurt said, "I checked the entire room and haven't found shit. I'm going to the next bedroom. How long have we been here?"

Zack leaned out of the doorway and checked the red LED readout on the clock radio sitting on the bookshelf in the living room. "About fifteen minutes." Then his eyes came alive. "Shit! I think we have something!" He sprang to his feet and hurried to the clock radio in the family room.

Kurt followed right behind him. "What is it?"

Zack pulled the clock radio off the shelf and examined it. He found what he was looking for. He pointed to a difficult-to-see dark spot on the clock face next to the LED readout. "This is a nanny cam. My wife bought a similar one for us. This little spot is a camera lens." He turned it around and saw the port for the memory card. He pushed on the card, and it popped out. "Let's load this memory card in my tablet." Zack unplugged the clock radio from the wall and headed for the door. They ambled down the stairs and hopped in the cruiser.

Zack pushed the memory card into his tablet and tapped on the icon to start the video. He ran the video back to the point where he and Mark were on the scene after the bodies were discovered. He saw the Desloge detective taking photographs of the victims. Zack ran the video back further until the girls were alive. They were sitting on the sofa watching TV when there was a knock at the door. Lindsay got up and opened it and invited someone inside.

"Fuck! That's Nick Pagano!" Kurt said.

They watched as Pagano handed Lindsay her laptop and apologized for taking it. He asked if they told anyone that he took it. After they said they didn't, he pulled a pistol and shot them both. He coldly finished them off with shots to the head.

"Damn, he's one evil bastard," Zack said. "I'm going to clip this and email it to the Sheriff, Sergeant Deer, and Herm Keller." Moments later, Zack hit send and called Blair.

Blair was sitting at his desk looking at his budget. He was trying to figure out a way to give his deputies a permanent pay raise before he was voted out of office. His cellphone rang. "Hello."

"Sheriff, this is Zack and Kurt. We got him. I just emailed you a video clip of Nick Pagano killing Lindsay Miller and Krista

Snyder. We found a nanny camera in the house that recorded the killing."

"Son of a bitch! OK, hold on a second." Blair opened his email account and clicked on the video.

Zack and Kurt listened to the audio of the video clip coming through the phone as Blair watched the video.

After it ended, Blair came back on the line. "I can't believe what I just saw. I've known Nick for twenty-five years. He certainly has his flaws, but I'd never have imagined he was capable of something this heinous. What was his motive for killing Lindsay and Krista? Taking the wrong laptop is not something you kill people over."

"Boss, now we know Pagano killed Lindsay and Krista with Lieutenant Close's Glock. It is reasonable to conclude Pagano must have killed Close because he had his pistol. Pagano probably killed Powers because he found out that Powers killed Hope. He was at Powers's trailer when Close arrived to investigate the missing person's report on Powers. So, Pagano killed Close to avoid being connected to Powers's disappearance. Then Pagano must have planted the Glock in Garza's truck to throw the suspicion onto him. Garza's fight with Powers gave him a possible motive to kill Powers," Zack said. The pieces had finally fallen into place.

"So, Powers kills Hope, and Nick finds out and kills Powers. Then Denny stumbled onto Nick at the trailer and Nick kills Denny. Then Lindsay Miller saw Nick steal her laptop on the nanny cam. She asked Nick to return it, and Nick kills her and

Krista Snyder," Blair said and then leaned back in his chair and rubbed his face.

"Can we go hook him up?" Kurt asked excitedly.

"No, the case belongs to the Major Case Squad. It wouldn't look right if I bigfooted them and started making decisions on the case without including Justin and Herm. Talk to them first and let them give you the green light. But I'm going to send a couple of deputies over to the airport to keep an eye on Nick's jet in case he tries to scoot. Good work, boys." Blair hung up.

"Justin probably left already; I'll call Herm." Zack dialed his cellphone. "Hey, Herm, it's Zack. Did you see the email I sent you a few minutes ago?

"No, I'm at the annex up to my ass in reports. What's it about?"

"Kurt and I found something interesting at the girls' house. Why don't you take a look?"

"OK, stand by. Hey, Justin, come here. Zack and Kurt found something."

"I guess Deer's still there," Zack said to Kurt. They sat and listened as Herm and Justin watched the video.

"Holy shit, that's Pagano!" they heard Deer say over the phone.

They heard the gunshots, then Keller said, "Jesus Christ, he just gunned them down!" There was silence on the phone for a few seconds before Keller asked, "Where did you guys find this video?"

"The girls had a clock radio on the bookshelf in the living room that was actually a nanny camera. If it wasn't recorded over, we may have Pagano stealing the laptop too," Zack replied. "Can we go arrest Pagano? We already talked to the Sheriff, and he said you guys should give the go-ahead."

"Hell yeah, hook him up! I'll call Missy Gilham. Herm, send a couple guys to back them up. Bring him back to the Sheriff's Station to book him," Deer said.

"Cody and I will go. Are you guys going to his farm or the training facility?" Keller asked.

"The farm's closer. We'll go there," Zack replied.

"OK, Cody and I will meet you guys."

Kurt and Zack raced up the driveway to the guard shack at Pagano's farm and came to an abrupt stop. Jeremy Soto came out of the shack. "Hey, man! Where's the fire?"

Zack stepped out of the cruiser and talked to Jeremy over the hood, "Jeremy, we're here to arrest Pagano for murder. You need to open the gate and tell his security detail to stand down."

"Shit! I can't do that, man. I mean, he's not here. He left this morning with his detail. I think he went to work at the facility. I can let you in, but the house is empty," Soto replied.

"Dammit! Kurt, let's get out to the facility." Zack jumped back into the cruiser.

"Just a minute," Kurt said. "Jeremy, you can't tell anyone about this. If you alert Pagano that we're coming, you'll become an accessory to any crimes he commits. If he kills someone, you'll be charged with Murder Second Degree. Do you understand?"

"Yeah, I got it. No worries. I ain't saying shit. I'll give you a call if he comes back," Soto said as he stepped back from the vehicle.

Kurt made a quick turn in the driveway and sped off toward Highway D. He flipped the lights and siren on as he turned onto the highway.

"I'll call Herm." Zack dialed his cellphone. "Hey, Herm, it's Zack. We just left the farm. He's not there. The gate guard thinks he's at the training facility. We're heading over there now." Zack listened to Herm's response. "OK, we'll get there as fast as we can. Listen, Herm, I know you have known Pagano for a long time, but don't let your guard down for a second. He's a stone-cold killer." Zack hung up. "Herm and Cody are in Bonne Terre on 67 turning around to head back south, so they have about a five-minute head start on us."

"Well, we'll see if we can't shave some of that time off en route." Sada smiled.

CHAPTER 35

Twenty minutes later, Zack and Kurt listened on the radio as Keller transmitted, "Central, two ten, 10-23 at the IMI training facility."

"Two ten, 10-23 at IMI," Peggy replied.

"We're still five minutes out; looks like we're going to miss it," Kurt said.

Two minutes later, the radio erupted, "Central, two ten, help, I'm shot! One fifty-two is down! Pagano is in a green IMI Jeep fleeing into the hills! Send Air Evac ASAP! One fifty-two is bleeding out! I can't stop it!"

Zack's eyes went wide at the sound of Herm's panicked voice. "Fuck! We gotta get there!" Zack said and then transmitted, "Central, ten oh five is three minutes out." Zack sat next to Kurt unable to do anything helpful for what seemed like an eternity. They listened to the excited radio traffic going back and forth as law enforcement agencies from the surrounding area reported they were responding to the call for help. "We have to stop this asshole before he kills somebody else," Zack said and then transmitted, "Central, ten oh five, 10-23."

Kurt skidded to a stop on the gravel parking lot next to the admin building. They ran into the building with their rifles at the ready and found Kristina sobbing hysterically under the reception counter.

"We're in here!" Herm yelled from Pagano's office.

Zack and Kurt entered the office and saw Herm kneeling next to Cody. He was using Cody's belt as a tourniquet to slow the bleeding from his left thigh.

"I think his femoral artery was hit! I can't stop the bleeding!" Cody's face was pale.

Zack opened the IFAK on his plate carrier and removed a CAT tourniquet. "Here let me get this on there, Herm." As soon as Herm let off the pressure, Zack could see the blood surging out under Cody's trouser leg with every pulse. He quickly applied the tourniquet. Cody screamed in agony. "Hang in there, Cody. We're going to get you out of here." Cody was completely out of it. Zack turned his attention to Herm. He was holding his abdomen. "Herm, how bad are you hit?"

"Pretty bad, I think. It burns like a motherfucker. I think I shit myself."

"Central, nine ninety, how long for the chopper?" Kurt transmitted.

"Nine ninety, the Air Evac helicopter from the Farmington Base is on a call. Another helicopter is responding from their Perryville base," Peggy replied.

"Kurt, that's too far from here. We can drive them to the hospital before the helo even gets here. Cody doesn't have time to wait, and Herm's probably bleeding internally. We have to get them to Parkland," Zack said.

"Alright, let's get them in the cruiser," Kurt said as he grabbed Cody's legs. Zack grabbed his arms, and they waddled outside to the cruiser and slid Cody across the back seat. Herm followed them, bent over and holding his gut.

"Here, Herm, take the front seat," Zack said as he helped Herm climb in and then reclined the seat to help ease the pressure on his abdomen.

"Zack, get in the back with Cody," Kurt said.

"I'm not going. Someone has to stop this asshole," Zack replied.

Kurt hesitated to think for a second, taking in Herm's and Cody's conditions. They were fading by the second. "OK, brother. Watch your ass. I'll get back as soon as I can." Zack stepped back, and Kurt sped off for the hospital.

Zack turned to head for one of the IMI Jeeps just as seven armed men in suits appeared from the kill house and started walking toward Zack with their M4s and Uzis at low ready. They were laughing and talking back and forth. Zack took cover behind an up-armored Escalade. He pointed his AR-15 at the group and yelled, "Sheriff's Department! Drop your guns and get on the ground, now!" Instead of complying, the men slowly started to spread out.

Their leader said, "Hold on a minute, Deputy. There must be some mistake. We're Mr. Pagano's security detail. He's in the office. He can vouch for us."

"Pagano is wanted for murder! He just shot two police officers and fled into the hills! Now, drop your fucking weapons and get on the ground or I'm gonna start shooting!" Zack ordered.

The leader looked over his shoulder. "Do what the deputy says, drop your rifles, and get on the ground." He lowered his own M4 to the ground and then proned out on the gravel. The other six followed his lead.

"What's your name?" Zack asked.

"Jesse Reeves," the detail leader said.

"Jesse, where were you guys when all the shooting was going on?"

"There are no clients here training today, so I asked Mr. Pagano if I could run the team through some drills in the kill house. We've been in there shooting for a couple of hours. We didn't realize anything was happening out here," Reeves said from the gravel.

"Your boss has killed four people and shot three cops. He took a Jeep up into the hills. Do you have any idea where he's going?"

"The trails lead to several different training areas, but none of them lead to outside roads. If he drove up in there, he'll have to walk out."

"Everybody, listen up. I'm going to get in this Jeep and follow him. More cops are coming. I'm ordering you guys to stay here until they tell you, you can go. Everybody stay on the ground until I'm out of sight on the trail. If you move, I'll assume you're a threat and light you up."

"OK, Deputy. Understood. We'll stay put," Reeves replied.

Zack climbed into the Jeep and sped off up the steep trail into the thickly wooded hills. About half a mile up the trail, Zack slammed on his brakes. Pagano's Jeep was stuck in a rut on the side of the hill, causing his driver's side tires to be six inches off the ground. Zack pulled the keys out of his Jeep and climbed out. He took cover behind his door and scanned the area through his Trijicon ACOG 4x32 scope. The scope cost him more than his rifle, but it was worth every penny. He had mounted it to his rifle after Mark was shot. He didn't see Pagano. He stepped off the trail into the brush and listened. Nothing. He slowly made his way through the brush parallel to the trail until he was even with Pagano's Jeep. The driver's door was open, and the front seat was empty. He crept up to the rear door, quickly checking the back seat. The driver's side mirror exploded, showering him with jagged pieces of mirror and plastic. Zack dove down the slope to the left of the Jeep and into the brush. He quickly low crawled behind a large oak tree. "Pagano, stop shooting, dammit! There's no way out. Give up and I'll take you in. Let your lawyers deal with this."

BOB ASHER

"Bullshit! Who do you think you're dealing with, kid? I was talking down shitbums when you were sucking your momma's tit. I know how this ends, and I'm not going to prison." Pagano fired another round in Zack's direction.

Zack tried to get smaller behind the tree. He wasn't sure where Pagano was, but Pagano knew exactly where he was.

"What happened to you? You were a cop for over twenty years and a respected leader in the community. Now you're a fucking low-life murderer?"

"The night Hope died, everything that was good in me died with her. Now that she's gone, nothin' matters."

"Why'd you do it, Nick? I mean, I get why you killed Powers, but why Close and the girls?" Zack asked as he looked for a way to get out from under Pagano's line of fire.

"That fuckin' bastard killed my daughter because he got her pregnant, and then he dumped her in the creek like trash. She was all I had left. I couldn't carry him to a creek, so I dumped him in the septic tank. Denny was an accident. I always liked him, but he showed up at the trailer at the wrong time. I knew if you guys found evidence in the trailer of a connection between Powers and Hope, I would be a suspect in his murder whenever you found his body, so I decided to burn the trailer. Denny showed up right after I poured gas on everything. I had no choice."

"Why didn't you burn the Jeep? We found Hope's prints and DNA in it."

336

"After shooting Denny, I had to get away from the trailer. I didn't know if another deputy was coming to meet him there."

Zack looked from side to side trying to think of a way to get in a better position. "What about the girls?" Zack asked, trying to buy more time.

"I took a laptop from the house that I thought was Hope's, but it turned out to be Lindsay's. She said she knew I had it because it had tracking software on it that showed the laptop was at my house," Pagano explained.

"Lindsay lied about that. They had a nanny cam that recorded you stealing her computer. It also recorded you coming over and murdering them in cold blood. You've known them since they were little girls and you shot them in their heads. What kind of evil bastard does that?"

"I told you, nothin' matters anymore."

"Look, man, you're a fuckin' billionaire. You can get the best lawyers in the country. You can still wriggle your way out of this. Just put your rifle down and come out. We've already started to surround the area, and soon they'll start closing in on you. You deserve to die for what you did, but do you want to? Because either you let me take you in or you'll die on this mountain."

He got his answer when another bullet smacked into the base of the tree he was lying behind. Zack fired a string of ten rounds back in Pagano's direction to keep his head down. Then, he saw glimpses of Pagano running away from him across the upside of the slope in the trees about fifty yards away. Zack sprang to his feet and fired another string into the brush ahead of Pagano, hoping to make contact. Zack loaded a fresh magazine and took off in pursuit. He tried to use the tactics he had been taught at the Basic School as a new second lieutenant. The terrain and vegetation on Iron Mountain was similar to that of Marine Corps Base Quantico in Virginia. He bounded from tree to tree, always trying to stay behind cover. Zack felt and then heard another bullet zip past him as he stopped behind a large white oak. He peeked out on the other side of the tree and fired another long string of rounds in Pagano's direction. He heard Pagano scream out in pain and go down in the brush. "Nick, are you hit? Throw your rifle out and I'll get you to the hospital."

"Fuck you! I told you, I'm not goin' to prison!"

"Well, OK! Go ahead and blow your fuckin' head off then! I'll wait!" Zack was trying to think of his next course of action when he heard another gunshot, but this one wasn't from the rifle. It sounded like a pistol shot. "Nick, are you OK?" He waited for five minutes but never heard a sound from Pagano's direction. Carefully, he continued forward, advancing from tree to tree. Eventually, he arrived at a tree about thirty feet from Pagano. He could see him lying on his back with a pistol in his right hand pointed toward his temple. Blood was all over his face and head, and blood covered his right pant leg. He wasn't moving. Zack figured he must have hit Pagano in the leg and then he killed himself rather than be taken in.

"Nick, are you alive? Throw the pistol away and I'll get you some help!" Zack yelled, but there was no reply. He approached with his rifle at low ready. About fifteen feet from the body, it suddenly came alive and pointed the pistol at Zack. He tried to move, but action is always faster than reaction. The pistol fired, and Zack felt the impact hit his chest. As he stumbled backward, he returned fire. Out of six rounds Zack fired as he fell, two struck Pagano: one in his chest and one in his throat. Zack hit the ground on his back. He couldn't breathe. He slowly rolled over and crawled behind a tree. He tried to take aim at Pagano again, but the wind had been knocked out of him. He took a quick look around the tree, and this time, Pagano's hands were empty. He slowly caught his breath and checked his chest for a wound. The bullet had struck a loaded magazine attached to the front of his plate carrier. He checked underneath, but there was no penetration. Then he noticed a piece of jagged copper stuck in his right forearm. Blood was running down the back of his arm to his hand. He got to his feet and approached Pagano with his rifle at the ready. He kicked Pagano in his bloody thigh, but there was no reaction. He kicked the pistol further away from the body and rolled it over to put handcuffs on it. He wasn't going to give this dead man another chance to hurt him. He sat down against a tree and plucked the piece of copper jacket from his arm with trembling fingers. It left a flowing half-inch gash. He pulled a bandage from his IFAK and wrapped the wound.

CHAPTER 36

DAY 14, THURSDAY, JUNE 18

After Zack knocked on the door to Mark's hospital room, Mark invited him in. "Good morning. How are you feeling today?"

"Morning. Better than yesterday. The doc said I can go home tomorrow. I'll need more outpatient surgery to repair my arm, but hopefully no more hospital stays. I heard you caught up with Pagano. I should have listened to you in the beginning. Lindsay and Krista would still be alive and the rest of us wouldn't have been shot up. How are you doing?" Mark asked.

"I'll be fine. My armor stopped the bullet. I have a softball-sized bruise on my chest, but it's not bad as long as I don't push it too hard. This is just a scratch on my forearm." He held up his bandaged arm. "He suckered me. I thought he was dead, but he was playing opossum."

"Remember law number six? Never trust a dead man, but that's not what I meant just now. You killed a man yesterday. He was a despicable murderer that needed killing, but he was still a man. Are you OK with that?"

"Yeah, I'm alright." He thought about Afghanistan. "He wasn't my first. Besides, he didn't give me much of a choice."

"Good. He must've been a sociopath. He didn't give two shits about anyone but himself. How are Herm and Cody doing?"

"Kurt got them to the hospital just in time. Herm lost about two feet of his small intestine, but he'll make a full recovery. Cody's femoral artery got hit and he lost a lot of blood, but he still has his leg. He'll need more surgery and a lot of rehab. They stabilized them here and then flew them up to St. Louis last night," Zack said.

"Are you working today?"

"No, the Sheriff gave me three days off because of the shooting."

"Yeah, that's normal. It gives you some time to calm down before going back to work, and it gives the department time to investigate the shooting. Of course, in this case, Pagano was paid for, so you're already in the clear. Just go home and enjoy the time off."

CHAPTER 37

DAY 17, SUNDAY, JUNE 21

I t was 0520 hours on Sunday morning, and Zack was sitting at
the front table in the squad room half asleep. He slept late on
all three of his days off, and it had screwed up his sleep pattern.
The Major Case Squad was closing out the investigation, and only
Sergeant Deer, Detective Weber, and Detective Lambert remained
to finish up the paperwork. Thanks to Pagano's refusal to
surrender, there would be no long, costly trial for the county to pay
for. After his three days off, Zack was told to report back to the
Patrol Division to work the day shift with Kurt Sada. He sat there
looking at an assortment of chocolate-covered candy bars and a
stack of mail he had retrieved from his department mailbox.

"Mornin', brother." Kurt sat down next to Zack.

"Good mornin'. Want a candy bar or five?" He slid the pile
of candy closer to Kurt. Kurt took a Baby Ruth. Zack picked up a
note from the stack. It was from the man who lived in the house
just down the road from Powers's driveway. The man wasn't home
when he and Mark did their area canvas after the trailer fire, so

Mark had left him a note asking him if he had seen anyone or anything unusual in the preceding days before the fire and to contact him or Zack when he returned. The note said a few nights before the fire, he had seen an old white Ford truck come out of the woods across the road near Powers's driveway and race off toward the highway.

"Hey, what sector are we riding today?" Zack asked.

"North, I think. Why? What's up?"

Zack handed him the note. "This guy saw a truck come out of the woods across from Powers's driveway a few nights prior to the fire. I think we should go talk to him."

"OK, but it's Sunday morning, so we should wait until around 1030 or so in case he sleeps late. If we wake him up, he might get pissed and not talk to us," Kurt said.

"Everybody, listen up, so Sergeant Krote and his squad can go home. Go ahead, Sergeant," Lieutenant McLeod said.

"Thank you, sir. Last night at approximately 1155, we had an attempted suicide at 127 Buzzard Rock Road. The resident, Todd Bennett, after being dumped by his girlfriend, decided life wasn't worth living, so he went out to his garage to kill himself by carbon monoxide poisoning. He hopped in his truck and ran the engine for about half an hour, after which he was so hot, he decided to go back into the kitchen to cool off for a while. Once he felt better, he went back out to the garage and started his truck back up again. He continued this cycle several times. Eventually, his ex-girlfriend read one of his suicidal texts and called 911. When deputies contacted him, he was beet red and sweating profusely after another session in the garage. He was transported by ambulance to the hospital on a 72-hour psychiatric hold. I guess he thought the truck's air conditioner would filter out the exhaust fumes," Krote said.

"The whole damn county's full of mouth-breathing idgits," Deputy Wainwright said from the back row.

"Speaking of mouth breathers, shut up, Bob. Thank you, Melvin, we'll take it from here."

"It's almost 1000. Are you ready for J4?" Kurt asked.

"Yeah, I'm always ready to eat," Zack replied.

"You want Granny Annie's?"

"Absolutely."

Before Zack could ask for lunch, the radio came alive, "Ten oh five, man down in the yard, possible electrocution, 7750 Hillsboro Road."

"Ten oh five, 10-76," Zack transmitted.

Ten minutes later, Zack and Kurt arrived on the scene. Big River Fire and the county ambulance arrived just ahead of them. The victim, wearing shorts and flip-flops, was lying in the grass unresponsive in about an inch of standing water. Zack approached the man's wife for a statement while the paramedics worked on him. "Ma'am, can you tell us what happened here?"

"Leroy had the sprinklers going all morning, so it soaked the lawn. Then he decided to fix those rotten boards on the bench. He was cutting the boards with the circular saw when the extension cord fell in the water and shocked him. I ran to the porch and pulled the plug from the socket, but he didn't wake up, so I called 911," she explained as she dabbed her eyes with a tissue.

Zack heard the paramedic call for his partner to charge the defibrillator. He turned and saw them kneeling in the water next to the victim. One had the paddles over his chest waiting for the charge to build.

Kurt grabbed the woman and Zack. "Let's back up a little."

As they backed away, the Big River battalion chief walked by and noticed them walking backward. Wondering why they were backing away, he noticed what was about to happen and yelled, "Stop! Get him out of the water and on the gurney over on the driveway before you defibrillate him." He turned to Kurt and angrily asked, "Why didn't you say something?"

"You guys are the experts. I didn't want to tell you how to do your jobs. I just thought we should back up so someone would be able to call for another ambulance."

Seconds later, Zack and Kurt watched as the paramedics zapped the victim and then put him in the ambulance. Behind them, a neighbor lady was talking to another woman who had just arrived. She said, "They was trying to jump-start Leroy, and he was jumping, but he just wouldn't start." Zack and Kurt exchanged a glance then hurried back to their cruiser, trying to hold in their laughter. They dove into the cruiser before they lost control.

"They was trying to jump-start, Leroy, and he was jumping, but he just wouldn't start," Kurt mimicked the woman. "Man, that's hilarious."

Zack tried to be professional, but he couldn't help but laugh. "How should I write this up, as an accidental death?"

"Nope, they were still working on him when he was transported to the hospital by ambulance. He's not dead until the doctor says so. We're 10-8, NRN," Kurt said.

"Central, ten oh five, 10-8, NRN, victim transported by county ambulance," Zack transmitted. "You want to head up to Rouggly Road before we eat?"

"Sure, I can wait a while."

Fifteen minutes later, Zack transmitted, "Central, ten oh five, 10-6, investigation at 3691 Rouggly Road."

"Ten oh five, 10-6 at 1045," Peggy replied.

As Kurt pulled into the gravel driveway, they saw a shirtless man of about sixty-five wearing faded blue denim overalls rocking on the porch under a ceiling fan. A half-empty pouch of Red Man chewing tobacco was sticking out of his chest pocket. His green camouflage John Deere cap was pushed back on his sweaty, balding forehead. He had a large glass of iced tea in his left hand and a fly swatter in his right. He was racking up an ever-increasing body count. A John Deere riding mower was parked on the driveway next to the porch. The yard had been freshly cut.

As they approached, Zack said, "Good morning, Sir. I'm Deputy Zack Goodson and this is Deputy Kurt Sada. It looks like you did a fine job on the lawn. Are you Ralph Young?"

The man slammed the swatter down on the porch rail and made another kill. He scraped the remains off with the swatter. "Mornin', and yes, I am. Would you boys like a glass of tea?"

"No thank you, Mr. Young," Zack replied.

"I found your note on the screen door. My wife and I've been out of town for more than a week visiting her family in Arkansas. I guess we missed all the excitement across the road. We left the morning of the fire."

"When did you see the truck come out of the woods?" Zack asked.

He narrowed his eyes and looked skyward. "That would have been Friday night, June 5th , around eleven o'clock. I watched *Blue Bloods* on channel four and then the news after my wife went to bed. I let the dog out one last time to do his business before I turned in. That's when I saw the truck. It came creeping out of the brush with its lights off until it turned onto the road. Then the driver turned on the headlights and hauled ass toward JJ."

"Can you describe the truck for me?" Zack asked.

"Yeah, it was a beat-up old white Ford F-250. It was jacked up and had those big knobby muddin' tires and a big roll bar in the bed behind the cab. It also had one of those rebel flag decals covering the back window." Young spit over the porch rail into the shrubs.

"Sir, how could you see all of that at night from back here on the porch?" Zack asked.

Young pointed his fly swatter at the tall wooden pole in his yard near the edge of the driveway. "See that dusk-to-dawn light? I had Ameren put it in about five years ago after my house got robbed. It lights up this whole area."

"Could you identify the driver if we brought you a photo array?" Kurt asked.

"Naw, the truck cab was too dark." Young spit over the rail again.

"Thank you very much, Mr. Young. You've been very helpful," Zack said. He and Kurt turned to walk back to their cruiser.

"You boys thinks he was involved in those killings?"

They turned back to Young. Zack nodded. "It's possible."

"Well, when you boys catch up to him, I hope you fry his ass."

"Thanks again, Mr. Young," Zack said as they returned to the cruiser and got in.

"That truck belongs to Grant Cunningham," Kurt said. "I've written him four tickets while he was driving it." Kurt backed out of the driveway and drove off toward Highway JJ.

"Cunningham was Hope Pagano's high school sweetheart. What if he came over here and killed her? Hope had a habit of coming to Powers's trailer and staying the night with him after he came home from drinking at the VFW. What if Cunningham became aware of their relationship and killed her out of spite? I just don't know how to prove it," Zack asked.

"Well, I have an idea. Maybe I can help you with that. Let's make some calls to get everything set up," Kurt said with a shit-eating grin on his face. "Then we'll find Grant and have a talk with him. It's time for lunch. How about we skip Granny Annie's today and go to Colton's?"

"Sounds good to me. I'm always up for a good steak," Zack said with a smile.

CHAPTER 38

"Hi, my name is Naomi. Welcome to Colton's. What can I get for you?"

"Hi, Naomi. I'll have the rib eye, medium, the loaded baked potato, green beans, and iced tea," Kurt answered.

She turned to Zack.

"I'll have the Hawaiian rib eye, medium well, with a double order of fries, and a Coke." Zack scooped a handful of peanuts from the small bucket in the middle of the table. "I hope the food comes soon. I'm starving."

Fifteen minutes later, their steaks arrived, and after another fifteen minutes, all the food was gone. Naomi came to the table. "Would you gentlemen like to have dessert today?"

"None for me, thanks," Zack replied.

"Me either, but could you tell me who's back there on the grill today? Is it Grant?" Kurt asked.

"Yes, he's back there," she said with a smile.

"Could you bring us the check and ask him to come out and talk to us? I want to tell him how much I enjoyed his work," Kurt said.

"Sure, no problem." She headed for the kitchen.

A minute later, Grant stuck his head out through the kitchen door. Kurt smiled at him and waved him over. Grant looked both ways like he was about to cross a dangerous street. He reluctantly walked over to the table.

"Can I help you, Deputies?"

"We just wanted to let you know the steaks were terrific. Why don't you have a seat so we can talk for a minute? Don't worry, we cleared it with your manager," Kurt said.

Cunningham took a seat.

"I guess you heard we caught up with Nick Pagano. We're just trying to tie up some loose ends before we close the case. When Deputy Langford and I talked to you, you said you were home all night on Friday, June 5. Are you sure about that?" Zack asked.

Cunningham remained silent but nodded his head.

"Really? Because we know that's not right because Trooper Murphy wrote you a speeding ticket that night on Highway 67 about a mile south of Highway Y." Zack slid a copy of the ticket across the table. He pointed to the bottom of the ticket.

Cunningham bent his head to look at it.

"That's your signature, isn't it? Murphy said you were heading southbound doing 80 in a 65. He also said you were

351

nervous about something. So, what's the deal? Why did you lie to us?" Zack asked.

"I guess I forgot." Cunningham pushed the ticket back across the table. He lowered his head and focused on his hands resting on the table.

"Have you ever been to Randall Powers's trailer?"

"No, I don't know him."

"Are you sure? Because your cellphone records indicate your phone was there." Zack slid another piece of paper across the table. "Here's another thing. Did you know Powers had trail cameras set up in the trees around his place pointed at his driveway and trailer? I guess he was kind of paranoid." Zack pulled a green camouflaged trail camera out of a paper bag next to his chair and placed it on the table. "They're really nice high-definition cameras with night vision capability. They show you coming to the trailer and later on leaving. Oh, and we have a witness who saw you drive out of the trees down the road from Powers's driveway with your headlights off around 11:00 p.m. like you were trying to sneak out without being seen. That was right before Trooper Murphy wrote your ticket. So, let's start over. Why were you at Powers's trailer?"

Cunningham didn't say anything, so Zack and Kurt employed an old cop trick to entice him to talk. They waited quietly and ate peanuts.

Eventually, he spoke. "That afternoon while we were working, Hope asked me to meet her at Powers's trailer. She said she was stressed out over school and work and wanted to get high.

She asked me to bring something for her. So, I did. I brought her some Ice, but she was fine when I left. I guess Powers killed her later after he came back."

Zack looked over Cunningham's shoulder and saw Sergeant Justin Deer and Corporal Doug Butler sitting at another table in civilian clothes. Butler held up what Zack recognized as a search warrant. Deer held up two clear plastic evidence bags with his gloved hands. One contained a roll of gray duct tape and the other a spool of black electrical cord. Then he pulled a red shop towel out of a brown paper bag. He pointed to a dried dark stain on the towel.

"Are you sure you didn't tie her to a chair with black electrical cord and then gag her with a red shop towel and duct tape before you beat the shit out of her?" Zack asked as he pointed over Cunningham's shoulder.

Cunningham turned to look. Butler and Deer held up the evidence again. Cunningham faced Zack and Kurt again. He licked his lips and swallowed hard.

"What do you think are the chances we'll find her DNA on that blood-stained shop towel?" Zack asked.

Cunningham kept looking down at his hands.

"Why'd you do it? Was it because she dumped you after you lost your scholarship? Look, I get that. You were the hometown hero, star athlete, a three-letter man with a full ride to Mizzou. You were the shit. You might've even played in the majors if you hadn't blown out your arm. Then She just shit on you and walked away," Zack prodded.

Cunningham's face reddened as he continued to stare at the table. Sweat was beading on his forehead. "It was her fault. I already had my scholarship. My arm was sore from throwing hard all season. I could have played third base instead of pitching that last game and let my arm heal, but we were in the playoffs. I told her my arm was hurting, and she told me to 'cowboy the fuck up.' You believe that? She didn't care about me. She said the team and the town needed me to win the game. So, I pitched and we won, but I threw my arm out in the sixth inning. After the surgery, I got hooked on the painkillers, and instead of supporting me, she dumped me. She thought she was too good to be seen with a washed-up jock. Stuck-up bitch.

"One night I fell asleep in my truck behind the restaurant after my shift. I woke up when a Jeep parked next to me. I saw her run out the back door of Colton's and get in. I looked down into the Jeep thorough the open sunroof. They were making out. Do you believe it? She was all over that old fucker. She threw her head back and saw me watching them. She smirked and pulled off her shorts and panties. Then she straddled him in his seat. She watched me the whole time she was fucking him. I dated her for three years in high school and she never even let me see it. She acted so happy with him. She thought he was some big war hero. The guy was a fucking drunk!

"So, I figured I'd teach her a lesson. See how she liked being addicted and not be able to stop. I gave her some Ice, but instead of showing me some understanding, she said she would tell Powers and her father what I did. She started laughing at me, so I hit her. Then she spit on me and said I hit like a bitch. I lost control and hit her some more. I put the rag and tape on her mouth to shut her up. I left a few minutes later. I figured her new boyfriend could deal with her. All I wanted was a little respect and compassion." Defeated, he raised his head. "What happens to me now?"

Zack was stunned by his callous disregard for his victim and total lack of remorse. "Now, you're under arrest. I do have one more question for you."

"What?"

"What kind of pussy hits a girl?" Zack asked rhetorically.

Kurt stood and dangled his cuffs in front of Cunningham. "Stand up and put your hands behind your back." He put the handcuffs on and pulled a laminated card from his shirt pocket. He started reading Cunningham his Miranda rights to make sure they got it on video. "You have the right to remain silent. Anything you say may be used against you in court. You have the right to an attorney before and during any questioning. If you cannot afford an attorney, one will be appointed for you free of charge before any questioning. Do you wish to waive these rights?"

"What? Fuck no! You didn't read me my rights before you questioned me! I'm gonna walk!" Cunningham said with a huge grin on his face.

Kurt smiled back. "You weren't under arrest yet, nimrod. Your statements were voluntary. Smile for the camera." Kurt pointed to Detective Weber sitting at the table across from them holding a small video camera. She smiled and waved as she continued recording. "Let's go." Kurt led Cunningham outside to his cruiser.

Deer and Butler approached Zack and shook his hand. "You did a great job getting to the truth on this, Zack. If it weren't for you, we never would've known Cunningham started this clusterfuck. He would've gotten away with it," Deer said.

"Well, thankfully, Mr. Young called us back with the information about Cunningham being at Powers's trailer. Without him, Cunningham would have gotten away with it. Did you guys have any trouble getting the search warrant for his truck?"

"Naw. Judge Buchanan came through big time. I called him and told him what you found out, and he authorized the search warrant over the phone and emailed it to me before we got here," Deer replied.

"That kid's gonna be royally pissed when he finds out you lied to him about the trail cameras. Where did you get the camera? I know Powers didn't have any," Butler said. As cops, all three of them knew the Supreme Court decided a long time ago that it was legal for the police to lie to suspects because the Court ruled cops couldn't convince an innocent man that he committed a crime.

"Normally, it's strapped to a tree next to my mother-in-law's chicken coop. I need to get back there before she notices it's missing," Zack replied.

Deer and Butler laughed.

"You guys can go book him into the jail. We'll wait for the tow truck to get here," Deer said.

CHAPTER 39

DAY 18, MONDAY, JUNE 22

"Ten oh five, respond to the station," Peggy transmitted.

"Ten oh five, 10-76," Zack responded. "I wonder what this is about?"

"You never know. Sometimes it's to take a report. Sometimes it's to get an 'attaboy.' Sometimes it's for an ass chewing," Kurt replied.

Five minutes later, they arrived at the station and Zack transmitted, "Ten oh five, 10-23." They parked next to the back door, but before they got inside, the sheriff came out.

"Kurt, I need to borrow your partner for a while. We'll call you when we're done. C'mon, Zack, let's take a ride," Blair said, and they climbed into the sheriff's F-150.

"Sir, is Mrs. Close gonna be able to keep that $500,000 donation?"

"Yep, I checked with the bank. The money for the cashier's check came from Nick's personal account and it already cleared."

"Did you tell her where the money came from?"

"Nope. If I did, I'm sure she wouldn't keep it, and I know she and her boys really need the money. Speaking of kids, I heard you have another little one on the way. Congratulations." Blair pulled out of the parking lot and drove down the road.

"Thank you, sir."

"I also heard your wife, Patty, wants to stay home with the baby for a while and that's going to put you in a bind. I'd hate for you to leave the department because you need more money. I can't give you enough of a raise to make a difference, but what would you say if I could find you a part-time job that could possibly double your income?"

Zack laughed. "I'd say it's probably illegal."

Blair chuckled as he drove into Farmington Regional Airport and parked next to the small terminal building run by the fixed base operator. He checked his watch. What started as a low distant rumble quickly became a roaring freight train. Zack recognized the sound and looked out his window. A dark green UH-60 Black Hawk helicopter flew over the terminal and made a low 180° turn before making a rolling landing on the edge of the empty concrete ramp. It taxied to a stop in front of the FBO's building. A crewman climbed down from the right gunner's window and placed yellow wooden chocks around the right tire. Within a minute, the engines were shut down and the rotors began slowing down. The pilots opened their doors and climbed out. They removed their helmets and survival vests.

"Right on time. C'mon, I'll introduce you." Blair opened his door. As they approached the helicopter, a tall gray-haired pilot stepped forward.

"Shakey, tell the folks in the FBO to top us off," he said to his copilot. "Hey, Don, good to see you." He held out his hand.

"It's good to see you too, Clark. Zack, this is Colonel Clark Pace. He's the state aviation officer for the Missouri Army Guard."

"Pleased to meet you, Colonel." Zack was clearly distracted by the helicopter.

"It's good to meet you too, Zack. C'mon, you can take a closer look." Pace turned back to the helicopter. "Climb in the right seat, and I'll take the left. Don told me you flew Super Stallions in the Corps."

Zack climbed into the cockpit and eagerly looked around. He couldn't resist the urge to put his feet on the pedals and hold the cyclic and collective controls. It had been almost a year since his last flight at the controls of a helicopter.

"Does anything look familiar?" Pace asked.

"The cockpit is set up like a mini 53," Zack replied.

"That's basically true. They're both Sikorsky helicopters. The cockpit layout is very similar. How would you like to fly this helicopter?"

"What do you have in mind, sir?" Zack asked suspiciously.

"Don told me about your situation. We could transfer your commission as a captain in the Marine Reserve to the Army Guard. It would only take a month or so. I have a handful of open captain billets right now. One is a company commander slot at Fort Leonard Wood. I think with your background, you would be perfect for it. Then we'd send you to Fort Rucker in Alabama or WAATS out in Arizona for the Black Hawk course and get you back home flying in the Guard part-time several months before your wife's due. If you attend all your monthly drills, annual training, and fly all your additional flight training periods, you could make over $30,000 a year. Have you kept up with your professional military education?"

"Yes, sir. I completed Expeditionary Warfare School before I got out of the Corps."

"Then you'd probably be promoted to major in a year or two, which would mean even higher pay. With your training and experience, you would excel in the Guard. Zack, Missouri needs high-caliber people like you to continue to serve right here at home. Every year in addition to our normal training flights, we respond to natural disasters like earthquakes, floods, and forest fires all over the state. We also do counterdrug missions. We've even dropped hay to stranded cows after blizzards."

"How long would I be obligated?" Zack asked.

"You're long past your initial eight-year obligation. If you don't like the Guard, you could transfer over to the Individual Ready Reserve or another service…or resign your commission."

"What about deployments, sir? The way I remember it, when I was deploying to Afghanistan in the Corps for seven months at a time, the Army was going over for a year."

"Well, of course, if the shit hits the fan, we're all going, but right now, after pulling out of Afghanistan, we aren't scheduled to go anywhere for over three years. We do have a few guys who volunteer to deploy individually to augment other units."

Zack nodded and said, "Thank you for the offer, sir. We could certainly use the money, but I'll need to talk this over with the boss."

"I'm sure it's OK with Don. He's the one who called me."

"No, I mean my real boss."

Pace laughed. "Oh, I get it. Talk to your wife and see what she thinks. There's no hurry. Take your time. If you're interested, give me a call. Since we're here, how would you like an orientation ride? We brought a spare helmet. You can take the right seat."

Zack looked at the sheriff like a kid asking his dad if he could go on the roller coaster.

"Go ahead, Zack. Give us a call when you get back, and we'll have Kurt come pick you up." He walked back to his truck and stood leaning up against the grill watching as the engines came to life and the rotors began to speed up.

Moments later, Zack lowered his helmet visor and saluted him from the right seat.

Blair waved back at him, and the helicopter rose from the pavement and nosed over to rapidly accelerate across the ramp before it climbed away from the airport. Zack was flying it like he stole it.

The End

Acknowledgements

To Gwenn, Bevy, Hillary, thank you to my beta readers, proofreaders, and armchair editors who volunteered their time to find and help me fix the mountain of errors I missed the first six or seven times I read it. Also, many thanks to Karen at Comma Queen Editing, who came in after all of us and still found copious mistakes.